Where Promises Endure

Cafe on Hope and Main ~ Book Two

Candee Fick

ISBN: 979-8-950859-00-7

Editing by Zero Alchemy

Cover Design by The Book Brander

Contents

“We have this hope as an anchor for the soul, firm and secure.” ~ Hebrews 6:19

“Let us hold unswervingly to the hope we profess, for he who promised is faithful.” ~ Hebrews 10:23

Chapter One

Clarissa Miller clutched the cardboard portfolio to her chest and sprinted down the concrete sidewalk toward Loveland High School, her breath forming small clouds in the crisp March air.

God, I promise I'll do a better job with the boys if You'll help me get in and out fast.

She couldn't afford to miss out on more tips than absolutely necessary.

If only she hadn't needed to make the extra stop at Brian's middle school to deliver his science report. But there'd been no way to ignore the tear-suppressing crack in his voice on the phone.

Or the fact it was her fault she'd accidentally grabbed his assignment off the printer along with her other work. Not to mention she'd also taken their only computer with her this morning so he couldn't print another copy.

Yet another failure in her role as guardian who was trying her best.

The heavy metal door groaned as she yanked it open, the familiar scent of floor polish and teenage angst hitting her in a nostalgic wave.

The halls were mercifully empty, classes already in session. Her footsteps echoed against the rows of red lockers as she followed the signs for the main office.

The quicker she delivered their new logo to the athletic department, the sooner she could return to her assigned section at Hope's Cafe.

Rounding the corner at full speed, Clarissa slammed into what felt like a brick wall.

"Whoa!" a deep voice exclaimed as strong hands steadied her.

Her makeshift portfolio wasn't as lucky. It hit the floor with a slap, spilling her carefully organized drawings across the polished linoleum in a cascade.

"I'm so sorry." Heat crept up her neck as she scrambled to gather the papers before they slid under the nearby water fountain.

"My fault," the wall—no, the man—said, crouching to collect several of her sketches. "I wasn't watching where I was going."

Clarissa looked up and her breath caught.

The man kneeling next to her was about her age and wore a red polo with the Loveland Red Wolves logo, his broad shoulders filling it impressively. But his eyes held her attention—blue as the summer sky, creased at the corners from what must be frequent smiling.

"These are incredible." He studied one in particular. "Your work?"

She glanced at the charcoal drawing she'd done of Timothy at bat last year. Back before everything changed.

"Yes." She bit her lip. Except they were her personal sketches, not the professional portfolio she someday hoped to show clients. "Just doodles, really."

"Doodles?" He raised an eyebrow, the corner of his mouth lifting in a half-smile that did strange things to her pulse. "If these are doodles, I'd love to see what you consider actual art."

The compliment warmed something inside her that had been cold for too long. When was the last time someone noticed anything about her beyond her ability to manage her brothers' schedules or remember extra pickles on a customer's burger?

When she reached out to accept the stack of drawings he handed her, their fingers brushed, adding to the tingling feeling coursing through her veins. She covered her reaction by tucking the papers back into her portfolio.

"Zeke Matthews." He stood, offering his hand to help her up. "PE teacher and coach. Are you new around here? I don't think we've met."

"Clarissa. And no." She shook her head, fully aware of the food-splattered T-shirt under her open jacket. "I work at Hope's Café downtown. I'm only here to deliver their updated team sponsorship form so the baseball program has the correct name and new logo."

Interest sparked in his eyes. "Baseball, huh? I'm always happy to see more sponsors. Can I see it?"

Clarissa sorted through her now unorganized portfolio, then pulled out the mostly unwrinkled sheet, now complete with the digital mock-up she'd added on the second page.

She'd spent hours on the design, working late after her brothers were asleep. The job might have been a favor to the new owners Joel and Lauren, but they'd been so good to her over the past few months.

And hopefully it might lead to future freelance work. The kind that would let her support the boys without running herself into the ground.

Zeke took the pages, glancing over the other information before focusing on the logo. "You said this is new?"

"It is. We used to be Dawson's Diner, but the new owners wanted to honor the family matriarch with a name change."

He glanced between the logo and the portfolio in her arms. "Did you draw it?"

"I did." She studied his expression. What would he think of it?

"Nice." Zeke's appreciation appeared genuine. "Modern but still classic at the same time."

His approval sent a surprising thrill through her. So far, outside her bosses, her clients had barely studied her designs before requesting arbitrary changes.

"Coach Matthews!" A voice called from down the hallway. A man in a suit waved impatiently. "The athletic budget meeting started five minutes ago."

Zeke grimaced. "Duty calls. Thanks for bringing this by, Miss..."

He hesitated. As if asking for her marital status?

Or more likely her last name.

Too bad it wasn't the former possibility because then he might also ask for her phone number.

Heat rose in her face at her misplaced assumptions. "It's Miller."

"Clarissa Miller," he repeated, as if committing it to memory, before glancing at the form again. "Well, Miss Miller, you have serious talent. And I might need to stop by the cafe to thank your employer in person for their sponsorship."

Meaning she might see him again, after all?

She scrambled to reclaim her professionalism, holding out a hand for the form. "Can you direct me to the office to turn that in?"

"I'm headed there now so I can take it from here." He flashed a smile that crinkled those deep blue eyes before jogging toward the waiting administrator.

She watched him go, an unfamiliar lightness in her chest. It had been so long since someone saw her—really saw her—for something beyond her responsibilities.

As she turned to leave, a bright yellow notice on the bulletin board caught her eye.

BASEBALL TRYOUTS TUESDAY.

Right. Timothy's tryouts were tomorrow.

A flutter of nerves danced in her stomach. He'd talked of nothing else for days, his lanky frame almost vibrating every time he mentioned baseball.

Her gaze drifted across the other details until they landed on a certain name.

Coach Matthews was listed as the head coach.

No wonder he'd been interested in the team's sponsors.

Which also meant her brother might wind up being coached by the same man who'd made her feel more like an artist than a waitress for the first time in months.

Unfortunately, there were probably rules about coaches and dating. Meaning their connection would end as quickly as it had begun.

Clarissa retraced her steps, pushing back through the heavy doors into the March sunshine. She glanced at her watch, calculating it would take about seven minutes to get back to the cafe.

Seven minutes to tuck away the lingering warmth of being seen as more than just Timothy and Brian's guardian. More than just the efficient waitress who never forgot an order.

Seven minutes to forget the way Coach Matthews' eyes lit up when he looked at her drawings—and, for a moment, at her.

Because nothing could ever come of it.

Tuesday afternoon, Zeke Matthews dumped the canvas bag of baseballs onto the infield dirt, the satisfying plunk and scatter bringing a familiar comfort as he surveyed the empty field.

This was his sanctuary. His place of purpose.

Because the field's chalked lines and measured distances created clear boundaries everyone understood and respected—unlike the messy complications beyond the diamond.

Life had enough variables outside his control.

Like the crisp breeze which held both the promise of spring and winter's lingering bite. The kind of breeze that made him thankful for the abandoned team jacket he'd found in the corner of the equipment shed and adopted as his own uniform.

Especially since it was embroidered with the word Coach.

He inhaled, savoring the unique blend of grass, clay, and chalk. Soon the air would also carry overtones of leather mitts and sweat along with the tang of possibility that always lingered before tryouts.

And this season he was in charge of the program.

God, help me impact these young lives. To be a father figure to those who need it–or at least a big brother. Help me to honor You in everything I say or—

"Hey, Coach!" Devon, one of his assistant coaches and a fellow teacher, jogged over , hands filled with a sheaf of papers and several clipboards. "I printed out the evaluation forms like you asked."

"Thanks." Zeke looked them over as he led Devon toward the home team dugout. "Good thing we both have the last period off to get it all set up."

"You'll find it comes in handy for travel days, too." Devon nodded to the equipment shed behind the home team bleachers. "What else do you want pulled out?"

"A few batting helmets and a couple bats for those who don't bring their own." Zeke set the evaluation forms down on the bench, relieved to see pens attached to each clipboard with a string. One less thing to worry about. "But first, can you help me carry out the pitching screen?"

Fifteen minutes later, his two other assistants arrived. He'd inherited the holdover coaches along with the job, but time would tell if they would gel as a staff.

Zeke was in the middle of assigning various stations to each coach with an emphasis on the skills he wanted tested and evaluated, when a harsh clang echoed across the infield.

He turned to find the school's suit-clad athletic director and assistant principal, Mike Vaughn, striding toward them, his leather dress shoes already collecting red dust from the warning track. Behind him, the metal gate swung, rebounding from being slammed open into the chain link fence.

"Matthews." Vaughn nodded a brisk greeting. "I need a word before the hormone horde descends."

It wasn't a request.

Zeke turned to his coaches. "Grant, you can help Dave set up the speed gun by the bullpen to clock our pitchers. And maybe grab the catcher's gear out of the shed while you're at it?"

His outfielder coach grunted before jogging off the field in one direction as their colleague headed another.

"And Devon—"

"What's this doing in my inbox?" Vaughn stepped between them, slapping a piece of paper against Zeke's chest.

Zeke took the offending page, instantly recognizing the cafe name. His lips curled at the memory of the lovely Clarissa Miller and her spilled sketches. "It's from one of our team sponsors. What's the problem?"

Vaughn huffed. "We have deadlines for a reason. It's too bad they missed it and won't—"

"No, she didn't." Zeke shook his head. "I handed the updated form to your secretary myself before our budget meeting. And this looks like a photocopy for your records. Besides, she said it's a name change for someone already on—"

"She?" Vaughn raised a bushy eyebrow. "You mean the pretty redhead you were talking to in the hall?"

Beside him, Devon chuckled. "A pretty girl? Where was I?"

Zeke's stomach clenched. Assuming she was single, he had no claim on the woman. But neither did he want to share her with anyone if there was even a chance he'd see her again.

He forced a casual expression on his face. "If you're referring to Miss Miller, then yes. I ran into her yesterday and offered to deliver the form myself since she needed to get back to work."

He glanced at the logo. There'd been something special about her. Something in her eyes.

Not just talent, though that had been evident in every stroke in her remarkable drawings, especially the one of a young baseball player. No, it was a depth of feeling. A quiet determination that intrigued him.

The type of commitment he recognized in the best of his players.

The type that made him want to give her an opportunity to shine.

Zeke took a deep breath as an idea took root. "However, while I'm thinking about budgets... I know you said we'd have to raise our own money for anything beyond the basics of game balls and umpires."

"True." Vaughn pursed his lips.

Devon blinked at the news.

Zeke rolled the sponsorship form and tapped it against his palm. "What if we had shirts designed with something unique, not just the standard mascot?"

"For the parents to buy?" Devon hummed. "The booster moms go crazy for customized merchandise."

"Exactly." Zeke bit his lip, letting the possibility grow. "Build team spirit and increase our budget at the same time. Bonus points if we keep the sponsors happy by putting their logos somewhere on the back."

"Perhaps." Vaughn crossed his arms. "But anything you create would have to look professional if it's got our school name on it. And you'll need to work fast to get something put together."

"Of course." Zeke nodded, then handed the now-curled sponsorship form back to the athletic director.

Vaughn frowned at the condition of the paperwork. "I did have another reason to come out here."

Devon cleared his throat. "I'll go help the guys while you two chat."

Zeke stared at Devon's departing back, then back at his boss. "Not sure why he'd run off just because you want to—?"

"No." Vaughn pulled folded papers from the inside pocket of his suit coat and held them out. "The school board forwarded it this afternoon. It's an update to our athletic department non-fraternization policies in the aftermath of the Brenner debacle."

Bile rose in Zeke's throat.

The former baseball coach had an affair with a player's mother. A married mother. And when it became public knowledge through the woman's divorce proceedings, the resulting scandal cost Brenner his job both in the classroom and on the field.

Positions Zeke had been hired to fill.

If only the man's poor judgment hadn't also upended the life of a teenage boy who'd since moved out of their district to live with his grandparents.

Zeke prayed the kid got a fresh start. The kind he'd always wished for himself but never got until college.

The papers crinkled as Zeke unfolded them. He skimmed the highlighted section, the familiar language making his jaw tighten.

No inappropriate relationships with player's family members. Strong recommendations to maintain professional boundaries at all times. Potential grounds for immediate dismissal.

"Not that you've given us any cause for concern after the wringer we put you through during your interviews..." Vaughn's tone suggested vigilance rather than confidence. "But it's fresh on everyone's minds."

"Understood."

"But I should warn you that these helicopter parents can be... let's say challenging. One perceived slight and they're in my office threatening lawsuits."

"Lawsuits? For what? I hope it's not for stuff like not playing their kid enough."

"Among other things." Vaughn's chuckle sounded forced. "I'll deal with most of that for you. Just make sure you get all your staff to sign the updated agreement and get them back to me ASAP so we're all covered."

Zeke swallowed the sour taste in his mouth. "I will."

A shrill ringing echoed from the building and moments later the doors burst open, spilling students outside. The majority headed to the parking lots or the line of waiting buses.

"I'll leave you to it." Vaughn jutted his chin. "Remember, while we love winners, it's about developing the whole student, Matthews. Mind, body, and—"

"Character," Zeke finished. "Always."

The first wave of hopeful players trickled toward the athletic fields, many of them awkward teenagers carrying equipment bags that seemed to weigh more than they did.

Zeke stuffed the policy forms inside his jacket and zipped it up, already focused on the task at hand.

The task of shaping these boys into skilled baseball players. And into men of integrity along the way like his coaches had done for him.

Forty minutes later, Zeke circled the edge of the diamond, clipboard in hand as he evaluated the thirty-two boys in numbered bibs going through fielding drills. He'd heard the bulk were returning players with a few promising freshmen added in.

His gaze kept drifting to a lanky redhead stationed at second base.

The kid moved with natural athleticism—quick reflexes, good instincts. But his form was inconsistent, his technique clearly self-taught. He fielded a hard grounder with surprising grace, then overthrew first base by a good ten feet on the next play. Raw talent without proper coaching.

Zeke marked notes on the kid's corresponding evaluation sheet. High potential. Needs fundamentals.

After the drill ended, he approached the redhead taking a water break, his freckled face flushed with exertion.

"Good hands," Zeke said. "You've played before?"

The boy's eyes lit up. "Yes, sir. Rec league through middle school. But never super competitive, you know? Just for fun."

"Your footwork needs adjustment, but you've got natural ability." Zeke demonstrated the proper fielding stance. "Bend from the knees, not the waist. That helps you stay balanced."

The boy mimicked him perfectly on the first try. Coachable. Another good sign.

"What's your name?" Zeke asked.

"Timothy Miller, sir."

The water bottle Zeke had been holding froze halfway to his mouth.

Miller. The same warm red hair, though the boy's was cropped short. The same determined set to the jaw.

"Miller," he repeated. "Any relation to Clarissa from Hope's Café?"

Timothy's face brightened. "That's my sister. Well, also my guardian—has been since our mom died last fall. Did you see the new logo? She worked super hard on it."

The pride in the kid's voice was unmistakable. As was the complication now facing Zeke.

"She did. It's excellent work." Zeke kept his tone neutral despite the sinking feeling in his stomach.

Guardian. Not just a sister, but essentially this boy's parent.

And the policy in his pocket couldn't be clearer.

"She's amazing." Timothy grinned, oblivious to Zeke's inner conflict. "Works like crazy, you know? The café, her design stuff, taking care of me and Brian. Don't know how she does it all."

Zeke nodded, stepping back. "Well, your sister's talent seems to run in the family. Head back out—we're doing batting practice next."

As Timothy jogged away, Zeke watched him with mixed emotions. The boy had potential that proper coaching could develop into real skill. And based on what he'd just learned, making the team would mean the world to him.

Meanwhile, the image of Clarissa's surprised face when their hands touched while gathering her drawings—the brief, genuine smile that transformed her tired features—lingered.

Zeke rubbed a hand along his jaw and blew out a slow breath. He'd spent his childhood watching his father break promises and rules with predictable, devastating consequences.

He was building his new career on being different—reliable, principled, trustworthy. Promised himself he'd be a better man than his father.

The wind picked up, sending a paper cup tumbling across the infield. Zeke caught it under his foot, then crushed it in his hand.

As surely as his chest squeezed with the unexpected difficulties in his upcoming roster decisions.

Timothy Miller should be evaluated fairly based on his abilities. And Clarissa, with her expressive eyes and remarkable talent, would have to remain what she was supposed to be: the guardian of a potential player.

Nothing more.

No matter how much he might wish otherwise.

Not if he wanted to keep his word. Or his job.

Chapter Two

His next task was the absolute worst part about holding tryouts, but he knew that going in.

Zeke tapped his pen against the laminated desk surface, the rhythmic sound punctuating the relative silence of the athletic department conference room.

Beside a collection of emptied fast-food wrappers, thirty-two stapled bundles of evaluation forms lay spread before him and his staff, each representing someone's son with a dream.

By tomorrow morning, twelve of those dreams would be officially deferred.

And of the twenty they kept, only half would play varsity.

He could almost hear the potential parent complaints, but as the head coach, the final decisions were his to make.

"Torres is still solid at shortstop." Devon slid a packet into the definite pile, then picked up another. "Henderson's good at second plus his bat speed improved over last year as a sophomore."

Zeke nodded, but his eyes returned to Timothy Miller's form.

The numbers didn't lie—inconsistent fielding percentage, throwing accuracy that varied wildly, batting mechanics that needed complete rebuilding. But there was something in the way the kid moved, an instinctive understanding of the game that couldn't be taught.

"What are you thinking about Miller?" Devon followed Zeke's gaze. "Overthrew first base twice, but he's got quick hands."

The fluorescent lights buzzed overhead as Zeke picked up Timothy's form again. "His fundamentals need work, but look at his reaction time. And his attitude—first to volunteer, last to complain."

"Agreed." Their pitching coach, Dave, jutted his chin toward the remaining players under debate. "You can teach the basic skills, but those intangibles are priceless."

Grant nodded. "As much as I'd love to have a kid like that in the outfield, given time he could grow into a game changer in the infield."

"Maybe, but I'm pretty stacked already." Devon raised an eyebrow. "Zeke, you showed interest in him during tryouts. Any particular reason to single him out?"

The question prickled Zeke's conscience.

Was he giving Timothy extra consideration because of one encounter with the boy's sister?

Zeke rubbed his jaw, feeling the day's stubble and fought for objectivity. "He's coachable. That matters more than natural talent sometimes. But I see potential. Raw, undeveloped potential."

The other three nodded.

Zeke returned the kid's evaluations to the tabletop. "Let's set him aside for the moment and look for the most obvious to cut."

Fifteen minutes later only three remained in the running.

The door opened with a squeak of hinges needing oil. Their athletic director entered, his heavy cologne arriving a second before he did.

"Had to come back and see how the roster is coming together." Vaughn pulled up a chair, its metal legs scraping across the linoleum.

"Down to the final decisions." Zeke resumed tapping his pen on the tabletop. "Should have it finalized in the next half hour."

He hoped.

"Well, how do you want to handle the announcements? Post a list on the website or make calls? I can have my secretary—"

"Absolutely not." Zeke sat up straight. "If anyone picks up the phone, it will be me. But there's no way on earth I'd ever get a kid's hopes up with a personal call only to dash them."

Vaughn shrugged. "Then only call the winners and text the others."

"Nope. Everyone who tried out this afternoon deserves equal treatment and respect, so like I told the boys earlier, I'll post a written list in the morning."

"Want me to make an announcement over the—?"

"No names. Just say that the team selections have been posted in the gym." Zeke waited for Vaughn's nod. "That settled, I'd like to get some information to the players before our first official practice."

Over the next few minutes, they debated a lunch meeting or basic handout to precede a parent meet-and-greet and worked out the logistics of assigning lockers and handing out uniforms.

Knowing not all the kids drove to school, Zeke fought for them to at least have a place to store their equipment the first day.

"Now that we've handled all that..." Vaughn's gaze fell onto the stacks of evaluations. "Who's left to decide on?"

"There's just Miller, Johnston, and Ramirez with two spots to fill." Devon pushed the remaining forms toward their collective boss. "All underclassmen. Johnston's father played minor league. Ramirez has the best arm of the three and might be a good relief pitcher."

Vaughn studied the sheets. "And Miller? What about him?"

"Loads of unpolished talent and an excellent attitude." The words burst from Zeke's lips and he glanced at the rest of his staff before tapping his pen again. "With coaching, he might become something remarkable."

At least the other coaches backed him up with grunts and head nods.

"Hmm." Vaughn raised an eyebrow. "If you want my opinion, it's always good to have guys who can also pitch. And a minor league player in the bleachers could help when it comes to fundraising."

The implication in Vaughn's tone was annoying at best.

Zeke let the pen drop and stared. "Not to minimize the minor leagues since I happen to know guys currently playing there..."

A phantom pain enveloped his shoulder, but he waited until he had Vaughn's full attention.

"We're basing today's decision on the actual players. On their athletic ability and contribution to the team. Nothing more. Not on their parents or any potential benefits they might bring to the program."

Advice he would do well to adopt when it came to a certain artistic redhead.

"Good." Vaughn shoved the evaluation forms to the center of the table and leaned back in his chair. "Just make sure we're being fair to all the boys. Wouldn't want anyone claiming favoritism down the line."

Zeke met his gaze steadily. "Every decision I will make is defensible based on skill and attitude. And that's a promise."

"Good to hear." Vaughn straightened his tie. "However, speaking of parents and potential benefits, did you get your staff to sign the updated fraternization policy? I need those ASAP."

"The what?" Devon's gaze bounced from Vaughn to Zeke and back.

"You only gave them to me a few hours ago. Tryouts ran a little long and we cleaned up in the dark then grabbed ourselves a bite to eat." Zeke reached into the briefcase near his feet and pulled out the folded forms he'd ignored in favor of the haphazard stack of evaluations.

"I despise excuses." Vaughn stood, frowning down at Zeke.

"You'll have them before we leave tonight. I promise."

Vaughn nodded. "And whatever players you pick will need current physicals on file, player contracts signed, and all fees paid by Monday or I'll cut them myself and promote a body from your reject list. Make Friday's parent meeting mandatory if you must."

"Heard." Zeke hid his clenched fists under the tabletop.

Seemed his boss was a bit of a control freak and might not have Zeke's back like he would have hoped.

"I trust you to make the right decisions here." Vaughn firmly clicked the door shut behind him, but his words left a heavy tension in the room.

Trust.

The word settled in Zeke's chest like a stone. His father had been the poster-child for untrustworthy, leaving a trail of broken promises. Which was why he vowed to be the opposite. Reliable. Principled.

Trustworthy.

A man worthy of respect. A man who kept his word.

Devon blew out a whistle. "What was that about?"

"Not sure. Well, except for the new policy I honestly forgot he handed me right before the first boys showed up today." Zeke passed them around. "Guess my predecessor's actions have resulted in tighter scrutiny and bigger consequences. We're supposed to sign saying that we've read it and agree."

He glanced at his own copy. "Looks like common sense stuff. Just avoid anything inappropriate and try to stay professional as much as you can."

Grant and Dave exchanged glances, but after a quick scan, both signed.

Devon read slowly, a grim expression settling over his face as he reached for a pen. "I had my suspicions last year and should have said something before it ended up costing the whole program. So, no offense to you Zeke, but I'm not going to make the same mistake again."

Dave grunted. "So now you're the morality police and our designated tattletale?"

Zeke held up his hands. "Enough. A little accountability never hurt anyone. And if we want to instill integrity in these boys, it starts with us. Agreed?"

He picked up his pen, pausing only for a moment before signing.

Fleeting attraction to a woman aside, he couldn't imagine any woman being worth risking his opportunity to mold and shape boys into ballplayers. And men.

With four signed forms ready to leave on Vaughn's desk, Zeke leaned back in his chair, the vinyl creaking as he exhaled slowly. "Now, all we need to do is finish this roster so I can get it typed up along with the handout."

Devon cracked his knuckles. "Then we can grab a beer to celebrate."

Zeke shook his head. "No beer for me, but I'm game for a Coke and nachos. I've got a good feeling about this season."

Grant nodded. "Same, coach."

Dave reached for one of the remaining three packets in the center of the table. "And we'll be stronger with Ramirez in our back pocket."

Zeke agreed.

Then there were two.

One with genuine potential to nurture and another with the athletic director in his corner.

The final decision was Zeke's to make.

And his to defend.

The numbers danced through Clarissa's mind with each plate she delivered, a mathematical rhythm that crescendoed alongside her anxiety.

Sixty-five dollars for baseball cleats. Eighty-five for registration fees. Forty for a practice jersey. And the same for new practice pants that actually fit after her brother's recent growth spurt.

Timothy's excitement last night about the team—a team he wasn't even on yet—had kept her awake long after her brothers fell asleep and her own assignments were done.

Except it wasn't anticipation that invaded her eventual dreams.

Just dread, along with its partners fear and worry, because their budget didn't have any wiggle room for extra expenses.

The bell chimed from the kitchen window, and the cafe's head chef Trevor slid more plates under the warming lights. A quick glance at the monitor revealed they were for a table in her section.

Clarissa balanced the meals on her arm, the weight grounding her in the present moment despite her wandering thoughts.

Every table served meant potential income to tip the financial scales.

Another reminder that working at the cafe had been a timely blessing even if it couldn't last forever.

The familiar scents of maple syrup and freshly brewed coffee enveloped her as she navigated between tables, delivering pancakes, eggs over easy, and a Denver omelet to a trio of retired regulars.

"Anything else I can get you?" She kept her smile professional. Friendly.

Roy's eyes crinkled with grandfatherly affection. "Just keep the coffee coming, sweetheart."

Clarissa nodded. The Great Minds Club—as Joel and Lauren liked to call them—would linger for another hour, debating and dissecting the local news.

At least they always tipped well.

Around her, the café hummed with Wednesday morning energy—spoons clinking against coffee mugs, snippets of conversation rising and falling, the cash register dinging as Joel rang up another customer, and sunlight streamed through the windows, catching dust motes in golden beams that warmed the checkerboard-tiled floors.

It was a place designed for the community to gather. And linger.

But only if the staff kept moving.

As Clarissa cleared a recently vacated table, her gaze fell on a discarded newspaper left open to the sports page. The headline "New Coach

Brings Collegiate Playing Experience to Loveland High" sat above a photograph that stopped her in her tracks.

Zeke Matthews stared back at her from the grainy newsprint, his expression serious yet somehow kind. Light hair, strong jaw, eyes that seemed to study her even from the flat surface of the paper.

The man she'd literally crashed into at the school—the man who treated her like a professional rather than another harried waitress or Timothy's stand-in parent.

The type of man who might star in her romantic dreams if it wasn't for the promise she'd made.

"Earth to Clarissa." Joel's voice broke through her reverie. He stood beside her, eyebrows raised in amusement. "That's the third time I've called your name."

Heat crept up her neck as she folded the newspaper and set it aside. "Sorry. Just cleaning up."

"Uh-huh." Joel's knowing look suggested he knew exactly what captured her attention. "But speaking of baseball, did you get our sponsorship form to the school on time?"

"I did." She busied herself wiping down the table to avoid his gaze. "Gave it to the coach himself."

"And Timothy's tryouts? You mentioned he was pretty nervous about them."

The memory of his animated face across their small dinner table brought a smile.

"He couldn't stop talking last night—said the drills were harder than he expected but that he thought he did okay. He's praying he'll see his name on the roster list later this morning." She glanced up at Joel. "Also told me like five times that 'Coach Matthews seemed really cool' and that he gave him some fielding tips."

Timothy hadn't known she had her own opinion of the coach.

A man who should have absolutely no place in her carefully organized life.

"Matthews, huh?" Joel gestured toward the folded newspaper. "The new guy is making quite the impression around town. One of my earlier customers was on the interview committee and said we were lucky he was available in the middle of the school year."

"Fascinating." Clarissa tried and failed to sound disinterested. "Oh, table five needs coffee."

As she moved toward the coffee station, a hollow feeling formed in her stomach—one that had nothing to do with missing breakfast.

If Timothy made the team, Coach Matthews would become a fixture in their lives. Meetings. Games. Practices. The prospect sent an unwelcome flutter through her chest while the financial implications triggered a chill down her spine.

The coffee pot trembled in her hand as she filled mugs, her exhaustion finally catching up with her.

Between her late-night study session and worries about baseball expenses, she'd fallen asleep mere hours before her alarm went off. Then she'd made the mistake of skipping breakfast in favor of a little graphic design work and had to rush to make it in time for the cafe's early morning prep shift.

Which meant she was operating on fumes and determination... and sips of watered-down soda from the cup tucked away behind the monitor.

"You okay?" Lauren appeared beside her, concern etched in her features. "You're looking a little pale."

"I'm fine. Just didn't sleep well."

Lauren gently took the pot from her hands. "Take five. I've got this."

"I don't need—"

"It wasn't a suggestion." Lauren's tone brooked no argument despite her smile. "Five minutes won't collapse the café, I promise."

Too tired to argue, Clarissa retreated to the office where she moved aside a box of old photos that used to grace the cafe's walls and sank onto one of the chairs in the corner. How many weary waitresses over the years found refuge around that same small table?

She closed her eyes for a second.

Timothy's voice echoed in her memory. "Coach showed me how to position my feet, Rissa! Said I have 'natural ability.' Do you think I might play college ball someday?"

The hope in his voice had been almost painful.

Their overworked mother had barely managed to get him to Little League games, often forgetting equipment or showing up halfway through. And it had only worsened after she'd gotten sick.

Now it seemed baseball meant even more to her brother. An escape? Or a connection to something greater than their cobbled-together family of three?

The door creaked open as Lauren entered with two steaming mugs. "Brought reinforcements."

She handed one to Clarissa.

The ceramic warmed Clarissa's fingers as she inhaled the rich aroma. "Thanks."

Lauren sat across from her. "So. Timothy might make the team."

"Mmm." Clarissa sipped her coffee, the bitter notes cutting through her fatigue. "Should find out soon."

"Under the very handsome new coach whose newspaper photo had you hypnotized while Joel tried to get your attention."

Clarissa nearly choked. "I was not hypnotized."

"Please." Lauren rolled her eyes. "I recognize that look. It's the same one I got every time Joel walked into a room before we started dating."

"It's not like that." Although the warmth in her cheeks suggested otherwise. "He might be Timothy's coach. Even if I had the time, I'm sure there are rules about those things."

"There are rules about a lot of things." Lauren shrugged. "But sometimes the rules don't account for real life."

The simple statement hung between them, loaded with Lauren's own experience of falling for her boss while trying to balance work as a waitress, family expectations, and personal dreams.

"Even if there weren't rules"—Clarissa stared into her coffee—"there's still reality. I have two teenage boys depending on me. Baseball equipment that will cost more than our weekly grocery budget. Graphic design clients I squeeze in between shifts and homework—both mine and theirs. I don't have room for..." She gestured vaguely, unable to name the flutter at seeing his photograph.

Lauren placed a hand on Clarissa's arm. "Juggling work and college and family is hard. But sometimes accepting help isn't a weakness. It's wisdom."

"I don't need help." Words she'd repeated to herself too many times to count. "I've managed fine so far."

Lauren's skeptical look spoke volumes. "The bags under your eyes suggest otherwise."

Clarissa drained the last of her coffee, then stood, eager to escape Lauren's too-perceptive gaze. "My break's over."

Lauren frowned. "I'm just saying there's no medal for martyrdom."

Back in the dining room, Clarissa slipped back into her familiar routine with mechanical efficiency. Take orders. Deliver food. Refill drinks. Smile.

At least until she caught sight of yet another discarded newspaper with Coach Zeke Matthews staring back from the page.

Her heart stuttered in her chest.

Everything in life had a cost. And ignoring her complicated emotions toward the man for her brother's sake might cost more than she had to give.

Any minute now she should hear if Timothy made the team, bringing him joy along with a slew of expenses. She'd need more design clients, which meant even less sleep, which meant more exhaustion, which meant no time for anything for herself.

Her shoulders drooped, but she shook her head.

Until the boys were grown, her family had to come first.

She'd promised.

Chapter Three

Clarissa's heart leapt at each ping from her phone—then plummeted when it was just another notification, another news alert, another anything-but-a-message-from-Timothy.

The roster should have been posted by now.

And the continued silence from her phone was deafening.

She tucked it back into her apron pocket and carried the dirty dishes from a cleared table to the designated tub under the counter, only to find it near to overflowing.

Well, any reason to stay busy.

She hoisted the load and pushed through the swinging door into the kitchen, stopping at the industrial dishwasher to sort plates, silverware, mugs, and glasses into the appropriate racks.

At the nearby prep counter, their resident baker and part-time waitress Greta sliced strawberries for their pie-of-the-day special. The knife's rhythmic thunk against the cutting board matched Clarissa's heartbeat.

"Checking that phone won't make it ring any faster." Greta swiped the strawberries into a bowl, then wiped the juice from her fingers onto a towel. "You've looked at it at least five times since you came in here."

"Have I?" Clarissa shoved her phone back into the apron pocket and turned to rinse the now-empty tub. "The roster will be posted this morning,"

"And?" Greta dusted the counter with flour and reached for a ball of dough.

"Timothy was so excited after tryouts..."

"But?" Greta's hands never stopped their practiced motions as she wielded the rolling pin.

"But baseball is expensive." The words tumbled out. "Cleats, jerseys, equipment fees. Not to mention the time commitment—practices every day, games on weekends. I want him to make it—he needs this—but I'm not sure how we'll manage."

Greta nodded, understanding softening her features. "I remember my brother complaining when Joel was younger. But there were dreams in his eyes and determination in that boy's swing. And later the same focus on football."

No wonder the cafe sponsored a sports team.

Clarissa hadn't worked with Joel's dad Frank before, but met him on several occasions. Enough to know the man liked to grumble and complain with the best of them. "So if it was hard, how did they make it work? Or justify the sacrifice?"

Greta paused, dusting more flour across the steel surface. "Trust me when I say, like my mother Hope used to say, some expenses pay dividends you can't measure in dollars."

"I know." Clarissa sighed, the sweet aroma of baking pies from the oven providing momentary comfort. "It's just—"

Her phone vibrated against her hip, the sensation like an electric jolt through her body. She wiped her hands on her apron and pulled it out, heart in her throat.

RISSA I MADE THE TEAM!!!

Relief and anxiety collided in her chest as she read Timothy's message. Joy for his accomplishment warred with the more practical calculations of the cost and logistics.

"Good news?" Greta's knowing smile suggested she'd already guessed.

"He made it." Clarissa smiled despite her concerns. "He actually made it."

"Of course he did," Greta replied matter-of-factly. "Not to say he doesn't have any natural talent, but if he's anything like you, that boy will do whatever he sets his mind to do."

"True." Which would be either good or bad as they navigated high school together.

Oh, God help me raise him right.

The ding of Trevor's bell broke into her thoughts. How long had she been lingering in the kitchen while her customers waited on food or coffee?

Clarissa grabbed the empty tub, nodded a goodbye to Greta, and retreated.

Back in the dining room, she moved between tables, delivering plates and refilling cups while her mind spun with adjustments that morphed from theoretical to reality.

They'd have to rearrange their after-school schedule. Find carpooling options. Budget for equipment immediately.

The bell above the door chimed as the mid-morning crowd trickled in. The familiar scents of coffee and bacon grounded her, but her thoughts remained divided between present tasks and future challenges.

Her phone buzzed again as she cleared a recently vacated table.

Coach handed out an equipment list. Need cleats that fit, gray practice pants (L), cup (TMI sorry), and maybe batting gloves. Can we go shopping after school? First practice tomorrow!!!

Clarissa bit her lip, tallying costs in her head. She'd been saving for Brian's new glasses, but that could wait for another paycheck. Maybe.

Or perhaps Saturday's rare extra shift would be a timely blessing. Unless Timothy had practice, and she also needed to pay someone to watch Brian...

"Table six needs coffee." Lauren passed by with a loaded tray.

"Right. Sorry." Clarissa grabbed the pot, moving toward a table she'd already visited twice this morning. Her usual focused efficiency had abandoned her.

On her return, she almost collided with Matt Simpson as he approached the counter from the area where the restrooms were, his tall frame blocking her path.

"Whoa there." He steadied her with a carpenter's calloused hand. The scent of sawdust and varnish clung to his flannel shirt. "You okay, Clarissa?"

"Fine." She clutched the still-warm coffee pot to her chest. "Just distracted."

Matt squeezed onto a stool beside Clay, another cafe regular, continuing what appeared to be an ongoing conversation with Joel about house restoration. His deep voice carried in the café's relaxed atmosphere.

"The original woodwork beside the staircase is salvageable, but it'll take time." He took a swig from his mug, then swiped a hand over his beard. "And your grandmother's buffet is coming along too. Those hidden compartments were tricky, but I should have it restored in a few weeks."

Clarissa swapped out the pots and moved to refill cups at the counter, her mind still on baseball expenses.

A month of additional graphic design work would cover all the basic equipment and fees plus Brian's glasses, but where would she find the time between shifts at the cafe, her final school projects, and her brothers' needs?

"Earth to Clarissa." Clay's gentle voice broke through her thoughts. "You just poured coffee into my water."

She looked down and gasped as dark liquid overflowed the ice water, spreading across the counter in a steaming puddle. "I'm so sorry!"

"No harm done." He used his napkin to stop the spread.

Embarrassment heated her cheeks as she set the pot aside and lurched to grab a cleaning rag.

Clay's eyes crinkled beneath his wire-rimmed glasses. "You seem a million miles away today."

"Timothy made his high school baseball team." She paused in mopping up the spill. "So I'm trying to figure out the logistics."

"Ah, baseball. America's expensive pastime." Clay nodded. "I swear my nephew's cleats cost more than my first car."

The small joke lightened her mood. "Tell me about it. I'm looking at a hefty shopping list before tomorrow's practice."

"Speaking of lists..." Clay's tone shifted to something more businesslike. "I saw your graphic design package in the fundraising auction next door and wanted to ask about it. Because my website hasn't been updated in almost forever. My youngest sister keeps telling me I need to 'get with the times' if I want to compete with the big box repair places."

Clarissa fetched Clay a fresh water glass, hope flickering to life. "I can help with that. Are you bidding in the auction or asking outright?"

Because while she'd do the work either way, only one would put money in her pocket. Why on earth had she volunteered to donate the proceeds, even if it was for a good cause?

"I'd rather help Frank by buying more of Greta's pie." He patted his stomach and grinned. "Which means I'm more than willing to pay your going rate."

Relief washed over her at the prospect of true income no matter the extra demands on her time. But still. "I can offer a friends-and-family discount..."

"Perhaps. But we can discuss the specifics later." Clay pulled out his wallet, extracting a hundred-dollar bill and a business card with his contact information. "Consider this a deposit."

"Clay, I can't—"

"You can and will." His tone brooked no argument. "My business needs this website. Your brother needs baseball equipment. Everybody wins."

Her throat tightened. The hundred wouldn't cover everything, but it would make today's shopping trip possible.

"Thank you." She swallowed hard as she tucked the money into her apron pocket.

"Just make me look good online." He winked, then lifted his half-empty coffee cup for a refill. "By the way, saw the picture of the new coach in the paper. Handsome fella. Single too, according to one of the town busybodies in my shop first thing this morning."

Heat rushed to Clarissa's cheeks. "He's Timothy's coach. There have to be rules about those things."

"Rules." Clay chuckled, shaking his head. "Life's too short for some of those, trust me."

Before she could respond, her phone vibrated again.

Oh yeah, there's a mandatory parent meeting Friday night at seven. Coach says no exceptions. I've got a study group so you'll need to get a babysitter for Brian.

Clarissa closed her eyes, adding another item to her mental checklist.

Another expense.

Another complication.

Although seeing Coach Matthews again wouldn't be a hardship.

The newspaper photo might have captured his strong jawline and a hint of a smile, but she still recalled the warmth in his blue eyes when he saw her scattered sketches in the school's hallway.

The admiration?

No.

She pushed the thought away.

Baseball season would be long enough without indulging inappropriate attractions to Timothy's coach. Keeping a professional distance would be essential—for Timothy's sake, for her sanity, and for the carefully balanced life she'd constructed.

Now if only her racing heart would get the memo.

And so it began.

Thursday afternoon, Zeke waited for the members of his newly-formed team as they jostled through the gate onto the field. "Drop your equipment in the dugout for now and join me at home plate."

Twenty eager teenagers buzzed with excitement as they gathered on the grass.

"Take a knee for a few announcements." Zeke pitched his voice to carry without shouting and the chatter died down immediately—a good sign of respect. "Congratulations, gentlemen. You're here because you demonstrated skill, potential, and the right attitude. Now the real work begins."

He surveyed their faces, committing each to memory. In the front row, Timothy Miller's lanky frame almost vibrated. The kid hadn't stopped grinning since he arrived.

"First things first." Zeke waved for his assistant coaches to distribute the papers he'd printed earlier. "You already received an equipment list and details for tomorrow's mandatory parent meeting. This is the rest of the season's schedule, at least as of today. Including our first game on Tuesday. If we have to reschedule any games due to weather or field conditions, I'll pass along the information as soon as I have it."

In college, he'd been spoiled with a lot of sunshine. But here in Colorado it was as likely to snow in the spring as rain. Even into May.

Zeke held up his own copy as the players began to scan the pages. "Your parents will get a similar handout tomorrow night, but I'm giving you the sneak peek. Because if you don't think you can make the commitment, I need to know now. There are a dozen others happy to take your place."

A couple of the older boys rolled their eyes, but most looked horrified at the possibility. Good.

Zeke nodded. "You'll see that unless we have a game scheduled, practices are every weekday after school, three to five. Saturday mornings, ten to noon. Missing practice could see you on the bench for a game."

On that note, he continued with his prepared speech, emphasizing the values he sought to teach through the game of baseball.

Values that were a complete opposite from his alcoholic father's destructive pattern. Values his mother had sacrificed to instill.

Noticing a few squirms and switching off the knee stance, Zeke folded the handout and stowed it in the inside pocket of his unzipped jacket. "A couple more things before we get to work. While I'm glad for the returning experience on our roster, playing time on varsity is up for grabs. And not only for the first games."

The murmurs began and Zeke held up a hand, waiting for silence. "I expect everyone to give me their best effort all the time. Consider junior varsity like the minor leagues. Work hard and you may get called up to contribute on varsity. Get injured, hit a lingering slump, or violate a team rule and know that someone might take your place for awhile."

He paused to make pointed eye contact again. "We'll use the next few days of practice to continue our evaluations and announce the starting lineups for Tuesday's games on Monday. But know this. I will always play who I believe is the best player for the situation and the good of the team. Understood?"

While some might see the competition for positions as unhealthy, he firmly believed that the team came first. And if some needed an added incentive—or the threat of a demotion—to inspire the necessary work, so be it.

Zeke clapped his hands once. "Now, let's see what you've got. Put your schedules in your bags and grab your gloves. Infielders with Coach Devon by second base. Outfielders with Coach Dave. Pitchers and catchers with Coach Grant."

They'd run their various warm-ups and drills for a bit, then start rotating through for batting practice. Hopefully by Saturday, they'd be able to add a combination hitting and fielding drill to get everyone involved and playing together as a team.

Except Zeke also needed to set aside time to go over base-running, signals, and strategy.

So much to do, but at least for now there was comfort in the familiar.

For the next hour and a half, his staff drilled the players on their fundamentals and Zeke's voice grew hoarse from delivering constant instruction and encouragement.

However, the crisp slap of balls hitting gloves, the grunts of effort as players stretched for difficult catches, and the occasional outburst of laughter when someone slipped on the dewy grass formed the soundtrack he'd missed.

At the conclusion of practice, he assigned the boys different tasks for field and equipment maintenance. With everyone pitching in, the necessary work was accomplished quickly with pride in a job well done.

Once dismissed for the day, most of the boys departed in clusters, voices loud with post-practice analysis and good-natured ribbing.

Timothy, however, lingered by the fence with his battered equipment bag.

"Need something, Miller?" Zeke kept his tone neutral as he tucked his clipboard and glove into his satchel.

The teen straightened his slim shoulders. "Oh. Um, yes, sir. I wondered about the equipment list and the fees."

"What about it?"

"Is all of it absolutely required?" Timothy shifted his weight, gaze dropping to the dirt where he traced patterns with the toe of his worn sneaker. "I mean, I've got the basic stuff to get me by for a while, but I saw other guys have their own bats and helmets. Do I need those, too?"

The hesitant question transported Zeke back a dozen years, to his own awkward conversations with a coach. The familiar shame of inadequate equipment, the dread of asking his mom for money they didn't have.

"The basics on the list are non-negotiable." Zeke paused, noting the tightening around the kid's eyes. "The rest you mentioned is optional. Everyone is welcome to use the team's helmets and bats."

Relief softened Timothy's features. "That helps. Thank you. It's just that my sister works really hard. I hate being another expense."

The simple loyalty in that statement tugged at something in Zeke's chest.

His instinct was to offer more, like the equipment stored in his garage from his own playing days. But as much as he longed to fill in the gaps for the fatherless, the fraternization policy loomed in his mind like a high fence.

Then he recalled something from the school handbook.

Zeke shouldered his bag and stepped closer, lowering his voice. "I believe the school also has resources to help with fees if that's a concern. Talk to the counseling office and I'm sure they can connect you discreetly."

At least he hoped so.

"Right. Thanks, Coach." Relief washed over Timothy's face. "My ride is probably waiting. See you tomorrow!"

Zeke watched him jog away, his equipment bag bouncing against his back.

A bag that had seen better days.

The baseball sketches from Clarissa's fallen portfolio flashed in his mind. Not only had her brother been playing for awhile, he clearly loved the game.

A unique image like those she'd drawn would be perfect on a team shirt sold as a fundraiser. Much better than a generic school logo.

The team needed to raise money. The booster club would need a quality design. And Clarissa needed money to provide Timothy with better equipment.

A legitimate business arrangement would solve all three problems at once. In fact, he'd make sure the booster club signed an official contract for the design work. That would help the Millers without having it feel like charity.

It would be completely above-board. Professional. Appropriate.

The side-effect of giving him another reason to interact with her was merely... coincidental.

Only for the sake of the kid and keeping Timothy on the team.

Zeke shook his head at his own rationalization. He needed to be honest with himself.

Following behind to ensure all his players departed safely, he rounded the corner of the field house.

In the parking lot, an older sedan idled near the curb, its faded blue paint catching the dwindling sunlight. His steps slowed as he recognized

Clarissa in the driver's seat, her head resting against the window while she waited.

From this distance, he saw the exhaustion in her posture—shoulders slumped, eyes closed before Timothy's approach startled her awake.

Zeke stopped when Clarissa got out of the car, her smile for her brother transforming her entire face. Meanwhile, Timothy's hands were flying in wild gestures as he talked.

His sister nodded, her attention focused on her brother despite the dark circles under her eyes.

Something twisted in Zeke's chest—a feeling that defied the neat categorization he preferred in his life. It wasn't mere attraction, though that remained an undercurrent he couldn't deny.

It was recognition. Respect.

The visceral understanding of what it meant to put someone else's needs and dreams above your own.

His mother had done that for him after his father left—worked double shifts to pay for his baseball equipment, fallen asleep in the car between her jobs, and still made time to listen to his excited recounting of games and practices.

Within a minute, Timothy tossed his baseball bag and a backpack into the truck and climbed into the driver's seat while Clarissa moved around to the passenger's side.

He guessed the teen had his permit and was racking up the required hours for his license. A fact reinforced by a few more gestures and the boy adjusting the mirrors before fastening his seatbelt and starting the engine.

Something else he remembered his mother doing while scrimping still more to help him buy his first car.

Zeke grinned. The rusty mess had been held together by more duct tape than he cared to recall, but still his. His to drive. And his to maintain.

He frowned. Was there someone in Clarissa's life able to teach the kid basic automotive maintenance?

As the Millers drove away, temptation to volunteer loomed.

God might be a father to the fatherless and a defender of widows or single mothers. But Zeke's hands were tied by the school's policy.

Any other involvement was too risky.

Chapter Four

Clarissa pulled into a space in Loveland High's parking lot, her ancient sedan protesting with a concerning rattle as she cut the engine. The dashboard clock glowed 7:08 in green digits that accused.

Late. Again.

Yet another sign she was falling short as a guardian.

She grabbed her notebook from the passenger seat and hurried toward the front door. Only to find signs pointing her around the building to the gymnasium entrance instead.

She picked up the pace, her feet crunching on leftover winter gravel as she rehearsed apologies for her tardiness.

The client call that should have taken fifteen minutes had stretched to forty-five, the man insisting on "just one more small change" to his website design. By the time she'd ended the conversation, modified the mock-up, and sent the revised files, she'd been out of time to fix dinner.

Meaning she'd had to ask Brian's babysitter to pick up something on her way, then used more of her precious cash at a drive-through to feed Timothy before dropping him off for his study group.

With no time—or money—left to feed herself.

At least she'd make up some of the deficit at the cafe tomorrow.

The heavy gymnasium door groaned as she eased it open, the sound drawing several heads in her direction. The cavernous space held a couple dozen parents seated in folding chairs facing a projection screen. Fluorescent lights buzzed overhead, casting everyone in the same unflattering pallor.

At the front, Coach Matthews stood with a clipboard in hand, his deep voice carrying through the room. "Discipline builds character. Character determines destiny. This isn't just about baseball. It's about developing young men."

Clarissa slipped into an empty chair in the back row, heat climbing her neck at the curious glances from nearby parents.

Coach Matthews continued without acknowledging the interruption, though she'd thought his gaze flickered in her direction.

In his red polo and khakis, Zeke Matthews cut an imposing figure, his shoulders squared with quiet confidence as he outlined the season's expectations.

"We have three core team values." He clicked over to a new slide. "Respect. Responsibility. Resilience."

Clarissa took notes as he elaborated on each value, finding herself unexpectedly moved by his passion. This wasn't rehearsed coach-speak. He truly believed in baseball's power to shape these boys' futures.

"Many of these young men will never play beyond high school. And for those who do, life has a crazy way of changing course." Zeke's tone softened. "But the discipline they learn here—showing up prepared, respecting authority, pushing through difficulty—those traits will serve them their entire lives."

The words settled in Clarissa's chest with surprising weight.

Wasn't that what she wanted for Timothy? Not just athletic skill, but the kind of character that would help him navigate life's complexities better than she could teach him alone?

She found herself studying Zeke. He wasn't just Timothy's baseball coach. He was a man who took his role in shaping young lives seriously.

"You have my word that all of my decisions will be made for the best of the team as a whole. That's why—like I told the players yesterday—the varsity and junior varsity rosters may be adjusted throughout the season for things like injuries, slumps, or even attitude."

The coach's words triggered a wave of murmurs that he ignored.

"Now that you've gotten to know the staff and my vision, let's move on to the necessary paperwork." He curled a sheet of paper over the top of his clipboard and referred to whatever lay beneath before advancing the slide.

"If your son did not play a fall or winter sport, they'll need a current physical on file before Monday. As well as their sports fee paid."

Between Timothy's football season—shortened abruptly by their mother's terminal illness—and the school's hardship scholarship he'd texted her about over lunch, at least they met those two requirements.

Charity left a sour taste in her mouth.

"You'll find another copy of our game schedule and travel expectations in your packet. Also make sure you got checked in on the attendance sheet before you leave and you can turn in your signed parent agreement at the same time."

Packet? Parent agreement?

Clarissa glanced at the closest parents to see they each held a stapled stack of papers.

Something they must have received when they arrived. Something she'd also have in hand if only she hadn't been late.

Her stomach chose that moment to remind her of a missed meal and she pressed a hand over her midsection as if that would quiet the rumbling.

"One last topic before we break into groups to get to know your son's position coach better. And I have to admit, I hate fundraising as much as paperwork since I'd much rather be playing ball."

Zeke waited for the crowd's laughter to fade, then clicked to a new slide. "As a staff, we've created a wishlist including an indoor batting cage to use in inclement weather, matching jackets for travel days, and a few other things as you can see here."

He scanned the room. "I understand we've got a booster club that I'm hoping to talk into helping host a youth skills camp as well as selling some team merchandise. I'd like to see a custom design that captures our team spirit. Something unique rather than the standard school logo."

A murmur of approval rippled through the parents.

Clarissa made a note, already wondering how to fit one or more special shirts into their budget. Because Timothy needed to match his teammates. And she and Brian could hardly show up to cheer for a game without one.

A woman on the second row raised a manicured hand, a gem-encrusted watch sparkling on her wrist.

"Yes, Mrs. Henderson?" Zeke acknowledged the woman with a nod.

Henderson. Clarissa recognized the name as that of a veteran player Timothy had mentioned several times already.

"As booster club president, I've called a meeting for Tuesday morning." The woman's haughty tone rubbed Clarissa the wrong way. "You should join us to discuss your ideas."

"Thank you. I'll see what I can do to make that work and hope to have a potential design or two to show you by then." Zeke's gaze swept Clarissa's direction before scanning the rest of the parents. "With that out of the way, let's break up by position. And make sure to turn in your forms to the position coach before you leave tonight. Now, Coach Grant will be to my left, Coach Dave..."

Forms. Right. She would do that.

As soon as she figured out where they were.

She craned her neck around the crowd, looking for a check-in table. Or a stack of papers on a nearby bleacher.

Around her, parents rose and began shuffling to various areas in the room. Clarissa hesitated, suddenly aware of her ignorance. She'd been so busy looking for the missing paperwork that she missed the announcement of where she was supposed to go.

Assuming she knew which coach to find having arrived after the staff introductions.

Tears pricked her eyes at yet another failure.

A woman who'd been seated in the row ahead, glanced back at Clarissa with raised eyebrows. "Are you not joining a group?"

"I will. In a minute. I..." What could she say that wouldn't reveal her cluelessness?

"Or do you like being late to things?" The woman slipped a designer handbag over her wrist, her voice rising until several others nearby turned to look. "Parents—or guardians—should set a proper example at home."

Clarissa blinked in shock.

The busybody huffed, then scooted out the end of her row. "Karen! Wait for me."

Her friend—a brunette with perfect highlights—stopped and glanced back at Clarissa and her casual wardrobe. "Who's that?"

She'd recognize the booster club mom's grating voice anywhere, and now she had a full name. Karen Henderson.

The first woman leaned toward her friend. "With that hair, she's gotta be Timothy Miller's sister. And his guardian, from what I heard."

Karen adopted a sympathetic expression that didn't reach her eyes as they drifted further away, her voice fading.

But not before Clarissa caught something about absent parents and the lack of a father figure.

Shame burned through her chest, followed by anger. Just who did these women think they were?

"Ms. Miller." Zeke stood at her elbow, clipboard in hand. "A word, please?"

Without waiting for a response, he guided her toward a quieter corner of the gymnasium. The scent of his cologne—subtle cedar and something clean she couldn't name—distracted her from her embarrassment.

He handed her a stapled packet and checked something off another list.

Guess that took care of two worries at once.

She found a smile. "Thank you."

"Timothy has excellent instincts for a second baseman, even if his double-play technique needs some refinement. Coach Devon has been impressed." Zeke jerked his head toward the group finding seats on bleachers to her right.

Gratitude washed over her. He'd rescued her from both awkwardness and ignorance in one smooth move.

Something flickered in Zeke's eyes, and he lowered his voice. "Speaking of Timothy, I got confirmation from the office that his fee has been taken care of."

Heat flooded her face, and Clarissa straightened. "We appreciate all you have done, but I should be able to handle the rest since I've lined up some additional work."

An awkward silence stretched between them, filled with things that couldn't be said in this context—her awareness of his kindness, his apparent understanding of her struggle, the strange current that flowed despite their efforts to maintain formality.

It was a complicated tangle of emotions she had no business feeling.

Gratitude. Respect.

And something warmer she refused to name.

Becoming aware of both their proximity and the stalled conversation, Clarissa took a step back. "Thank you, again. Timothy's lucky to have you as his coach."

"The team is lucky to have him." He held her gaze a moment longer than necessary. "And he's fortunate to have such dedicated support at home."

The simple acknowledgment of her efforts—so at odds with the judgmental whispers from the other mothers—caught her off guard.

Zeke turned and strode away toward a different group of waiting parents. Reminding her that she needed to do the same.

She slid onto a bench in the bleachers, mere moments before Timothy's coach called the infielder's meeting to order. Ignoring the dirty looks from the queen bee Karen and her swarm of followers, Clarissa opened to a new page in her notebook.

She might not know all the baseball terminology or have the right clothes or enough hours in her day. But she would learn.

For Timothy's sake.

And perhaps, just a little, to prove to a certain coach that his faith in her dedication wasn't misplaced.

So far, his first parent meeting had gone better than expected. And with the first position groups starting to disperse, Zeke couldn't wait to get home.

It had been a long week learning to juggle his teaching and coaching responsibilities. It would get easier with time and experience, but that didn't change the fact he wanted nothing more than to put his feet up and catch a game on television.

Except across the gymnasium, Devon's infield group was still going strong.

Zeke's attention drifted to Clarissa Miller who sat slightly apart from the rest.

Unlike the other parents who checked watches or scrolled on their phones, she was absorbing every word—her posture attentive as she scribbled notes in a worn spiral.

A notebook that looked as tired as the exhaustion etched in the shadows beneath her eyes.

Her casual jeans and a T-shirt stood in sharp contrast to the fashionable attire of several mothers or the suits of fathers who'd come straight from work. Her hair in a messy bun only reinforced the youthful impression.

A scorn-filled impression he'd overheard earlier, courtesy of two gossiping mothers.

"She looks like she should be in high school herself, not raising two boys. No wonder the Miller boy seems...rough around the edges."

Karen Henderson's sanctimonious tone had set his teeth on edge. But unfortunately he'd need to appease the woman's sense of entitlement if he wanted the booster club's support.

However, her words had triggered a memory so vivid Zeke could almost smell his childhood kitchen—dish soap and burnt toast, his mother's drugstore perfume as she hurried to get him to Little League practice after her second shift.

Followed by the whispers from other parents when she showed up in her waitress uniform, too tired to pretend she had the energy to bake cookies or coordinate carpools but determined that her son would have every opportunity despite their circumstances.

Clarissa reminded him of his mother in ways that made his chest ache—the same quiet determination, the same dignity in the face of challenges, the same fierce prioritization of her child no matter the personal cost.

"Coach Matthews?" A parent's question pulled him back to the present. "About the away game schedule..."

For the next fifteen minutes, Zeke fielded questions about uniforms, transportation, and the myriad minutiae of baseball season. All the while, his awareness of Clarissa remained, like a knuckle ball finding the strike zone.

She finished with Devon's group and now waited on the periphery, clearly hoping to speak with him but unwilling to interrupt.

When the last parent finally moved away, she approached, her notebook clutched against her chest.

"Ms. Miller." He kept his tone neutral despite the inexplicable acceleration of his pulse.

Her smile was tentative but genuine. "I do have a few logistical concerns that weren't covered in the group."

The gymnasium had emptied considerably, their voices now carrying in the cavernous space. The distant squeak of the janitor's cart echoed from the hallway.

"Of course." Zeke gestured to a nearby bench. "It'd been a long day and I'd love to get off my feet. What can I help with?"

She remained standing, her fingers nervously tapping against the spiral binding of her notebook. "The Saturday practices. They're mandatory?"

"They are. Especially for building team cohesion."

"I see." She made another note, her handwriting small and precise. "And there's no flexibility? I sometimes have to work Saturday mornings—like tomorrow—and Brian—our younger brother—has his own activities."

The conflict in her expression was clear—wanting to support Timothy while struggling with the logistics of a single guardian's limited time and resources.

"The schedule is firm, but players don't need supervision during regular practices. Just transportation."

She nodded, jotting something else down. "About that, the information packet mentions early dismissal for away games?"

"The team travels together by bus." Why hadn't those details been explained in Devon's group? Or had she been too intimidated to ask in front of a veteran mom like Karen? "Players are excused from their afternoon classes but responsible for making up missed work."

Relief softened her features. "That helps. One less problem to solve."

"You're juggling quite a few." He couldn't stop the observation.

Her gaze snapped to his, surprise evident in her widened eyes—green with flecks of amber. Why did that detail seem important?

"We manage." Her voice carried a quiet pride that reminded him again of his mother. "Timothy's really good about helping with Brian, and my café schedule is consistent during school hours."

She consulted her notes. "And the team dinners? The packet mentioned pregame meals..."

"The booster club handles those," Zeke said. "Parents can contribute either food or a small donation, but it's optional."

The gymnasium's industrial heating system kicked on with a mechanical groan, sending a rush of warm air through the space and blowing around wisps of Clarissa's auburn hair that escaped the confines of her bun.

She tucked a strand behind her ear, the simple gesture drawing his eyes to the delicate curve of her neck.

Dangerous territory, Matthews.

"One last question," she said. "About practice jerseys—Timothy mentioned they need to bring cash for those tomorrow?"

The perfect opening to present his idea.

Zeke leaned forward, his voice lowering. "Actually, I wanted to talk to you about something related to team merchandise—"

Movement near the entrance caught his attention. Assistant Principal Vaughn stood watching them, arms crossed and eyebrows raised.

The comfortable rhythm of their conversation faltered. Zeke took an instinctive step backward, suddenly aware of how they must appear—alone in the nearly empty gymnasium, standing closer than was necessary.

"However, it's getting late. If you have additional questions, Ms. Miller, I'd recommend emailing them." He shifted to a formal tone that sounded harsh even to his own ears. "My address is in the packet and we hope to keep team communication primarily electronic to respect everyone's time."

Confusion flickered across her face. "I understand. Thank you for clarifying the—"

"Coach Matthews." Vaughn's voice boomed as he approached. "Productive meeting?"

"Very." Zeke took another step away from Clarissa. "Just answering some final questions."

Vaughn's gaze moved between them with thinly veiled speculation. "Ms. Miller, isn't it? Timothy's guardian?"

"Yes." Clarissa extended her hand with a polite smile that didn't reach her eyes. "Nice to meet you, Mr...?"

"Vaughn. I'm the athletic director and an assistant principal." He shook her hand. "Coach Matthews comes to us highly recommended. Timothy's in good hands."

"So I'm learning." She tucked her notebook into her bag. "I should be going. I need to pick up Timothy from his study group and then pay the babysitter. For Brian, so I could be here tonight."

"Of course," Vaughn said with practiced sympathy. "Guardianship must be quite the challenge, especially at your age."

The comment, though innocuous, carried an undercurrent that made Zeke's jaw tighten.

Clarissa's spine straightened.

"We manage." She turned to Zeke. "Thank you for your time, Coach Matthews. I appreciate your thoroughness in answering my questions."

"My pleasure, Ms. Miller." The words tasted like clay in his mouth.

She nodded once, then walked toward the exit, her footsteps echoing in the space. Zeke watched her go, aware of Vaughn's scrutiny beside him.

"Dedicated guardian," Vaughn said as the door closed behind her. "Quite attractive too. Single, I assume?"

The casual question carried a trap that Zeke recognized immediately.

"I wouldn't know." He moved away to disconnect his laptop from the projector and stow everything away.

"Really?" Vaughn's tone suggested disbelief. "I thought I detected. ..interest."

"As you pointed out, Ms. Miller is Timothy's guardian." The phrase was turning into a flimsy shield. "Any interest I may have in supporting a players' home environment is so they can then focus on the game. That's coaching 101."

"Of course." Vaughn's smile didn't reach his eyes. "Just remember how easily professional interest can be misinterpreted. Or lead to gray areas and a slippery slope. Coach Brenner learned that lesson the hard way."

The inference hung between them, impossible to ignore.

"You've made the school policy abundantly clear." Zeke kept his voice steady despite the discomfort crawling up his spine.

He zipped his satchel closed, hoping to also close the conversation.

"I hadn't been worried about you falling for any of the moms, but a guardian about your age is another story. So, stick to your principles and don't disappoint me." Vaughn clapped him on the shoulder, before walking away.

Zeke clenched his fingers around the handle of his bag.

He should never have stepped in when Karen Henderson made those comments about Timothy's absent parents. Should have directed Clarissa back to Devon for all her questions. Should have maintained more physical distance during their conversation.

And worse, he'd missed his opportunity to ask about the T-shirt designs. The one legitimately professional reason he'd had to speak with her privately. Now he'd need to find another way to approach her about the fundraiser, something that wouldn't trigger Vaughn's suspicions or violate his own boundaries.

Perhaps email, as he'd suggested. Impersonal. Professional. Safe.

Yet as he walked toward the dark parking lot, the memory of her quietly determined "we manage" followed him.

His mom had managed, too.

Until she hadn't.

Chapter Five

Saturday morning at Hope's Café felt wrong.

The light hit differently—brighter and more insistent through the windows. The customers moved at a different pace—lingering over their meals rather than rushing to work.

Even the interactions of the staff sounded off without Joel's baritone voice calling out the kind of reminders that triggered Lauren's answering laugh from behind the counter.

Clarissa balanced three plates along her arm, the action a poor distraction from the fact that while the extra income was a blessing—and she was happy to pitch in when asked—she still wished she were somewhere else.

Saturdays were supposed to be for Timothy and Brian—grocery shopping, laundry, catching up on her college coursework and design clients.

Instead, she was here, covering for Joel and watching the clock tick toward Timothy's ten o'clock practice that she'd need to leave for by nine-thirty.

Trevor slid another plate through the pass-through window and tapped the bell.

"I've got it." Monica's teenage exuberance was both refreshing and exhausting as she bounded past.

Kitchen helper Debbie's daughter worked the weekend shifts as a waitress in Clarissa's place, and her son was on dish duty, making today's overlap another jarring note in an already off-key morning.

For a moment, the aroma of country gravy and freshly-baked biscuits grounded her in the familiar.

And then she caught a glimpse of Lauren leading a young woman with a small child on her hip toward the office. The "Help Wanted" sign that had appeared in the window last week was gripped in Lauren's hand.

A spasm of anxiety tightened Clarissa's chest. They were already hiring her replacement, even though she'd told them she wouldn't leave until summer.

What if the new person trained quickly? Would they cut her hours? The life insurance policy might have paid off the mortgage on the tiny house she shared with her brothers, but the rest of their budget required every penny she could scrape together.

"You look like you've seen a ghost." Greta paused beside her with a half-filled pot of coffee. "Everything okay?"

"Just busy." Clarissa transferred the plates from her arm to table seven.

"It's nice seeing you on a Saturday." Greta followed her back toward the counter. "Though it feels strange being out here instead of in the kitchen."

"I heard Frank's coming back on Monday." Thank God for the change in subject. "Doctor cleared him?"

Greta's face brightened, the fine lines around her eyes crinkling with genuine happiness. "Part-time only like we'd discussed, but yes. He's going stir-crazy at home, driving my sister-in-law crazy, herself."

"Speaking of changes, I'll bet Clay will be thrilled for you to be back out here." Clarissa grinned.

"That man's been proposing to me for years." Greta laughed, the silver streaks of her hair catching the light. "He can wait until Tuesday for his weekly rejection."

The familiar teasing loosened some of the tension. Maybe this weekend shift wasn't entirely foreign territory after all.

"Where is Joel?" A customer at the counter accepted his check from Monica. "Never known him to miss a Saturday."

"Consulting work of some kind for Mr. Graham." Monica laid a small flyer alongside the check. "Lauren's dad realized his future son-in-law has an MBA for a reason."

Clarissa grinned. Joel's pursuit of creative ways to repay the diner loan faster had led to extra cash in her pocket, too. In fact, thanks to the breakfast crowd, she had enough from tips to pay for Timothy's practice jersey on time, after all.

The customer glanced at the colorful flyer. "What's this?"

"A reminder about the bake sale and silent auction happening next door," Monica said. "Proceeds go to help with Frank's medical expenses. So you'd better hop to it."

Clarissa rolled her eyes at the girl's joke. With Easter tomorrow, there'd been enough egg puns to last another year.

And yet, the fundraiser was just another example of how the Hope's Cafe community took care of their own. And like today's extra shift, she did her part.

Hopefully whoever won her donated image package would point additional clients—paying clients—in her direction.

The bell above the door clattered and Clarissa glanced up, the friendly greeting freezing on her lips as Zeke Matthews walked in, followed by his assistant Devon.

They chose a booth along the windows—prime real estate during the breakfast rush, and definitely in her section.

"You've got to be kidding me," she muttered under her breath.

"What was that?" Greta followed her gaze to where they pulled menus from the condiment rack.

"Timothy's coach." As if that explained everything.

"And that stops him from needing to eat?" Greta's smile held too much understanding for comfort. "Better not keep him waiting."

Clarissa grabbed her order pad and the coffee pot, taking a steadying breath as she approached the booth.

Zeke glanced up from his menu, a smile flickering across his features before his expression settled into something more neutral.

"Good morning, gentlemen." She kept her voice steady. "Welcome to Hope's Café."

"Ms. Miller."

Zeke gave a formal nod that felt ridiculous after their conversation at the parent meeting just last night. At least before the principal showed up.

Guess it was now her turn to act like a professional in the workplace.

Zeke glanced around. "Is it always this busy on Saturday mornings?"

"I wouldn't know, since I'm just covering for a colleague today. Any takers on coffee?" At their nods, she poured two cups. The rich aroma filled the space between them.

"Timothy will still be at practice later, right?" Devon stirred cream into his cup.

"Of course."

Although it had taken a little begging on her part to arrange the transportation on short notice. Basically, she'd be using her break to drive him there and hope to skip out in time to pick him up.

All while leaving Brian unattended.

Zeke remained oddly silent, his attention focused on the menu.

She rested the pot near the edge of the table. "Are you ready to order or need a few minutes?"

"I'll have the breakfast special, over easy with bacon," Devon said.

Zeke looked up, his gaze not quite meeting hers. "Western omelet, hash browns extra crispy."

"Perfect." She made a note, then retrieved the coffee pot. "I'll put that right in."

As she turned toward the kitchen, she caught Monica's raised eyebrow and knowing grin. Heat flashed up Clarissa's neck as she entered their order into the system.

"So that's the guy?" Greta stopped beside her. "I didn't realize he was so handsome."

"It doesn't matter. He's Timothy's coach." The phrase was becoming her deflection shield. "Nothing more."

"Uh-huh." Greta's expression said she wasn't fooled.

For the next fifteen minutes, Clarissa managed to avoid direct contact with Zeke's table, even sending Monica with their food while she focused on other customers. But the weight of his presence remained, drawing her attention like a magnet no matter how she tried to resist.

Especially when she caught him looking at her a few times.

However, when she approached with their check and a fresh pot for refills, she found the pair deep in discussion and studying what appeared to be a typed list of names.

"...so I say start Torres at shortstop and Henderson at second while Miller gets some experience on JV." Devon tapped the paper between them, then took another bite.

Clarissa's heart sank. Timothy would be disappointed.

"I'll defer for now." Zeke's quiet authority sent an unexpected shiver down her spine. "But his coordination is already improving. He'll earn a spot by the end of the season."

Warmth bloomed in her chest at his defense of her brother, colliding uncomfortably with her awareness of him as a man.

She stopped at their table and he looked up, his expression softening for only a moment.

"Thank you for the excellent breakfast, Ms. Miller." Something warmer lurked beneath the words.

"I'll pass your compliments on to the chef." She smiled politely, too conscious of both Monica and Greta pretending not to watch their interaction as she laid their check down near the roster along with a flyer about the bake sale and auction. "I'll be your cashier when you're ready. But in the meantime, how about a refill?"

She was in the middle of topping off their mugs when a laptop closed with a definitive snap from the corner booth.

"Coach Matthews!" Kyle, the local reporter who practically lived at the café, materialized beside their table, notebook in hand. "Just the man I hoped to run into. Any comment on the team's prospects as you start the season? Word is you've assembled quite the roster."

Zeke's gaze met Clarissa's—a glance that sent another unwelcome flutter through her chest—before he turned to the reporter. "The team is coming together well, but it's too early for predictions."

Clarissa retreated to the safety of the counter, leaving Kyle to his journalistic pursuit.

Greta joined her at the coffee station. "That man can smell a story from three blocks away."

Clarissa grinned, then spotted the time on the ordering monitor.

Timothy and Brian should be arriving in a half hour and then she'd have to split her role as waitress and guardian for the rest of the morning. Starting by finding Brian a spot to work on his homework.

"You like him." Greta's knowing gaze followed Clarissa's toward Zeke, now answering Kyle's rapid-fire questions.

"It doesn't matter if I do." The truth of Clarissa's words stung more than expected. Because Timothy needed the man's influence and she refused to mess that up for her brother.

A customer down the counter signaled for Greta's attention and Clarissa welcomed the interruption.

"I should check if Lauren's done with the interview." She headed toward the office. "Brian will need somewhere to study while Timothy's at practice."

As she reached the swinging door to the kitchen, she glanced back once more at Zeke, now caught between Kyle's probing questions and Devon's amused expression. Despite his obvious wish to escape, the poor man was holding up admirably.

And looked oh-so-attractive in the process.

Not that she had the time or energy to date anyone right now. Between work, her brothers, and her growing design business, her life held enough complications. The last thing she needed was feelings for someone firmly in the "off-limits" category.

But as she pushed through into the kitchen, Clarissa couldn't quite ignore the small voice whispering that maybe, just maybe, complicated wasn't always the same as impossible.

The reporter finally retreated to a corner table and Zeke sighed.

Now where were they before being interrupted? Right. Varsity lineup decisions, then Clarissa had refilled his coffee. But now it was cold.

He scanned the interior of the cafe, finding their waitress and waiting for her to glance their way.

"Maybe try being a little less obvious," Devon muttered. "I'm pretty sure everyone in the room has noticed you staring at her."

Zeke tore his gaze from Clarissa, irritation flickering through him. "I wasn't staring."

"Right." Devon's amused expression hardened. "Just remember what happened to Brenner. Small towns have long memories and short fuses."

Forgetting about his cold coffee for a moment, Zeke focused on the roster between them, the names blurring as he pushed thoughts of Clarissa Miller's green-flecked eyes from his mind.

"Henderson's parents are pushing for us to add more batting practice." Devon mercifully changed the subject. "Kid already got off-season coaching."

Zeke frowned. "Some parents think more is always better, but in my experience, too many voices can cause confusion when it comes to technique."

The bell above the café door rattled, and Zeke glanced up.

Two red-headed boys entered—Timothy Miller and a younger version who had to be the Brian Clarissa had mentioned. The family resemblance was striking, though the youngest's face held a constellation of freckles beneath a mop of unruly curls.

Clarissa approached, her face lighting with surprise. "I wasn't expecting you for another half hour yet."

"Mrs. Winters had a few errands to run and asked if she could bring us early. I figured it would be okay." Timothy adjusted his baseball cap. "And I talked to Jake. His mom said she'd take me to and from practice today so you don't have to leave work."

Something in Clarissa's expression softened—relief, gratitude, and a flash of what might have been wistfulness. "That's...actually really helpful. Thank you for thinking of that."

"I'm not completely useless." Timothy grinned, the teenage sass earning him a gentle swat on the arm.

"Did you bring your homework?" Clarissa asked the younger boy, who held up a backpack in response.

"Math and science. It's stupid." He wrinkled his nose, making his crooked glasses list a bit more to one side.

"It is not stupid." She shook her head. "Find a table and get started. I'll bring you chocolate milk in a minute."

"Can I say hi to Coach first?" Timothy already looked toward their booth.

Zeke straightened, preparing his "coach face" while his heart warmed at the unexpected window into the Millers' family dynamic. Something about their easy affection and mutual support in the mundane logistics of daily life drew his attention.

"They're having a meeting." Clarissa's tone brooked no argument. "You'll see Coach at practice soon enough."

As if to emphasize her point, she nudged the boys toward an out-of-the-way corner, then approached Zeke and Devon's table. "Anything else I can get you gentlemen?"

"Just a new cup with some hot coffee? Mine seems to have cooled during that impromptu interview." Zeke kept his smile friendly but polite, aware of Timothy watching from across the room and his assistant across the table.

Devon pulled out his wallet and some cash. "My treat today. And keep the change."

"Thank you." Zeke nodded.

"I'll be right back with the receipt and some fresh coffee." Clarissa gave no hint of the woman who'd let her guard down with her brothers.

She had just returned with both when the café door opened again. A man entered, his tailored suit and styled hair marking him as distinctly out of place among the café's casual clientele.

A man Zeke had met last night.

A man with clear ambitions for his son. And one Zeke would have around for another year since his kid was a junior.

"Matthews!" Richard Henderson spotted him, changing course to approach their table. "Just the man I wanted to see."

Zeke slid the roster beneath his notebook, something telling him the over-involved parent did not need another reason to voice his opinions.

Devon raised an eyebrow at Zeke.

"Mr. Henderson." Zeke nodded in greeting, then picked up his fresh coffee. No way would he let this second cup go to waste. "You know Devon?"

"Of course, of course." Henderson shook Devon's hand before turning back to Zeke. "Any chance we can discuss Andrew's development plan? Karen seems to think you might be considering infield adjustments."

Before Zeke could come up with a response, Assistant Principal Vaughn appeared beside Henderson, briefcase in hand. "Sorry I'm late, Richard. Traffic on Main Street."

Their principal and a parent were meeting off campus? Now that didn't scream anything near a potential conflict of interest.

Vaughn nodded to Zeke and Devon. "Gentlemen. Team meeting on a Saturday? That's dedication."

Something in his tone suggested the question wasn't as innocent as it appeared.

Zeke kept his expression neutral despite the crawling sensation between his shoulder blades. "Just grabbing breakfast before practice. Hope's Café is one of our sponsors, and I can now honestly say, they might have the best omelets in town."

"So I've heard." Vaughn's gaze swept the room before landing on Clarissa, now delivering chocolate milk to her younger brother. "Shall we find a table, Richard? I believe we have athletic donations to discuss."

As the two men moved to an empty spot across the dining room, Devon leaned forward. "That guy sure is keeping tabs on your location. Think he has your office bugged or a tracker on your car?"

"Probably just a coincidence." Except Zeke didn't quite believe it. Vaughn's appearances were becoming too frequent to be accidental.

Across the room, the teenage waitress—Monica, according to the nametag he'd seen earlier—leaned against the boys' table, twirling her hair as she talked to Timothy.

The younger brother made a gagging face while Timothy straightened, his posture suddenly more adult.

Clarissa approached, her brow furrowed at their interaction.

The expression was the same look *his* mother had worn when girls first started calling their house. Mom had laughed as she called it the dating advice stage of parenting.

Devon followed Zeke's gaze, then chuckled. "Might need to talk to the team about maintaining focus during the season. Hormones and baseball don't always mix well."

"Noted."

Zeke watched as Clarissa gently shooed Monica back to work with a look that promised a conversation later.

The easy authority she wielded, the natural way she balanced discipline with understanding... She was a remarkable guardian despite her youth.

Devon stood, picking up the small flyer delivered with their bill. "I think I'm going to check out the bake sale setup next door. Might pick up a cherry pie for our Easter dinner."

"Let me finish this coffee first, but I'll meet you there in a minute. Might find something for my own sweet tooth." Zeke remained seated, his gaze fixed on Clarissa as she moved between tables.

He'd missed his chance to ask her about the T-shirt designs last night. Now, with Vaughn and Henderson both present, the timing seemed equally problematic.

But the booster club was meeting on Tuesday and her designs were exactly what the team needed.

A legitimate reason to speak with her.

Nothing inappropriate about that at all.

He waited until she approached the register, timing his move to intersect her path. "Ms. Miller?"

She looked up, surprise flickering across her features. "Coach Matthews? Did you need something else?"

The overhead lights caught the auburn highlights in her hair, distracting him for a moment. Focus, Matthews.

"Actually, I wanted to discuss a potential project with you." He kept his voice professional despite their proximity. "After last night, you know that the booster club will be planning team merchandise as a fundraiser. We need someone like you to design our custom shirts."

Her eyes widened. "You're asking me?"

"I saw the sketches that fell out of your portfolio. You have real talent and I particularly liked the baseball-themed ones."

A flush crept up her neck. "That's...unexpected. But flattering."

Aware of Vaughn watching from across the room, Zeke tugged on the hem of his coaching jacket as if it were a suit of armor shielding his reputation. And intentions.

"I'd make sure to draw up a proper contract through the booster club so you can get paid for the design. It would be a business arrangement."

Understanding dawned in her expression—she'd caught his meaning and the careful wording. Had likely also noticed Vaughn's presence in the cafe. "I'd be interested. Perhaps you can email me the specifics?"

"Of course." Relief mingled with something warmer and he fought to contain his smile. "You have my contact information from last night? For purely professional purposes."

"Purely professional." The hint of a smile touched her lips.

From across the room, Henderson's voice carried. "Matthews! Can you spare us a minute? We were just discussing a potential donation for equipment."

Vaughn's gaze moved between them, his expression unreadable.

Zeke felt the weight from both, creating a tightrope he'd need to walk carefully for the sake of his future.

Clarissa shifted under the scrutiny, her mask slipping to reveal discomfort. "I should get back to work. But I'll email you later about the design project."

Still aware of their audience, Zeke nodded. "Thank you, Ms. Miller. I look forward to seeing your concepts."

After taking a deep breath, he reinforced his own professional mask and approached the next conversation. At least this time he had the excuse of a waiting Devon and impending practice to ease his escape.

"What was that about?" Vaughn frowned. "Didn't look like you were paying your bill."

"I heard you like to keep business in the community." Zeke tilted his head back at Clarissa, then shrugged. "So I secured our shirt designer."

Nothing inappropriate about helping the team, right?

Even if it also helped a fatherless player–and a weary guardian–at the same time.

Just doing his Christian duty like Jesus would.

At least that was all he'd admit to.

Vaughn just rolled his eyes.

Chapter Six

You have real talent...a proper contract so you can get paid...a business arrangement.

Days later, Clarissa still couldn't shake the whirlwind of emotions Zeke's request had triggered. Only the initial compliment had made the rest seem like a legitimate deal when it might have come across as thinly disguised charity. Or code words for something beyond her comprehension.

Yet only a fool would turn down paying work.

Clarissa rubbed her tired eyes, the glow of her laptop screen the only bright spot in the dimming café thanks to the overcast sky outside.

She'd always been tempted to linger in the afternoon after closing with the gentle hum of the industrial refrigerator and occasional clink of dishes from the kitchen creating a soothing backdrop.

Then today, as additional thanks for her extra Saturday shift, Joel had let her off a couple hours early.

She smirked at the memory of his face when she'd begged to stay and use a vacant table for her freelance work. Because the scary truth remained that if she headed home, she'd be tempted to take a nap instead of doing something productive before Brian got out of school.

Yesterday she'd kept her promise to Mom to get the boys to church, especially on Easter. She'd even tried her best to make it a day of rest despite her never-ending to-do list.

Which was why today—at 1:43 according to the clock on her screen and minutes until the cafe's actual closing—she was playing frantic catch up and still debating her font selection for the Johnsons' anniversary invitation ahead of tonight's deadline.

Meanwhile, her sketchbook lay nearby, open to one of three potential baseball shirt designs. Her fingers itched to continue adding small details to each—or keep playing with ideas for Clay's website and now Peterson Hardware's auction winning logo package—but the cloak of responsibility weighed her down.

She shifted her attention to the silver-themed invitation on her screen. It was almost there, elegant without being ostentatious. Just a few more tweaks to the border element and—

Her phone buzzed, skittering across the table.

This is Mrs. Evans. Cameron invited Brian to our house after school to work on a project. He can stay for dinner, and I'll bring him home later if that's okay with you.

A simple text forcing another adjustment to her schedule. One less person to feed, though she'd miss seeing Brian at dinner. It seemed like that was the only time they were able to connect as a family before diving back into homework and other tasks.

Clarissa typed her thanks and permission, then set her phone aside. Twenty minutes of uninterrupted work—that's all she needed to finish the Johnsons' invitation.

"Making progress?" Joel's voice startled her. He stood beside her table, two mugs of fresh coffee in hand. The rich aroma distracted her from the design.

"Some. And thanks." She accepted the offered mug, the ceramic warming her fingers.

Joel glanced at her screen, then settled into the chair opposite her. "That looks amazing."

"It's getting there. I just need to finalize this and then focus on the baseball shirts."

Joel raised an eyebrow. "I heard about that. Quite the opportunity."

She couldn't prevent the warmth that crept into her cheeks at the memory. "Coach Matthews is arranging the job through the booster club. Timothy's thrilled and full of opinions."

"I bet." Joel studied her for a moment. "You look exhausted, Clarissa."

"I'm fine." The automatic response came easily after months of practice.

"That's why I wanted to let you know we've hired another waitress."

Clarissa set her cup down. "The same woman Lauren interviewed on Saturday?"

He nodded. "Yes. Her name's Amanda, and Lauren said she also has some accounting experience, which I plan to take advantage of. Can start training next week. So we could make your early exit—like today—a regular thing if you want."

The casual comment landed like a stone in Clarissa's stomach.

Next week? She'd assumed she'd have at least another month of full shifts before any changes. Her graphic design business was growing, but not fast enough to replace steady café income if her hours were cut.

"Great." She forced a smile, but the word sounded hollow.

Joel frowned. "Hey, this was your plan, remember? More time for your design work, more flexibility for Timothy's baseball and for Brian this summer? We're just helping make it happen."

"I know. It's just—" Clarissa stopped herself, unwilling to voice her fears. "It's happening faster than I expected."

"Nothing's changing immediately." Joel took a swig of his coffee. "Unlike you, Amanda needs at least a week of training, and she can only work part-time because of her daughter's special needs."

"Okay." It would be okay. It had to be.

Joel stood. "I'll let you get back to it, and even bring you a refill before we dump the pots after closing."

She nodded her appreciation. While she tried to avoid caffeine after noon, today she'd make the exception if only to make a dent in her looming deadlines.

With renewed focus, she polished off the anniversary party invitation, the silver script gleaming against the pearl background. A few clicks sent the file to her client for them to forward to the printer.

With that weight lifted, she shut down her laptop and flipped through the pages of her sketchbook instead.

Taking advantage of the rare creative outlet, she'd hand-drawn three concepts, each with a different approach.

The first featured a stylized baseball diamond with silhouettes of players in action positions. The second showcased the team name in a dynamic, graffiti-inspired font. The third, her favorite but the least conventional, depicted a baseball stitched with words representing the core values Zeke had emphasized—Respect, Responsibility, Resilience.

She dug her graphite pencil out of her bag, twirling it between her fingers as she considered additional details.

Coach Matthews—Zeke—had been professional but enthusiastic about her taking on this project. So she wanted to deliver something that exceeded expectations, something that would make Timothy proud.

Something worthy of the trust placed in her talent.

"Need a refill?" Trevor, of all people, had ventured from his kitchen domain and stood holding a coffee pot.

"Sure." She held up her near-empty cup. "What brings you out here? Want to see how the other half lives?"

Their chef rolled his eyes, as if finding her joke lame. "Needed the caffeine. Mom had a rough weekend and then today I didn't realize how hard—er, weird or awkward—it would be working with Frank again."

True. There had been a few raised voices filtering through the pass-through window earlier.

"I never actually worked with him before so I don't know what he's like."

Trevor sighed. "He used to be more bark than bite, but let's just say it will be an adjustment and I'm glad Greta is still around to run interference. And Debbie."

"I'll be praying for you. For all of you." And her own sanity and strength while she was at it.

"What are you working on? Baseball stuff?" He jutted his chin toward her sketchbook.

"Shirt designs for Timothy's team." She sipped the fresh coffee. "I'm stuck between concepts."

Trevor studied the sketches. "That one." He pointed to her favorite, the stitched ball with values. "It's different. Shows what the team stands for, not just what sport they play."

"You think? The booster club president seems like more of a snob with really high expectations."

"You're not designing for her." He shrugged. "Design for the players. Design for the coach who hired you."

"Good advice."

Her phone vibrated again, rattling on the tabletop. Timothy's name flashed on the screen, this time with an incoming call rather than a text.

And during school hours.

She snatched it up, immediate concern tightening her chest. "Timothy? What's wrong?"

"My glove is at home!" His voice held the particular panic reserved for teenagers facing catastrophe. "Practice starts in less than an hour."

"Why isn't it in your bag? Never mind." She shook her head. They'd sort out routines later to avoid a repeat. "Where are you now?"

"Brian said he wants to play baseball this summer, so I let him try it on for a minute and he must not have put it back like I told him to."

"Timothy."

"And then Henderson got new batting gloves so he gave me his old ones. But when I went to put them in my bag, I saw my mitt is missing and figured Brian left it by the door when he—"

"Timothy. Calm down." She raised her voice.

"Mom-mode activated." Trevor smirked, then saluted before retreating.

"And if I don't have my glove, I can't practice, which means I can't play tomorrow, and it's our first game and Coach will be so disappointed in me and—"

"Timothy! Where. Are. You. Now?"

He sucked in a breath. "In the bathroom so I could call you, but I have to get back to biology class."

Clarissa checked the time. Practice started at three and if she factored in the drive home and then on to the high school—and actually located the glove quickly—she might make it on time.

But might not...which meant interrupting practice for the delivery.

"Practice might have started before I can get there. Do you really want me to embarrass you in front of the team?"

He hiccuped. "Maybe see if there's a way to sneak it to me? Or give it to Coach? Or..."

"I'll do my best." The only thing she knew to do.

And adding this extra errand to an already overpacked day meant another late night of work while her brothers slept. Ha. Who needed sleep when coffee existed?

After hanging up, she drained the rest of the liquid energy and began to pack her things. She paused with the sketchbook in hand.

If she was going to be at the school anyway, perhaps she could find a way to get Zeke's opinion early? Just to confirm she was on the right track?

Joel appeared at her side. "Trevor said there's an emergency?"

"Timothy doesn't have his glove." She slung her bag over her shoulder. "Practice in an hour. I need to swing by home first."

Understanding crossed Joel's features. "Hey, you're already taking some time off for the baseball booster meeting tomorrow, so how about you just come in at eleven."

"I can't ask—"

"You didn't ask. I offered." His tone was kind but firm. "Lauren and I can handle the breakfast rush, and you can finish your designs tonight without worrying about a five a.m. wake-up call."

"Thank you." Her throat tightened at the simple kindness.

Maybe things were looking up.

Maybe her graphic design business would flourish enough to support them.

Maybe she'd get caught up on her coursework and graduate on time.

With a hint of hope in her heart and the incentive of a lazy morning, Clarissa rushed to her car eager to get Timothy's errand done and a head start on her chores.

Except, she'd barely gotten inside her sedan when the sky chose that moment for a spring deluge.

God, why can't I catch a break?

Rain. Why did it have to rain the day before their first game?

As the hosts, Zeke would need to monitor their field conditions to ensure a safe competition. Or else have to postpone and create a re-scheduling headache for Vaughn's secretary before the season even began.

Between the winter's drought, their infield grass, and a stockpile of quick dry clay to sprinkle on the baselines, he prayed today's moisture soaked in fast.

Assuming tomorrow's weather cooperated.

Because despite a slim chance in the forecast, this storm had rolled in without warning, forcing him to move practice inside to the gym while rain lashed against the high windows in relentless sheets, occasional thunder punctuating the steady drumming.

Tugging his damp coach's jacket close, Zeke glanced at the exposed overhead lights and the unused section of floor space beyond the far bleachers. What he wouldn't give for an indoor batting cage about now, but hopefully this season's fundraising efforts would make that perk possible for next year's team.

The doors to the locker room burst open, followed by the squeak of multiple tennis shoes on the hardwood. Good. Devon had passed along the message for the boys to leave their cleats behind.

Zeke lifted the whistle hanging around his neck and blew a sharp blast that echoed off the cinder block walls. "Leave any water bottles on the bench, grab a partner and a ball, then form two lines. Easy tosses back and forth as a warm-up."

He nudged the five-gallon bucket of balls forward with his toe. "And do me a favor today. Focus on control. Aim well. Then make the catch. I don't want to get called to the principal's office for dented bleachers or broken light bulbs. Deal?"

As expected, the guys responded with a mixture of laughter and good-natured digs at their friends as they followed his instructions.

Given the constraints and the amount of space, they couldn't practice batting, pitching, or even catching fly balls. Which meant they'd need to work on the mental game and strategy instead.

He already had a list of unique situations on his clipboard with the intention to add one thing per practice, but maybe they'd take on a few more today. Starting with what to do if a runner got caught in a pickle between bases.

As the thwack of balls hitting leather echoed in the room, Zeke glanced up and down the lines of boys counting heads.

Wait. The pair at the end were just standing around while Timothy Miller fidgeted, no fielding glove in sight.

"Miller. A word, please." Zeke called out for the boy's attention, then waved for Grant to step into the vacancy.

Timothy approached slowly, back hunched beneath his practice jersey. "Coach, I can explain—"

"We discussed equipment responsibility on Saturday." Zeke kept his voice low but firm, mindful of nearby players. "Part of being on this team is being prepared for every practice."

"I know, sir." Timothy glanced at the outside door, the tips of his ears reddening. "I thought I had it in my bag this morning, but I must have left it at home after showing it to my little brother."

Zeke suppressed a sigh. The explanation was probably true, but that didn't change the team's expectations.

"Actions have consequences, Miller. Without a glove, you'll have to observe today's drills from the sidelines and the lack of practice will have an effect on playing time. Even on junior varsity."

Timothy nodded, the disappointment evident in his posture.

Zeke tucked his clipboard under his arm, then rested a hand on the boy's shoulder. "It's only the first game, so learn from this. Today, study the other's techniques because mental rehearsal can be valuable too."

He waved the boy toward the bench. As he turned to supervise the rest of the players, he caught movement beyond the gymnasium's side entrance.

Through the rain-streaked glass, a figure sprinted across the faculty parking lot—a flash of auburn hair instantly recognizable despite the downpour.

Clarissa.

Running full-tilt through the storm, clutching something against her chest.

"Devon, keep an eye on things for me." Zeke said, already moving. "I'll be right back."

He pushed through the door just as Clarissa reached the entrance, rain hammering the metal overhang above them.

She stood before him, breathless and soaked, water streaming from her hair down her face in rivulets while her clothing was plastered to her body.

He frowned. "What are you doing here?"

"Timothy needed his glove." She unwrapped a very-wet sweatshirt from around a baseball glove and what looked like a leather-bound sketchbook.

Both were remarkably dry despite her otherwise drenched state.

"You didn't—"

"I would have gotten it here sooner except for an accident on Garfield and then after I'd parked on the street out there, Timothy texted you were in the gym today but a stupid—okay not stupid, just inconvenient—bus blocked this entrance and so I had to run—"

He held up his hands against the verbal onslaught. "Slow down, there."

"Is he in trouble?" She blinked up at him.

"Nothing serious."

She shivered as a gust of wind caught the rain, spraying them both despite the minimal shelter.

Without thinking, he shrugged out of his coaching jacket and handed it to her. "Here."

"I couldn't—"

"You're freezing." It was a simple observation.

She hesitated, then accepted the jacket with a grateful nod, handing him her belongings so she could slip it over her shoulders. The material dwarfed her frame, making her appear smaller and more vulnerable than usual.

Zeke juggled everything in his arms, then held up the glove. "You drove through the storm for this?"

"I was at the cafe when he called in a panic." She pushed wet hair back from her forehead, leaving a smudge of what looked like graphite across her temple. "Said something about fielding drills and being benched. But based on where I finally found his glove... Let's just say that I'll be having a talk with Brian later about taking things that don't belong to him."

Interesting that Clarissa believed Brian was at fault and yet Timothy hadn't cast blame. Only shouldered the consequences like a man.

She shook her head. "Timothy's worked so hard and didn't deserve to pay for his brother's mistake. And if it wasn't for the rain and having to move from where I'd first parked, I might have gotten it here before practice started."

What was he supposed to say to that?

"Oh, I can take my stuff back." She held out her hands.

Keeping the glove and his clipboard, he handed back the wet sweatshirt and then paused to wiggle the sketchbook. "I can see why you'd bring his glove through the rain. But this?"

"Right. I've got three shirt concepts for tomorrow's booster club meeting." She flipped open the book in his hand to the middle, revealing several pages of hand-drawn illustrations. "Since I'm here, I thought you might like a preview. Offer an opinion or two?"

Zeke rested the sketchbook atop the other items and slowly turned the pages as he studied the images, finding not rough sketches but detailed drawings.

She'd put a lot of work into her art and he'd made the right choice—professionally speaking—in asking her.

"These are excellent, especially this one." He tapped the page featuring a baseball stitched with the team's core values.

Her face brightened despite her bedraggled appearance. "That's my favorite, too. I wasn't sure if it was too conceptual for a team shirt."

"It's perfect."

She started to respond when a violent shiver interrupted her words.

Without thinking, Zeke reached to adjust the collar of his jacket around her neck, his fingers accidentally brushing her skin. The contact, brief and innocent, sent an unexpected jolt through him as her rain-cooled skin somehow still radiated warmth.

Their eyes met, the moment stretching.

For a heartbeat, neither moved.

The gymnasium door banged open behind them.

"Hey, Coach?" Devon paused in the opening. "How long do you want them to keep playing catch?"

Zeke stepped away from Clarissa, then shuffled the things in his hands until he looked at the clipboard with his scribbled practice plan. "Have the infielders roll and field balls to each other while the outfielders do the same but with a higher toss. Just not high enough to hit the lights. I'll be right there."

"Sure thing, Coach." Devon pulled the door shut with a firm click.

"I should go." Clarissa glanced back the way she'd come, then started to remove his jacket.

He raised a hand. "Keep it. You can return it later."

The offer was practical, nothing more.

At least that's what he told himself.

"Thank you." She clutched the sweatshirt—the one she'd used to protect her things from the downpour—to her chest like a shield as she prepared to dash back to her car. "And good luck with practice."

A moment later, she darted into the downpour, hunched against the weather, his bright red jacket a blur against the gray curtain of rain.

Zeke waited until her headlights flickered on before returning to the gymnasium, Timothy's glove in hand. The warmth hit him immediately, along with the realization that he might wish for his jacket in a few hours when it was time to leave.

But for now, he was indoors and dry.

"Miller." He strode toward Timothy on the bleachers. "Looks like today's your lucky day."

The boy's face transformed as Zeke handed him the glove. "She brought it? In this weather?"

"Your sister cares about your commitment to the team so don't waste her effort." Zeke dropped his paperwork onto the bench. "And while she said she's going to lecture your brother, it might be wise to double-check your equipment before you leave home in the mornings."

"Yes, sir." Timothy grinned.

"Now, get to your position. You've got fielding drills to make up."

As Timothy jogged to join his teammates, Devon approached, his expression curious. "What happened to your jacket? And why is Miller back in the lineup?"

"His sister brought the glove the youngest took from his bag." He kept his tone neutral, though the lingering sensation of Clarissa's skin against his fingertips remained a distraction. "Then she got caught in the downpour so I lent her my jacket."

"Ah." Devon's knowing smirk spoke volumes. "Just being a gentleman, right?"

"Of course." Zeke reached for his whistle, signaling an end to the conversation. "Let's get back to practice."

Because he needed to get his focus back on the things that mattered most.

His players and his job.

And not the fact he'd see her again tomorrow.

Chapter Seven

Clarissa leaned against the hallway wall for a moment, the empty laundry basket an anchor on her hip and fatigue weighing on her like a physical presence in the quiet house. She closed her eyes and breathed deep.

Both boys were asleep, the day's chaos settling into stillness.

Could she call it a night herself?

Clay's website mock-up sent? Check. Start on her Advanced Web Design final project? Check. Dinner cooked and kitchen cleaned? Check and check.

Laundry done and delivered? Check.

The latest load might not have included Timothy's pair of muddy, grass-stained practice pants thanks to the rain-induced indoor practice, but the funky smell of the game uniform he'd been given had desperately needed attention.

Brother disciplined? Also check.

She sighed.

Brian had stumbled through the door from his friend's house, taken one look at Timothy's face, and started backpedaling while begging for forgiveness.

Suffice it to say, Brian would be doing both boys' chores for two weeks.

And she'd be delaying his new glasses yet again in order to register him for the Loveland Baseball Association's recreational league. Plus finding him a glove to use at the tryouts on Saturday.

As if she had an abundance of money. Or time.

No. She couldn't think that way, couldn't give those kinds of intrusive thoughts room. God would provide all they needed. Like He'd been doing for months now.

He'd dropped Clay's job in her lap just in time for Timothy's equipment shopping, so maybe the balance would come in time for Brian? Assuming she had time to incorporate his feedback.

And then there was the promise of payment for the baseball team's T-shirt designs. Designs she would present to the booster club in the morning while praying snobby Karen Henderson and the other parents would approve. Maybe she should add a few more embellishments to be sure.

She pushed away from the wall, moving to the kitchen table where her papers were spread in organized chaos near the shared laptop Timothy had used to finish his homework assignments. The sketchbook should be right there, beside her planner.

But it wasn't.

A prickle of unease crawled across her skin.

Between her college courses, fledgling design business, and personal creative outlet, she thought better on paper sometimes. Which is why she kept the sketchbook with her other materials.

Always.

Had it somehow fallen out of her backpack in the car?

The night air carried a chill as she stepped outside, the scent of damp earth enveloping her. Stars glittered overhead in the clear post-rain sky, offering just enough light to navigate the short path to her car.

Clarissa opened the door, the dome light dimly illuminating the interior for her search.

Not on the passenger seat or floorboards where her backpack often rested. Not under the seats either. Panic began to rise, a steady tide of dread washing through her chest.

She moved her search to the backseat, catching a glimpse of red hidden beneath Timothy's sweatshirt.

And memory rushed back—standing in the rain, the borrowed jacket, showing Zeke her designs, the unexpected warmth of his fingers adjusting the collar around her neck, the interruption from Coach Devon, and the rush back to her car in the rain...

Caught up in the moment they'd shared, she must have left her sketchbook behind.

Now what?

Back inside, Clarissa tossed the sweatshirt into the laundry room, then sank onto a kitchen chair, Zeke's jacket still in her hands.

She checked the clock over the stove: 10:38 PM. Much too late to call the school office or even use the email listed in the parent packet. And the booster club meeting was at 10:00 AM tomorrow.

What were her options? One, hope her sketchbook would be found and returned before then. Unlikely and out of her control. Or option two: recreate the designs from memory tonight.

Sleep was overrated anyway.

Clarissa retreated to her bedroom for a fresh sketchpad, then started a pot of coffee. As it brewed, another thought nagged at her.

The jacket. She needed to return it, of course, but how? Sending it with Timothy to practice seemed the obvious choice, but somehow too likely to trigger teenage embarrassment or misinterpretation from the other players.

She could drop it off at the school office anonymously before the booster club meeting. Avoid any awkward personal interactions. Problem solved.

However, as she stirred sugar into her mug of coffee, her gaze fell on a new bag of chocolate chips she'd bought hoping to celebrate Timothy's first game with homemade cookies.

If she was baking anyway, why not include a few for the coach as a simple thank you for his kindness? Surely that wouldn't cross any lines.

With that decided, she started to draw. The hours blurred together, marked only by the occasional adjustment of her position to ease her cramping fingers and the steady depletion of her coffee mug.

By 1:17 AM, three re-created designs lay complete before her—not identical to the originals, but close. Good enough that only she would know the difference.

She finally collapsed into bed, setting her alarm for six—enough time to bake cookies, pack lunches, and get the boys to the bus before dropping off the jacket and heading to the meeting.

Thank God Joel had given her the morning off.

Not enough hours later, Brian watched her mix cookie dough. "Mom always said you'd wash away in the rain because you're so sweet."

"Very funny. And you're still on the hook for the dishes." Clarissa stifled another yawn. "Did you finish packing your lunch?"

"Almost." He swiped a finger into the batter, then darted away. "But why are you making cookies? Are they for breakfast?"

"I needed some as a thank you gift." Hopefully he'd buy the vague answer.

Timothy appeared in the doorway, hair still wet from his shower. "For Coach Matthews? Because he lent you his jacket?"

Clarissa almost dropped her mixing spoon. "How did you—"

"When he came back inside yesterday with my glove, he wasn't wearing his jacket. Which never happens. He's, like, superstitious about it or something." Timothy glanced across the room. "And it's sitting right there in plain sight."

Her face heated and she turned away to preheat the oven. "He's a gentleman. And this is just a polite thank you. Nothing more."

"Whatever." Timothy crossed to the fridge and pulled out sandwich ingredients. "Want me to make the delivery?"

"No!" She'd answered too fast and now aimed for nonchalance. "I mean, I'll drop them at the school office since I already have to be there."

"Will you save any for us or are they all for Coach?" Timothy smirked.

"These were originally for you, but now I'm not so sure." She glared, then changed the subject as she scooped balls of dough onto the baking sheets. "Bus is in twenty minutes. And double-check your backpacks and bags before you leave. No forgotten anything, especially on a game day."

"Yes, ma'am." Timothy and Brian spoke in tandem, then high-fived each other.

At least they'd put their differences aside.

Once they headed out to catch the school bus and the cookies cooled on the rack, Clarissa collapsed at the kitchen table, cradling her third cup of coffee and savoring the rare quiet.

Maybe after she finished her degree and left the cafe behind, she'd have more mornings like this to enjoy? But until then, something would always demand her attention.

Something to do for the boys as she kept her promise to hold their family together at all costs.

Her phone vibrated, an unknown number lighting up the screen. Probably a telemarketer, but she answered anyway.

"Is this Clarissa Miller, the graphic designer?" The woman on the other end got down to business.

"Yes, speaking." She set her coffee aside, fatigue forgotten.

"One of our staff members overheard a conversation about you designing logos and websites."

"Yes, I'm building my client base and portfolio." That sounded professional enough, right?

But who on earth had been talking up her business? Someone at the cafe? Or someone who saw her silent auction package?

Oh, please, God? You know I need more clients to replace the cafe income.

"I'll get to the point. We're in the market to upgrade our website. And given our unique constraints, we're willing to double the industry's going rate."

Double? Why that could cover all of Brian's expenses plus get an extra pair of practice pants for Timothy so she didn't have to scrub out the stains every night.

The rest of the mystery woman's words sank in.

"Unique constraints?"

"I'll let my boss explain his requirements if you're available to meet later today."

"Not today." She already had enough going on. "But I can make time tomorrow afternoon, if that works."

She could only hope Joel would let her off early again. But then again, if she had to beg, she would. Anything for a job at double her rate.

The woman sighed. "I can squeeze you in at three o'clock and hope Mr. Ridge understands."

"Perfect. Thank you." After getting the address for the Rocky Ridge Development company's offices, Clarissa ended the call and made a note in her planner.

She glanced at the clock, then allowed herself exactly thirty seconds to savor the moment before standing to wrap up a dozen fresh cookies for Timothy's coach.

The booster club meeting still loomed. She still needed them to approve—and pay for—her designs. And her original sketchbook filled with other ideas was still missing. But somehow with a single phone call, the weight seemed more manageable.

With the clock ticking, Clarissa added a small note to the brown paper package containing both the jacket and baked goods, then gathered her other things and headed out the door.

She had a package to deliver, designs to present, and for the first time in weeks, a genuine reason to feel hopeful about her professional future.

Hopefully today's encounter with Karen Henderson wouldn't spoil her mood or sabotage her opportunity.

"Hit the showers." Zeke punctuated the command with a sharp blast from his whistle.

His first-period freshmen boys shuffled to the locker rooms, their sneakers squeaking against the polished floor.

He checked his watch—thirty minutes until the booster club meeting.

The parents might be mostly interested in their own children's playing time, but he had plans for any money they raised. Especially if he leveraged yesterday's storm to convince them to invest in an indoor batting cage before the other items on his list.

Zeke headed toward his office, a glorified storage closet off the main gym with just enough space for a desk and filing cabinet.

"Coach Matthews!"

He turned as one of his fifth-period students jogged over with a brown paper package.

"This was dropped off at the main office for you." The kid extended the parcel, then left just as quickly.

Tied closed with twine, it felt surprisingly light for its size but it gave under his fingertips. A faint, sweet aroma wafted from whatever it contained.

Inside his office, Zeke opened the wrapping to find his neatly folded coaching jacket alongside a small bag of chocolate chip cookies and a handwritten note: *Thank you for your kindness. —Clarissa Miller.*

The simple message, written in neat, precise handwriting, carried more weight than its few words suggested.

He lifted his jacket, the familiar red fabric now carrying the faint scent of spring rain and something distinctly feminine—perhaps her perfume or shampoo. Something it must have picked up in the brief time she'd stood before him, soaked to the skin yet determined to deliver her brother's glove.

Zeke slipped on the jacket, feeling more prepared for Karen Henderson's inevitable opinions and Vaughn's watchful eyes at the booster meeting.

He opened the cookie bag, the aroma intensifying as he took one and bit into it. The perfect balance of chocolate and buttery dough transported him to another place—to a kitchen with warm light and his mother's laughter. To the kind of home where people baked for each other simply because they cared.

His own apartment remained spartanly functional, meals practical rather than pleasurable. No one had baked for him since his mother passed away three years ago.

The simple gesture—cookies, a returned jacket, a polite note—shouldn't affect him this way. Yet the care behind it resonated in a place he usually kept guarded.

He'd see her at the meeting and the thought sent an unexpected current of anticipation through him, inappropriate but undeniable.

Forcing his focus back to work, Zeke sorted through the papers scattered across his desk, then pulled out his budget proposal, reviewing the numbers one last time.

A larger object beneath his clipboard caught his attention. Not his. Smooth brown leather, worn at the corners, with a small coffee stain on the cover.

Clarissa's sketchbook.

In the chaos of yesterday's rain and indoor practice, he must have accidentally kept it, then set it aside with his coaching materials.

Zeke opened it and inside found the quality he'd remembered.

Pencil drawings of everyday scenes like Timothy at bat, Brian hunched over homework, and what might be cafe regulars captured mid-conversation. Each detail conveyed the determination, frustration, or camaraderie of the subject.

Flipping toward the back, he came across a few sketches of kitchen appliances. And a well-stocked toolbox. Interesting choices but she must have a reason.

And then more baseball drawings.

Horror washed through him. The booster meeting was minutes away and she was supposed to present her designs.

Designs she no longer had because they were sitting on his desk.

Had she noticed they were missing? Of course she had. She was nothing if not thorough, which meant she'd been scrambling to recreate them.

Hopefully he could catch her before it started and ease her mind.

Zeke gathered the sketchbook, budget proposal, and his notes, grabbing another cookie for internal fortification, then headed out. He almost collided with Devon in the crowded gym outside his office.

"Whoa there." Devon took a step back. "Someone's in a rush."

"Can't keep the booster club waiting." Zeke juggled his materials. "Sure you're okay covering my next class along with yours until I get back?"

"No problem." Devon nodded toward the cookie in Zeke's hand. "Perks of coaching, huh? Henderson's mom brought me a store-bought fruit basket last year when I helped Andrew with his batting stance. Guess you rate homemade goods."

"Something like that."

Devon gaze took in Zeke's jacket, his grin suggesting he wasn't fooled about the source of the baked goods. "Do me a favor? Tell Karen Henderson I said her son's looking good at second base. Keeps her off my back when she thinks her precious Andrew is getting special attention."

Zeke nodded, already moving toward the main office. The hallways were empty, the only sounds his footsteps against the linoleum and the murmur of voices behind classroom doors.

When he reached the conference room, several booster club members were already there.

Karen Henderson held court at the head of the table, her designer handbag claiming territory beside her. Her husband sat to her right, scrolling through something on his phone.

Three other parents whose names Zeke still mixed up occupied the remaining seats while Vaughn lurked near the coffee machine, probably there to represent the school's interests.

"Coach Matthews." Karen greeted him with the practiced smile of someone accustomed to always being the most important person in the room. "Now that everyone's here, we can get started."

"Actually..." Zeke scanned the room. "We're still waiting for—"

"We don't want to waste your time." Karen raised an eyebrow, as if reminding him of her position as club president in charge of the meeting. "Let's start with your fundraising requests. We can discuss the more trivial stuff like meals and parent volunteers at the end."

Zeke set the sketchbook on his lap. He'd have to wait for Clarissa's arrival to return it to her.

"As I told Richard..." Karen glanced at her husband who finally looked up from his phone. "Merchandise has always been our strongest revenue source. Last year's generic shirts sold well, but if we took your unique design idea and required it for all players..."

"The school provides game uniforms and we already require the players to purchase practice jerseys," Zeke said. "Additional items should remain optional for families with budget constraints."

Karen's rebuttal was cut short as the door opened and Clarissa slipped in.

"I apologize for being late." She headed for the only remaining chair across from Zeke.

Zeke grasped the sketchbook on his lap. "You're right on time. We just started to discuss the design I asked you to develop."

"Perfect timing despite the line at the copy machine." She distributed a stack of printouts around the table, then took her seat. "These are three ideas for consideration, but I'm open to suggestions."

He studied the images in front of him. Although a little less detailed than her originals, they captured the same essential elements with remarkable skill considering they were recreations from memory.

But based on the dark circles still shadowing her eyes, she was short on sleep as a result.

"I'm impressed, especially with this one and the way you've depicted our team values." Might as well start the discussion off right with a vote for his favorite.

Karen set the pages down and wrinkled her nose. "Are these... hand drawn?"

Clarissa's spine straightened. "Yes. I prefer the hands-on approach over digital tools. Not to mention the result is sufficient for this meeting, putting a sample on your order form, and honestly, even for delivery to the screen printer."

Karen sniffed, then glanced at Vaughn. "I heard Coach Matthews requested we pay the designer as a part of our expenses, but I believe we should hire a professional instead of an amateur."

The not-so-subtle dig wasn't lost on anyone present.

Zeke sat forward. "I say Ms. Miller's work speaks for itself. And we're not the first group to use her services."

The Hope's Cafe logo she created should count for something.

"Is that so?" Karen raised a judgmental eyebrow. "Then please enlighten us as to your credentials. Where did you receive your training?"

Zeke caught his breath. He couldn't risk continuing to defend Clarissa without reinforcing Vaughn's suspicions.

Clarissa lifted her chin. "Assuming everything continues according to plan, I'm a month away from receiving my fine arts degree with a graphic design concentration. And as for my most recent client portfolio, you can ask Hope's Cafe, Hogan Appliance Repair, or Peterson's Hardware for their opinions."

Guess that explained the other random sketches he'd seen. But thankfully, several frowns around the table relaxed at the mention of her degree program.

The revelation seemed to satisfy even Karen, who shifted tactics. "Well, regardless, I'd still like to see more of a polish before production."

Clarissa only nodded.

Karen turned to the group. "Shall we vote on which design to use?"

To Zeke's satisfaction, the baseball with team values won by a significant margin. And thanks to his suggestion seconded by Clarissa—probably because of the recent mention of her employer—they'd agreed to add mentions of the team's sponsors on the back.

Might even sell a few extra shirts to those very same sponsors. Win-win.

"I'll have order forms ready by tomorrow's game at the latest and push for a quick turnaround. And as usual, all the money will funnel through the athletic secretary." Karen set her printout aside, then slid Clarissa a business card. "Which means if you want to collect your fee from her, you must deliver the final version—in an electronic file—to the screen printer by Friday evening."

Clarissa glanced at the card. "No problem."

His plan to help her earn a little cash to offset her brother's team expenses had worked, and any extra they raised for the baseball program was a bonus.

Seeing an opportunity to shift the focus, Zeke shuffled his papers. "With our merchandise fundraiser underway, do we have time to discuss hosting a skills camp for elementary and middle school players? It's a way to build community connections while raising additional money."

The idea sparked immediate interest and the discussion flowed into further logistics and potential scheduling as the meeting progressed.

When they finally adjourned, Clarissa stood. "I need to get to the cafe."

A moment later, the door closed behind her with a soft click. While Zeke still held her forgotten sketchbook.

He gathered his papers, then slid them atop the sketchbook as he rose. Maybe he could catch her in the parking lot? Spend a moment talking before heading back to class?

Vaughn stopped Zeke halfway to the door. "Seems you knew what you were doing when you recommended her for the shirts. And good work on the skills camp idea, too." He squeezed Zeke's shoulder. "I'll see what I can do to help you get that indoor batting cage."

Zeke could only nod his thanks.

Because Vaughn's comments, delivered without the usual undertone of suspicion, suggested a temporary reprieve from scrutiny.

Meanwhile Clarissa's leather-bound book remained like a forbidden treasure in his hands. Just like the home-baked cookies waiting in his office.

Both symbolized what he couldn't have.

Not if he wanted to keep his job.

Or even more, keep his promise to live with integrity.

It was the least he owed his mother's memory.

Chapter Eight

Clarissa's face tingled as the elevator doors parted with a soft pneumatic hiss, revealing a reception area that screamed money in every polished surface and designer detail.

With a fluttery stomach, she stepped onto plush carpet that swallowed the sound of her footsteps, keenly aware of her practical flats and simple black dress in a space designed for power suits and Italian leather.

A space that reinforced her imposter status.

"Miss Miller?" The receptionist's refined tone matched her immaculate appearance. "Mr. Ridge will see you now."

Clarissa smoothed her skirt, wishing she'd also had time for a quick shower after her cafe shift. The faint scent of coffee clung to her skin despite her best efforts with perfume. Nothing like the aroma of breakfast service to boost one's confidence.

The receptionist led her down a hallway lined with framed architectural renderings—sleek high-rises and sprawling commercial complexes that transformed landscapes into monuments of glass and steel. Each bore the distinctive Rocky Ridge Development logo, a stylized mountain peak that managed to suggest both nature and its conquest.

"Is this the designer you recruited?" A deep voice startled her as the receptionist opened the corner office door.

A man she recognized from the company's current website rose from behind a massive mahogany desk, his tailored suit complemented by the office's calculated opulence.

Everything about Brock Ridge radiated practiced charm overlaid with the unmistakable air of someone accustomed to getting whatever he wanted.

"Thank you for meeting with me, Mr. Ridge," Clarissa said, accepting his handshake.

His grip was firm to the point of discomfort, his palm dry and cool against her skin.

"Please, have a seat." He gestured to a leather chair positioned slightly lower than his own. A power move she recognized from design psychology classes. "Coffee? Water?"

"No, thank you." She perched on the edge of the chair, ankles crossed with her hands folded in her lap.

Through floor-to-ceiling windows, Loveland spread out below, the mountains a distant backdrop to the rooftops. From this height, Hope's Café would be just another indistinguishable speck.

"I'll get straight to the point." Mr. Ridge settled back into his chair. "We've grown, and our website has become outdated. My team suggested a complete overhaul to better reflect our current projects as well as showcase our various divisions of acquisitions, construction, leasing, and property management."

Wow. Guess they covered everything from beginning to end.

"Is that something you can handle?"

Clarissa nodded. "I have reviewed your existing site. And there are certainly opportunities for improvement in user experience and visual impact."

He narrowed his eyes. "I know I asked for someone with immediate availability, but I expected someone...more established."

The dismissive assessment stung, but Clarissa maintained her professional demeanor. "My client list includes several local businesses. I'd be happy to provide references."

"That won't be necessary." He waved off her offer, the cufflink at his wrist catching the light. "This project is quite extensive. Complete redesign, content management system integration, showcases with interactive elements. With an aggressive timeline—six weeks maximum."

He named a figure that made Clarissa's breath catch.

Three months of expenses. Maybe four.

The kind of payment that changed everything.

Baseball expenses covered without worry. A proper emergency fund.

Maybe even enough left over for that used car she'd been secretly researching for Timothy—something reliable for when he eventually got his license, allowing her more flexibility with her own schedule.

She worked to keep her expression neutral, deflecting her reaction from the compensation back to the monumental task. "That's a substantial project with a tight timeline."

"I expect excellence delivered promptly." Mr. Ridge slid a folder across his desk. "Our branding guidelines, content requirements, and technical specifications are all outlined here. We'll require weekly progress reviews and will release the payment in stages as benchmarks are met."

Clarissa leafed through the materials, her mind already cataloging the work involved. Complex but not impossible. She'd need to adjust her other deadlines, possibly pull a few all-nighters to get them done and out of the way first, but the payoff would be worth it.

In fact, some of the very things she was learning in class could also be applied here.

"There are, of course, certain conditions." Mr. Ridge tapped his fingertips on the polished surface of his desk. "Given the proprietary nature of our projects and client information, you'll have to work on-site during our business hours. My assistant will provide workstation access each session."

Clarissa blinked. "On-site? I usually work remotely. Why not use secure file transfers?"

"Non-negotiable, I'm afraid." His tone suggested boredom with the topic. "Corporate security protocols. I'm sure you understand the value of protecting intellectual property."

The implications cascaded through her carefully balanced life.

"That does present some scheduling challenges." She admitted, already calculating the ripple effect on her other responsibilities. "My current commitments include—"

"Miss Miller." Mr. Ridge leaned forward. "If my requirements are too demanding, I can certainly find a more... established professional. One with the infrastructure to accommodate a serious client."

The dismissal in his tone triggered something deep and defensive. The familiar voice that whispered she wasn't enough, couldn't manage, should give up.

The same voice she'd been proving wrong since her mother first got sick.

"That won't be necessary." She fought to maintain her professionalism. "I can adjust my schedule to accommodate on-site work, but only in the afternoons."

At least that way she'd still keep the bulk of her waitressing income and tips. And with the new waitress starting Monday, her bosses shouldn't be too upset if she needed to leave early from time to time.

Satisfaction flickered across Mr. Ridge's features. "Excellent. I have a contract already drawn up. We'll expect you to begin next Monday, nine to three."

"Monday should be fine, but I'll be available from *noon* to either four or six depending on the day." She held her gaze steady.

He finally nodded.

That was one battle won.

Now, she needed to get Joel onboard with her new hours. Then convince her neighbor Mrs. Winters to watch Brian after school. Clarissa would have to race from the cafe here daily, then rush to pick up Timothy from after practice unless it was a game day.

Her personal coursework and other clients would have to wait until late into the nights or on weekends.

Every waking hour would be accounted for, leaving precious little time for sleep, let alone the normal interactions with her brothers.

But only for the next six weeks.

Mr. Ridge opened a new folder, made a few changes on the paperwork inside, then slid it toward her along with a pen.

Clarissa accepted the documents and scanned the written terms. The heavy paper stock felt expensive against her fingertips, embossed with the same mountain logo that decorated the building's façade.

She signed, then as she waited for his secretary to make her a copy of the executed contract to add to the folder of website specifications, the weight of everything she'd just agreed to settled onto her shoulders.

Mr. Ridge stood and reached out for another firm handshake. "I expect you to deliver excellence, Miss Miller. Rocky Ridge Development accepts nothing less."

"You'll have it."

The receptionist appeared to escort her out, and Clarissa followed, clutching the paperwork to her chest like a shield.

In the elevator, she sagged against the polished brass railing as the numbers descended. The contract would be life-changing if she could deliver—and she would deliver, no matter what it took.

Adding twenty-plus hours a week to her already stretched schedule was daunting.

And exhausting.

But she'd survived worse. They all had.

Clarissa stepped out of the air-conditioned building into the afternoon warmth, blinking in the brightness as she walked to her car.

She wouldn't count on the income before it arrived—life had taught her that lesson too often. But for the first time in months, she allowed herself to imagine a future with slightly fewer edges. Slightly more cushion against life's inevitable hard landings.

The boys would understand the temporary sacrifice.

They'd forgive her the missed dinners, the distracted conversations, and the late nights hunched over her overworked laptop after they went to bed.

At least she hoped so.

Clarissa slipped into the metal bleachers, wincing at the screech of her sneakers on the aluminum. Several players' uniforms were smudged with fresh stains—evidence of plenty of action while she'd waited for Brian's bus.

"What did I miss?" she whispered to the closest mom, a forty-something woman with a Loveland Red Wolves sweatshirt.

"Scoreless so far." The woman never took her eye off the field. "Timothy got thrown out at first. Swung at a high fastball."

Clarissa nodded as if she understood the significance, settling onto the uncomfortable seat.

A dozen parents scattered across the home team bleachers—most at least a decade older than her—cheered as a Loveland player connected with the ball. The sharp crack echoed across the field, followed by the collective groan when an opposing outfielder made the catch.

From his perch at the end of the bleachers, Brian huddled with two boys near his age who appeared more interested in a handheld video game than watching their brothers play.

Although Brian seemed to be splitting his attention between the two activities.

"Strike him out, Jason!" A man in the front row on the visitor's side bellowed.

All around her, other parents shouted instructions to their sons with the confidence of lifelong baseball aficionados. Meanwhile, the afternoon sun cast shadows across the field, and the spring air carried the unmistakable scent of freshly mowed grass mingled with hot dogs from the small concession stand.

A slight breeze jostled the colorful banners lining the fence, each displaying the logo of a different team sponsor. Banners she'd snapped a picture of at yesterday's game and happily showed both Joel and Lauren this morning before the cafe opened.

It all formed the backdrop to a world Clarissa was still learning to navigate. After Brian's tryouts on Saturday, she'd have two boys in this sport, making this her life for the foreseeable future.

A gray-haired man to her right pointed to the field. "Martinez is up for his second RBI opportunity."

Clarissa nodded again, adding "RBI" to the list of terms she needed to Google later. The specialized vocabulary made her feel like a foreigner in a country where everyone else spoke the language fluently.

Her gaze drifted to the dugout, where Coach Matthews leaned against the chain-link fence, focused on the field. Wearing his apparently trademark red jacket paired with baseball pants like the team, he carried himself with the easy confidence of someone completely in his element. Not so much older than her, but occupying a different realm of authority and assurance.

He called something encouraging to the player at bat, his voice carrying just enough to be heard without the shouting of the more excitable parents. The contrast wasn't lost on Clarissa.

The game progressed with a steady rhythm she slowly began to understand. Loveland pulled ahead by two runs, lost the lead, then reclaimed it with a well-placed hit that had the hometown crowd on their feet.

"Miller's up," someone announced, drawing Clarissa's attention back to the game.

Timothy approached the plate, his stance mimicking what he'd practiced in their tiny backyard. His expression carried the intense concentration she recognized from his homework sessions—determined but overthinking.

"Choke up on the bat, Miller!" shouted one of the dads. "You're swinging too low!"

Clarissa clenched her fists at the unsolicited advice. Who did this armchair coach think he was? She bit her tongue to keep from suggesting where he could choke up.

From the dugout, Coach Matthews called something—too quiet for her to hear, but whatever was said made Timothy adjust his grip. The pitch came, Timothy swung, and connected with a sound less decisive than ideal.

The ball dribbled between first and second base.

The second baseman fumbled the pickup, and Timothy safely reached first with a sprint that showcased the hours of conditioning the coaches had put the team through. Clarissa found herself on her feet with the other parents, surprise and pride bubbling up.

"That's how you hustle!" The woman beside her cheered, then turned to Clarissa. "Your boy's got good speed."

"Thanks." Warmth spread through her chest at the simple acknowledgment.

Two pitches later, Timothy slid into second base in a cloud of red dust, barely beating the tag. The white uniform pants she'd washed after last night's game now bore the distinctive stain of the baseball diamond's clay.

"Not again." She'd have to find time to soak and scrub before adding them to the washing machine. "I should make him wash them himself."

The woman beside her laughed. "First season?"

"That obvious?"

"The look of dread gives it away. Pick up a bar of Fels Naptha soap in the laundry aisle. A quick pre-scrub works wonders on clay stains before you toss them in the wash."

"Quick is great. I'll try that, thanks." The simple exchange—parent to parent rather than guardian to authority figure—was blessedly normal.

The next batter struck out, and the teams switched sides.

The Loveland pitcher headed to the small hill in the middle of the field, while Zeke jogged to home plate. The sun caught the planes of his face, highlighting his strong jawline and no-nonsense expression.

But then he dropped into a catcher's squat with athletic ease, his muscular legs and broad shoulders suggesting he hadn't lost much since his own playing days.

Clarissa forced her gaze elsewhere, uncomfortable with the direction of her thoughts. She shouldn't be ogling anyone, let alone Timothy's coach. Talk about how to make things awkward in a hurry.

Especially when he seemed determined to keep firm boundaries in place.

The memory of last night surfaced unbidden.

After the game, Timothy had delivered her sketchbook with the casual words "Coach asked me to give this to you." Taped inside was an unsigned note: *Didn't notice I'd accidentally taken this until right before the meeting. Sorry. Hope the design fee helped.*

Any momentary hope that chivalry in the rain and baked goods might lead to something had been swiftly extinguished by the terse tone.

They were coach and pseudo-parent. Nothing more.

Exactly as it should be.

Would have to be.

By the fifth inning, the bleachers began filling with additional spectators—parents in business attire coming straight from work, teenagers gathering in noisy clusters, and most notably, a wave of varsity team mothers arriving with the air of sports royalty.

Karen Henderson led the group, designer handbag swinging from her arm as she air-kissed her way through the crowd. Her voice carried over the game noise: "Perfect timing! Junior varsity's almost finished, and the varsity boys are warming up on the practice field."

The dismissal of the current game—of Timothy and his teammates' efforts—sparked fresh irritation in Clarissa. She noticed similar expressions on other JV parents' faces.

Karen began distributing papers throughout the bleachers. "Merchandise order forms, everyone! Due Friday morning at the athletic office."

She paused at Clarissa's row. "The families of the returning players already have a lot of school gear, but we really want everyone to get one of our special T-shirts to wear at every game. Plus one for your son." Her practiced smile didn't reach her eyes. "It supports the team, shows school spirit. The newest design is quite... creative."

Clarissa accepted the paper with a tight smile, acknowledging the barely veiled reference to her work. As Karen moved on, repeating her Friday deadline announcement loudly enough to distract from a crucial play, Clarissa examined the order form.

Her eyes widened at the prices. Twenty-five dollars per shirt? The booster club meeting had discussed fifteen as a reasonable price point with five dollars going to the team. But definitely no more than twenty. This markup was outrageous.

And counterproductive to a fundraiser.

Two shirts for her brothers plus one for herself would cost seventy-five dollars—almost half of what she'd be paid for the design work.

Around her, other parents studied the forms with similar dismay, particularly a mother with three younger children who chewed her lip like it was her last meal.

However, after securing the website project with Mr. Ridge just hours ago, the windfall felt like a sign.

For once, Clarissa could do more than just scrape by. She could be generous. The design fee had been unexpected income and they'd survive without it. But for other families, purchasing these shirts might represent a genuine hardship.

A plan formed. She'd talk to the athletic secretary, donate her fee back to cover her family's shirts, and maybe buy a few extras for others who might be struggling.

An anonymous gift. The kind her mom would have appreciated during their tougher times.

As the junior varsity game came to a close, Clarissa watched Timothy high-five his teammates, his face alight with the simple joy of being part of something bigger than himself.

Their coach moved among the players, offering personalized feedback and encouragement to each boy. When Zeke reached Timothy, he demonstrated something with his batting stance that made her brother nod with understanding.

For the first time in months, something loosened in her chest.

Experience taught her to be wary when everything seemed too good, but for today—this evening—she intended to rest in God's rich blessings.

A prestigious design project. Financial breathing room. The opportunity to give back.

A place for Timothy to belong. To shine. And to shake off his grief.

And maybe baseball could do the same for Brian.

While the varsity team took the field for another warm-up, Clarissa mingled with the JV parents near the gate to greet their players once they exited the dugout.

After last night, she already knew Timothy would want to stay and watch the varsity game, but she'd much rather run Brian home and do a little work on her class project.

Hopefully by the time she returned to pick Timothy up, Karen would be done posturing among the varsity parents.

And Clarissa would have a decent plan to survive the next six weeks.

Chapter Nine

Zeke shouldered his bag as the last rays of Friday evening sunlight slanted across the field.

His whistle still hung around his neck, a weight that matched his fatigue after three straight game days followed by today's grueling practice.

He rolled his shoulders, trying to release the tension that had built throughout the week. The boys had needed the intensive drills after their performance against Riverside, but he'd pushed them hard.

Perhaps too hard.

But at least next week's games were more spaced out and they could use the weekend practice to relax a little.

As he crossed toward the parking lot, a solitary figure on the sidewalk caught his attention. Timothy Miller sat on a bench, both a baseball bag and backpack between his knees, checking his phone.

He'd dismissed the team over twenty minutes ago.

"Miller? Everything okay?"

Timothy looked up, concern straining his features. "Coach. My sister's late and she's not answering."

"Try calling her again." Zeke set down his bag. The cooling evening air carried the scent of distant rain clouds—a spring storm brewing.

Timothy nodded, phone already at his ear.

After several rings, Clarissa's voice became audible, the pitch higher than usual even from a distance. "I know, I'm sorry—the car won't start and I'm stuck at the sporting goods store and the shirt design has to be delivered in twenty minutes or Karen will kill me and—"

"Rissa, slow down." Timothy held up a hand, as if she could see him. "Coach Matthews is still here so I'm not alone. At least for now."

A pause, then more frantic words that he couldn't quite make out.

"Let me talk to her." Zeke extended his hand.

Timothy surrendered the phone with a half-smile.

"Ms. Miller? This is Coach Matthews."

"Zeke?" Her voice caught and something in his chest tightened at the raw vulnerability in that single word. "I'm so sorry about Timothy. I'm trying to find someone to try to jump my car, but that's not working out so well and the design has to get to the print shop before they close at six or else they won't rush our order and Karen specifically said—"

"Whoa. Hold on a second." While he already wanted to help, Karen's power trip was nothing to ignore and Clarissa's errand directly affected his team. Or at least their fundraising efforts. "Where are you?"

"Eastside Sporting Goods on Washington."

"We'll see you soon." He ended the call, already pulling out his keys. "Come on, Miller. Let's go rescue your sister."

Timothy grabbed his gear, following Zeke to his SUV with the calm acceptance of someone who'd had to adjust on the fly before.

As they pulled out of the school parking lot, Timothy fidgeted with his phone on his lap. "Please don't think badly of Rissa. She never flakes like this. It's just been a crazy week."

"I don't think badly of her at all." Zeke navigated a left turn. "Everyone has car trouble sometimes."

Timothy nodded, staring out the window at the gathering dusk. "Last time our car died, Mom was still around. That was rough—she was pretty sick by then."

The casual reference to loss created an opening Zeke hadn't expected. "Cancer?" he asked quietly.

"Yeah. It sucked." Timothy's voice held the forced casualness of someone who'd learned to state painful facts without emotion. "Rissa moved home from college to help when Mom first got diagnosed. Then stayed after...you know."

Zeke nodded, memories of his own mother surfacing unbidden—not of her death, still fresh three years later, but of her determined single parenting after his father checked out. "Your dad wasn't in the picture?"

Timothy shrugged. “Nah. He split when I was like five. Brian barely remembers him. Just...gone one day.” He glanced sideways at Zeke. “Yours, too?”

The perceptive question caught Zeke off guard. “Yeah. Alcohol was his first love. We were a distant second.”

A moment of understanding passed between them, transcending coach and player, adult and teenager.

The boy sighed. “Mom always said that God is a father to the fatherless. That He promises to never leave us.”

Zeke’s heart leapt at the familiar verse. Something his mother had also quoted numerous times. A father to the fatherless. A defender of widows.

And one who placed the lonely into families.

“Anyhow, Rissa gave up a lot,” Timothy said, pride evident in his voice. “She was on some art scholarship at CSU. Had to switch to online classes. But she never complains.”

Zeke absorbed this new information, adding another layer to his growing understanding of Clarissa Miller.

Not just a talented young woman thrust into guardianship, but someone who chose family over opportunity long before it became a legal necessity.

They found her pacing outside the sporting goods store, clutching a flash drive in one hand and her phone in the other. Her hair had escaped its usual ponytail, copper strands catching the fading light.

Zeke pulled up alongside the curb and rolled down the window, gesturing to the back seat as he hit the unlock button. “Hop in.”

Relief washed over her features and she quickly buckled in. “You actually came. Thank you.”

“Where’s this printing place?”

“Murphy’s on Third street. We have—“ She checked her phone. ”—twelve minutes.”

Zeke pulled back into traffic, heading downtown with practiced efficiency.

From the front seat, Timothy peppered his sister with questions about her day, her stranded car, and how long she’d been waiting.

"Let's just focus on getting this design delivered." Her voice was steadier than it had been on the phone but still stretched thin. "Then we can figure out the rest."

Murphy's Printing occupied a narrow storefront wedged between a coffee shop and a tax preparation office. As they arrived, the owner was flipping the sign to "Closed."

Zeke jumped out before either Miller had even unbuckled.

The bell jangled as he entered, catching the owner mid-lock.

"We're closed," the man said.

Zeke extended his hand. "Zeke Matthews. Baseball coach at Loveland High."

Recognition softened the man's expression. "Coach Matthews. I'm Joe Murphy. My nephew plays ball so I've been following you in the paper. Good program you're building."

Zeke nodded. "Appreciate that. I'm here with the designer for our team shirts—Clarissa Miller? Karen Henderson said you needed the files by six."

Joe checked his watch with a sigh. "Cutting it close. Karen's been calling every hour asking if they've arrived."

"Technical difficulties." Hopefully that was enough explanation to smooth things over. "But we're here now."

Joe nodded toward the door, where Clarissa stood clutching her flash drive. "Come on in, then. Let's get this transferred so I can start production tomorrow."

As Clarissa uploaded her files to Joe's computer, the printer examined her work with professional interest. "Clean design. Good spacing on the text elements. And a balanced layout for the back too. Very nice."

"Thank you." Clarissa's posture relaxed.

"I'll have the first batch ready by Monday afternoon. Fifty shirts at twelve dollars each, just like Karen requested."

Clarissa's head snapped up. "Twelve? Each?"

Joe nodded, oblivious to her reaction. "Standard rate for the two-color design and quality she specified, plus the rush. Would have been ten if you'd reached the bulk order threshold."

He saved the file and started to shut down his computer. "Selling them for twenty is a decent margin for a fundraiser."

She accepted the returned flash drive, then stepped back. Her muttered words about overpriced shirts and absurd markups weren't quiet enough to escape Zeke's notice.

A flicker of concern registered. Karen had been pushing for a higher price point at the booster meeting, but he'd tried to rein her in. Had something changed?

He'd save that conversation for another time and place since Joe appeared eager to lock up.

Once back in the SUV—this time with Clarissa in the passenger seat and Timothy in the back—her professional facade cracked further. "I can't believe I came that close to messing up the team shirts. But at least I kept my word unlike someone else. We really should have been able to place a bigger order than that."

She pressed her fingertips to her temples. "Too late for that now. Meanwhile Brian's home alone, probably starving because I'm not there and I still need to figure out what's wrong with the car before parts stores close, and—"

"Breathing helps," Zeke said gently.

She exhaled a sound halfway between a laugh and a sigh. "Sorry. It's been a day."

"How was practice?" She turned her attention to Timothy in the backseat, clearly attempting to shift focus from her own concerns.

"Brutal." Timothy's exaggerated shudder reeked of teenage dramatics. "Coach made us run extra sprints for every unforced error in the games."

"Team accountability. Part of taking responsibility." Zeke met Timothy's eyes in the rearview mirror with the hint of a smile.

Timothy rolled his eyes. "Plus the varsity guys hogged the batting cages again. Hard for me to improve if we never get reps."

Zeke filed away the complaint, making a mental note to address the practice structure. The JV players deserved equal development opportunities, not leftovers from the varsity.

"Is he really struggling with his hitting?" Clarissa glanced at Zeke, the simple question carrying layers of parental concern.

"He might be struggling a bit at the plate." Zeke chose his words with care. "But I'm confident he'll hit his stride. Especially since he's one who actually listens to the coaches."

The flash of gratitude in her eyes told him he'd struck the right balance between honesty and encouragement.

Back at the sporting goods store, Zeke tried to start Clarissa's sedan himself just to listen, then took a look under the hood.

He straightened just in time for a raindrop to land on his forehead. He shook it off. "It's most likely your battery or alternator but could be a starter motor or something more serious. It will take a bit of time to diagnose and fix it, but stores are closing and it's starting to rain."

"Can't you just try jumping it? I have cables."

He hated to burst her bubble of hope. "As do I, but I'd hate to have you end up stranded again another time. I'll just give you both a ride home, and you can deal with fixing it tomorrow."

Her shoulders slumped, but she retrieved a shopping bag from the trunk and locked the car. "At least I got Brian's glove. I was already cutting it close."

"If it's new, it will need breaking in." Zeke plugged their address into his GPS and started driving. "What's happening tomorrow?"

"Recreational league tryouts." Clarissa sighed. "Brian's bouncing off the walls. But also nervous, because the coaches will hold a draft next week to pick the actual teams.

"A draft for a kids' rec league?" Zeke snorted a laugh.

"Apparently it's a big deal." Her first genuine smile of the night appeared. "Welcome to small-town sports politics."

As they approached the Miller residence—a modest single-story home with neatly trimmed hedges—Zeke made an impulsive decision. "I can give Timothy a ride to practice tomorrow morning. And afterward, we can take a look at your car, see what it needs."

After all, nothing inappropriate about giving a player a ride in an emergency. Right? Or teaching him how to jump-start a car.

"Really?" The surprise in her voice suggested she wasn't accustomed to such offers.

"My mom's cars were always breaking down so a neighbor taught me basic maintenance. Good life skill for him to learn, too."

"That would be amazing. Teaching him to drive has been challenging enough."

"Then it's settled." Zeke fought back a yawn, the long week catching up with him. "Eight o'clock pickup tomorrow, Miller. Be ready."

As the Millers gathered their things and headed up the walkway, a light came on in the front window. Brian's silhouette appeared, the door opening before they reached it.

Even from the car, Zeke saw the relief on the younger boy's face.

Family. Connection. Belonging.

He drove home in silence, the emptiness of his SUV now palpable where it hadn't been before. His apartment waited, clean and orderly and utterly devoid of the chaotic warmth he'd just witnessed. No one would have a light on for him. No one would open the door before he reached it.

For the first time in years, the solitude he'd once craved felt less like independence and more like isolation.

And now he had tomorrow to look forward to.

Or to dread.

After practice Saturday morning, Zeke glanced over his shoulder before ushering Timothy into his SUV, feeling ridiculous at his own furtiveness.

Like a spy in a bad movie, not a coach giving his player a ride.

"Why are we being so weird about this?" Timothy tossed his bag into the backseat.

"Don't want the other players thinking there's favoritism." Zeke started the engine, the partial truth tasting sour in his mouth. "Baseball teams run on perceived fairness."

The real reason—avoiding Devon's knowing looks and inevitable report to Vaughn—felt too complicated to explain. And too personal to admit, even to himself.

As they pulled away from the deserted practice field, Zeke stifled a yawn. He'd regretted his impulsive offer almost immediately after arriving home last night, the weariness of the week settling into his bones as he'd stared at his empty refrigerator.

But a promise was a promise.

"Everyone knows that varsity players are the favorites." Timothy huffed out a breath. "And life is never fair. So why did you volunteer to give me a ride and stuff?"

The memory of his mother's face flashed before Zeke's eyes. "Just taking what someone did for me—and my mom—in the past and paying it forward. Being a good Samaritan."

Loving his neighbor like—

Nope. Not going there. Especially not with that particular word.

"Okay." Timothy turned his attention to finding a radio station.

Ten minutes later, Zeke pulled into the Millers' driveway, surprised to find another car pulling out—an aging red sedan with a dented bumper. "Who's that?"

"That's Mrs. Winters." Timothy was already halfway out the door. "Rissa and Brian must be back from tryouts."

Zeke followed Timothy up the walkway, this time noticing the frayed net on the basketball hoop above the garage, the weathered paint on the trim, and the abundance of weeds and volunteer grass surrounding a few yellow tulips in the sparse flower beds flanking the front door.

Everything about the property spoke of delayed maintenance and limited resources. Especially time.

The door opened before they reached it.

Brian burst out, a baseball cap askew on his head and his freckled face alight with excitement. "I think I'm going to make a team! The coaches said I did good in right field!"

"Congratulations." Timothy stole the cap and ruffled his brother's hair.

Zeke nodded. "Right field's an important position."

"That's what they said!" Brian beamed, then snatched his cap back.

Clarissa appeared in the doorway, her smile warm with pride and affection. "Tone it down just a notch, okay bud?"

"Rissa, can I show Timmy the drills we did?" Brian bounced on his toes as if about to explode with energy.

Clarissa rested a hand on his shoulder. "Let your brother put his stuff away and grab a snack for him and his coach. But maybe later after we get the car working again."

As the boys disappeared inside, Clarissa leaned against the door frame. "Thanks again for last night's ride. And for today. You really didn't have to do this."

"Happy to help." Zeke meant it despite his earlier reluctance. "Car troubles never happen at convenient times."

"Speaking of which..." She reached into her pocket and produced a set of keys. "We're tagging along."

"That's not necessary—"

"It is, actually." The gentle determination in her voice stalled any argument. "Brian should learn the basics too, I need to pay for the parts, and legally, I should be the one driving it home when you get it running."

His hesitation must have shown on his face.

"Don't worry." She retrieved a small purse from just inside the door with a teasing smile. "I have my license as well as complete faith in your mechanic abilities."

Something about her easy confidence—both in him and in general—disarmed his protest. "Practical, I guess."

"I'm all about practical." The simple statement seemed to carry more weight than its brevity suggested.

Not much later and they were headed toward the sporting goods store, the Miller family filling his usually quiet SUV with conversation and life. Brian dominated the backseat dialogue, regaling his brother with a detailed play-by-play of his tryout performance.

"Did they make you do the throw-in from the outfield drill?" Timothy asked. "The one where you have to hit the cutoff man?"

"Yeah! The coach showing us the stuff said my arm's decent but I need to aim better."

While the brothers talked baseball, Zeke glanced at Clarissa in the passenger seat. "What were you doing during the big tryout? Watching to pick up a few tips for backyard practice later?"

"Hardly. I took advantage of some uninterrupted laptop time and my phone's hotspot to finish a website for one of the café regulars." She offered a self-deprecating smile. "Hogan Appliance Repair desperately needed to join this century."

"And anything else?"

"Then I wrapped up the logo package for last weekend's silent auction winner. I totally worked the laptop to the point it started to overheat, but it feels good to get stuff off my plate for a change." She turned toward him, the morning sunlight catching the natural highlights in her hair. "Now I'm clear except for classwork until Monday, when my big new project starts."

"Classwork for your design degree?" Zeke recalled her mentioning it at the booster meeting and then Timothy had brought it up again. "What made you choose that path?"

Something softened in her expression. "I've always loved creating beautiful things. Wanted to be a painter when I was little."

Hadn't Timothy said something about an art scholarship? Maybe he'd ask to see one of her paintings sometime.

She glanced out the window, her voice taking on a wistful quality. "But I needed something practical. Not everyone can sell in galleries, but there's design work everywhere you look. Logos, websites, packaging—it's all art in disguise."

"Commercial art with a purpose." He raised an eyebrow.

"Exactly." Her smile returned. "Plus the switch let me transfer to online classes when Mom got sick. Flexible enough to fit around real life."

"Must have been a difficult time."

"It was." She tucked a loose strand of hair behind her ear. "At least Mom's life insurance paid off the house. Only way we've managed on café wages since then."

The simple statement, delivered without self-pity, revealed volumes about her financial reality.

As they pulled into a spot next to Clarissa's old sedan, Zeke thought of his comfortable coaching salary, his simple but secure life, and the absence of dependents. The contrast humbled him.

Under the careful observation of six additional eyes—and the assistance of two of the extra hands—Zeke was able to jump-start the stranded vehicle. That at least ruled out anything wrong with the starter and put the repair more firmly within his knowledge base.

He followed Clarissa to the closest auto parts store and soon they were all inside. While they waited in line for a sales associate to test the battery and alternator, Brian bounded ahead to examine the display of air fresheners shaped like pine trees. Timothy trailed behind, then stopped at the row of specialized tools.

"Your brothers are a lot alike." Zeke grabbed a shopping basket since he might as well pick up more oil and washer fluid for his vehicle while here.

"Sometimes I think they're twins born three years apart." Clarissa matched his stride down the aisle. "Same mannerisms, same interests. Brian hero-worships Timothy, tries to mirror everything he does."

"And Timothy?"

"Pretends to be annoyed but secretly loves it." Her voice held the warm insight of someone who knew her family's hearts completely. "He's stepped up more than any fifteen-year-old should have to."

Before long—after a trip outside with a diagnostic tester—they were browsing the batteries.

Zeke was too aware of Clarissa beside him from the subtle scent of her shampoo to the way she scanned packages for price comparisons.

If things were different…

But they weren't.

She was Timothy's guardian. His player's sister. Off-limits in every way that mattered if he stuck to professional interactions. And he should because his signature on Vaughn's form meant something.

Zeke diverted his attention back to the boys and his automotive mechanic task.

They weren't the only customers in the parking lot with a hood up as he showed the Miller boys how to clean the terminals and install the new battery.

Timothy carried the old one back into the store with his sister to get a refund on the core deposit, then returned whistling at the receipt in his hand. "Over a hundred bucks for a battery? That's crazy."

"And that was the cheapest one." Zeke chuckled.

"Welcome to car ownership." Clarissa took the receipt. "Insurance, tires, fluids, repairs—it adds up fast."

Timothy groaned. "I'm gonna need a job just to afford driving."

"We'll figure something out." A secretive smile flickered across Clarissa's face, there and gone so quickly Zeke might have imagined it before she stashed the receipt in the glove compartment.

"Shall we give this job a test run?" Zeke gestured for Timothy to get behind the wheel. "Keep it in park, but see how she starts."

The engine roared to life and Clarissa breathed a sigh of relief. The weight that lifted from her shoulders was almost visible.

Yes, she was out a hundred dollars, but it could have been a lot worse.

"That deserves a celebration." She turned to her brothers. "Hot fudge sundaes for successful tryouts and a resurrected car?"

The boys whooped their approval before she pivoted to Zeke, her invitation clear. "You're welcome to join us. My treat—least I can do after your rescue services."

His heart and mind battled for a moment. It might not be inappropriate to give a player a ride or teach them auto mechanics. Or to spend time with a single woman either.

But ice cream crossed some sort of invisible boundary.

He really needed to pray about how close he could get to the Miller family and still keep his integrity intact.

"I should get going." The responsible answer won out.

He didn't imagine the flash of disappointment in her eyes, though she masked it in a blink. "Of course. Thanks again for everything."

As the Millers piled into their newly functional car, Zeke trudged back to his SUV.

Alone.

Too close to past walks of shame to the dugout after striking out.

Chapter Ten

Clarissa fumbled at the coffee maker in the pre-dawn darkness of the kitchen, her mind already racing through the day's meticulously scheduled minutes.

Tuesday meant waitressing at the café until eleven-thirty, Rocky Ridge Development until four, then a rush to Timothy's away game—assuming traffic cooperated.

Oh, how she hated sliding into the bleachers in the second inning or later, but some–most–days it couldn't be helped. At least she'd eventually be there to cheer him on.

The familiar gurgle of brewing coffee provided momentary comfort as she reviewed her mental checklist. Finish Clay's website feedback during her lunch break. Complete her online discussion post during Brian's homework time.

Just more of the rhythm of perpetual motion that defined her life.

She glanced at the kitchen clock: 5:17. Just enough time to check her email before heading out the door.

Moving toward the table, Clarissa reached for her laptop and touched something sticky beneath it. She lifted the computer to find a puddle of neon blue liquid spreading across the wood surface.

"No, no, no..."

Her stomach dropped as she examined the laptop's underside, the sports drink having seeped into the vents and keyboard. She hit the power button, praying for the familiar startup chime.

Nothing.

She tried again, holding the button longer, desperation building with each silent second.

Her college assignment—the one due Thursday that was almost done after hours of work. Clay's website files. Her budget spreadsheets. Her entire collegiate and professional life lived on this machine.

Okay, a few things were backed up in the virtual cloud, but only enough to keep her safely qualified for a free account. She really should have upgraded her storage before now, but there'd always been another bill to pay.

A different emergency to handle first.

"Come on." She connected the charger with trembling fingers. The charging light remained dark. "Please."

The magnitude of the disaster crystallized in her mind. Without her laptop, she couldn't complete her coursework and graduate. Couldn't finish her freelance projects. Couldn't earn the income needed to support her family.

The kitchen clock's relentless ticking reminded her she had no time to deal with this now. Already running late. Always running late. Never enough time.

Clarissa stuffed the laptop and charger into her bag, wiping sticky blue residue from her fingers onto her jeans before heading out into the chilly morning, her chest tight with building panic.

Inside her car, the first tears escaped—hot and unwelcome against her cheeks. She swiped them away with the back of her hand, angry at her momentary weakness. Crying solved nothing. Fixed nothing. She knew better.

But the weight of the new problem atop her precariously balanced life crushed her resolve. For one shameful moment, she yearned for someone beside her in the passenger seat. Someone to share her struggles. Someone whose strength she could lean on when her own faltered.

Zeke's face flashed unbidden in her memory. Mostly his relieved-to-escape expression masked with a veneer of polite regret as he declined the ice cream invitation. She'd read too much into his kindness, as usual.

He was Timothy's coach, not someone to shoulder her burdens.

Cast your cares on me, for I care for you.

The verse surfaced from previous quiet times, a whispered reminder in the silence of her car.

"I'm trying," she murmured, starting the engine. "Sorry I keep forgetting that You're here."

The prayer felt inadequate, but it was all she had to offer as she drove toward Hope's Café and whatever else the day might bring.

As Clarissa entered the cafe kitchen's warmth, a few of the staff were busy chopping ingredients for the day's menu.

Trevor tipped his head at the oven. "Greta already popped blueberry muffins in to bake and coffee's brewing."

"Thank heavens." Clarissa hung her jacket on a free hook by the back door. The rich aromas surrounded her, momentarily displacing her worries.

"Rough morning?" Lauren stopped beside her with a concerned frown. "You look like you've been crying."

"It's nothing." Clarissa brushed off the observation, retrieving her apron from another hook. "Where do you need me?"

"Check to make sure we've got enough silverware rolled, then circle back here and Trevor will put you to work prepping." Joel stood in the office doorway, the empty cash register tray propped on his hip. "Dad's coming in at eight, and Amanda starts her second day. Should be a full crew today."

Clarissa nodded, moving toward the dining room where she plugged in her laptop behind the counter. Perhaps with some rest and charging time...

The next hour passed in the familiar choreography of café preparation. Napkin bundles rolled. Condiments filled. The daily chef's special written on the small white board near the entrance.

The routine offered a comforting normalcy that almost let her forget the crisis waiting behind the counter.

Just minutes before opening, Clarissa checked her laptop. The charging light remained dark. She pressed the power button and held her breath.

A faint crackling sound emerged, accompanied by the acrid scent of electrical burning. She yanked the plug from the wall, her heart racing.

"That can't be good." Greta poured a cup of coffee nearby.

"Not good at all." Clarissa's throat tightened as she pulled out her phone to text her brothers.

What happened to my laptop last night?

Timothy's response came almost immediately: ***It got super hot while Brian was using it. Shut down by itself. But I'm sure it was off when my Gatorade spilled.***

She blew out a slow calming breath. ***Next time, clean it* all *up! And TELL ME if there's a problem so I'm not caught by surprise. BTW, the laptop is fried.***

She silenced her phone and shoved it into her pocket.

The confirmation of what she suspected did nothing to ease the knot in her stomach. The laptop was old, a refurbished model she'd bought when starting college. It had been slowing down for months, occasionally overheating during complex tasks.

But she'd needed it to last just a bit longer. Just until she finished the Rocky Ridge Development project and had financial breathing room.

"It's dead," she whispered. The full reality sank in. "Everything's gone."

The first sob caught her by surprise, bubbling up from somewhere deep and unguarded. She pressed her hand against her mouth and hurried toward the semi-privacy of the kitchen, but it was too late.

The dam had broken.

Tears streamed down her face as her body shook with the force of her suppressed distress.

Greta's arms encircled her, steady and warm, guiding her into the office. "Let it out, honey. It's okay."

"It's not okay." Clarissa collapsed onto a chair and struggled to speak between sobs. "My assignment was on there—twenty hours of work down the drain. And Clay's website. And all my billing records. So much stuff that wasn't backed up to the cloud. Plus I don't have time to deal with this today. I have work to do for a new client and there's Timothy's game, and—"

"Breathe." Greta edged her own chair closer and rubbed small circles on Clarissa's back.

"Why is God letting this happen?" The question escaped before she could censor it. "On top of everything else? It's too much, Greta. I can't..."

"You know," Greta said gently, "when my dad died, my mom asked the same questions. The letters Matt found in the old buffet are like the Psalms that way—full of honest cries for help. God doesn't mind when we tell Him exactly how we feel."

The simple permission to acknowledge her pain eased something in Clarissa's chest. Her tears slowed, leaving her hollow and spent.

"What happened?" Lauren asked from the doorway, concern etched across her features.

"Laptop disaster," Greta said. "Everything's gone."

Joel appeared behind Lauren, his expression shifting from employer to friend. "What do you need, Clarissa? How can we help?"

The simple questions—and the genuine care behind them—brought fresh tears to her eyes. "I need to get it to a tech, see if anything's salvageable. Especially the web design project that's half my grade and due Thursday. But taking time for that errand, means missing Timothy's game, and Brian will be alone after school, and—"

"I know a computer nerd from my speech class last semester. I'll see if he's available." Lauren pulled out her phone, then slipped past Joel into the kitchen.

Greta tightened her arm around Clarissa's shoulders. "And I can pick up Brian, take him to the game, and bring them both home. Except I might need to leave here before the delivery—"

"I can stay late to put the rest away," Debbie volunteered from behind Joel, a flush coloring her cheeks. "If... if that would help."

The offer wasn't as casual as Debbie might have hoped. Clarissa had seen the woman's secret interest in the handsome delivery driver.

Lauren returned, phone in hand. "My friend can pick up your laptop in an hour. He'll assess it and give you options before this evening." She squeezed Clarissa's hand. "And if you need a couple days off to redo your class project, we've got you covered."

"I can't ask you all to—"

"You didn't ask." Joel narrowed his eyes. "We offered. That's what family does."

Family. The word lingered in the air, warming the space between them.

"Let me make sure I understand." Clarissa took a steadying breath. "Lauren's friend will check my laptop. You guys will cover my shifts if needed. Greta will get Brian and take both boys to today's game. And Debbie will handle the grocery delivery."

"See?" Greta smiled gently. "You're not alone in this. Not even close."

"Group hug." Lauren pulled Joel and Greta toward Clarissa in a circle of support.

"Father God." Greta rested a steady hand on Clarissa's shoulder. "Shower our girl with Your peace today. Remind her that You see her struggles. Your word says we can hold onto hope because You are faithful to keep Your promises."

Greta's voice cracked. "You promised to carry Clarissa. To provide for her needs, to never leave her alone. You never lie so we know Your promises endure."

As they moved apart, Clarissa wiped her eyes, trying to absorb the comfort of Greta's words.

She wanted desperately to believe. To trust that even a fried laptop would somehow work out.

But as the café's front bell clattered, signaling the arrival of the first customers of the day, the weight of her responsibilities settled back onto her shoulders.

While she was grateful for her café family and their practical help and spiritual encouragement, ultimately, the problems remained hers to solve.

And she had never felt less adequate for the task.

Clarissa shouldered the front door open, fumbling with her keys while balancing the oversized box against her hip.

Six o'clock and exhaustion already pulled at her limbs like gravity gone wrong. The day's trials had left her wrung out, and evening loomed with hours of work still ahead.

She set the box on the kitchen table, wincing at the bright orange price sticker she hadn't yet removed.

The emergency credit card—the one she'd promised herself was only for a true crisis—now carried a balance that would take months to erase. Especially since she'd made the difficult decision to also upgrade to the necessary speed and features required for her future work.

Earlier that afternoon, Lauren's computer expert friend had delivered the bad news with apologetic efficiency. Between the perpetual overheating that had fried internal components and the power grid shorted by a sports-drink-soaked battery, resurrecting her old laptop would cost almost as much as replacing it.

Worse, he'd confirmed her greatest fear: most files on the hard drive were corrupted beyond recovery, including the nearly-finished Advanced Web Design project due in just two days.

The one she was going to upload when it was done.

A rookie mistake she wanted to blame on her perpetual lack of sleep.

She dropped her backpack beside the box, then surveyed the kitchen table where sticky residue still marked the scene of the crime.

This wouldn't work any longer. They needed a different homework spot. Plus stricter rules about beverages.

First, she'd need to set up the new laptop, reinstall her software programs, and see what she could salvage from cloud storage. The boys' school assignments should be accessible through their online classroom platform, and the client files not already backed up might be retrievable from email attachments.

Time consuming but possible.

But the custom coding for her class project? She'd have to recreate it from scratch and had already texted to accept Joel and Lauren's offer of time off.

Her phone buzzed with a text from Greta: ***Bringing the boys home with burgers. What's your order?***

A small mercy. ***Anything works. Thank you.***

With dinner handled, Clarissa hauled the card table up from the basement and set it up in the living room, away from food and drinks. The new laptop's box opened with a satisfying hiss of vacuum-sealed packaging, revealing gleaming hardware that smelled of plastic and possibility.

As she connected cables and followed startup prompts, she also calculated the fallout from the day's disaster.

Instead of enjoying a financial cushion or a chance to surprise Timothy with a car, she'd be focused on paying off the debt. Which meant she'd have to accelerate the Rocky Ridge Development project to reach the first payment benchmark sooner.

Sleep would become an even more distant luxury.

Headlights swept across the living room window, followed by car doors slamming and the sound of boys arguing about something indecipherable. The front door burst open, bringing with it the scent of fast food and the chaotic energy of her brothers.

"Food's here!" Brian brandished paper bags spotted with grease.

Greta followed with drink carriers and a sympathetic smile. "Computer situation update?"

"Replaced and getting set up." Clarissa gestured toward the addition to their living room. "Thanks for taking on the boys today."

"Anytime." Greta squeezed her shoulder. "Call if you need anything else."

As Greta departed, the boys gravitated to the kitchen, spreading food across the table.

"How was the game?" She unwrapped her burger, glad to see both bacon and lettuce.

"We lost." Timothy frowned. "Four to two."

"We had runners on base in the eighth." Brian was already halfway through his burger. "But Timothy struck out."

Timothy shot his brother a venomous look. "Thanks for the reminder."

Clarissa recognized the seeds of a deeper frustration. "You'll get it next time. Everyone has off days."

"It's not just today." Timothy jabbed a fry into ketchup with enough force that it crumpled. "I'm in a slump. Can't connect with anything. I'll never make varsity if I can't hit."

The melodrama of teenage catastrophizing tested Clarissa's frayed patience. After her day of actual crises, Timothy's baseball struggles seemed trivially manageable—yet she remembered fifteen all too well.

Every setback felt like the end of the world.

"Slumps don't last forever." She softened her tone. "And Coach Matthews seems to believe in you."

"How would you know?" Timothy's words carried an accusatory edge. "You weren't there."

The barb landed with precision. "I wanted to, but I had an emergency, Tim. My laptop—"

"You're always having emergencies." He wadded up his burger wrapper. "There's always something. Some excuse. Some complaint about how much you have to do. Work. School. Cooking. Laundry."

Tears pricked her eyes as guilt twisted beneath her ribs. "That may be true, but sometimes there are true emergencies that have to be taken care of right away no matter what else I'd rather be doing. It's kinda like doing your homework when you'd rather play a video game. Responsibilities are part of growing up."

She took a deep breath and blew it out slowly. Taking her stress out on a grumpy Timothy or a wide-eyed Brian was far from how she'd envisioned the night going.

"It might be hard to believe me right now, but I promise I'm going to do everything I can to be at your game on Thursday." Even if she got no sleep between now and then.

Timothy grunted as he reached into his backpack, pulling out a soft package. Glimpses of red fabric with black and white lettering showed through the plastic wrapping.

She'd forgotten the first batch of team shirts were being delivered.

"These made everything worse." Timothy opened one side long enough to pull out the paper inside, then tossed it all on the table

Clarissa recognized her handwriting on the order form, but written across the top in bold ink were the words "Paid by Sponsor."

"Henderson's mom made a big deal about how a *generous anonymous donor* allowed some kids to get free shirts." His voice dripped with humiliation. "Might as well have a neon sign saying *charity case* above my head after the school paid my registration fee."

Clarissa unfolded a shirt and held it up, admiring how they'd turned out. Timothy might be annoyed, but had the others reacted the same? "Were you the only one who got a sponsored shirt?"

"No." Timothy's lower lip jutted out. "I think Martinez got one too. At least, his mom was crying and I heard his dad lost his job last month."

Something warm unfurled in Clarissa's chest. Her spontaneous gesture had helped another family in genuine need.

God knew. He'd prompted her generosity before she needed those funds to repair her car or replace the laptop. The promise Greta had reminded her of earlier—that God would provide—suddenly felt less like wishful thinking and more like tangible truth.

"Did anyone say who sponsored the shirts?" She bit her lip to suppress a smile.

Timothy shrugged. "Some people thought it was the Ramirez family since they own that big restaurant. Or Coach. He'd do something like that."

"Or..." Clarissa said slowly. "Maybe it was your sister."

Two sets of eyes snapped to her face.

"You?" Timothy's disbelief morphed into understanding. "Wait—because you designed them?"

"I donated my design fee back to cover shirts for families who might struggle with the cost." She glanced at the order form. "I didn't know how the secretary would label the forms. But... you're welcome for your new shirt."

Timothy's expression cycled through confusion and embarrassment before landing on reluctant amusement. "You could have just told me."

"And miss your dramatic reaction?" She raised an eyebrow. "Besides, I didn't expect Mrs. Henderson to make such a spectacle of it."

"So you paid for our shirts." Brian's gaze bounced between the two of them. "Even though you needed money for a car battery. And a laptop."

"I didn't know we'd need either of those when I made the decision. And since I'd just signed a contract for that big project, it was a good time to be generous." Brian's simple observation had created an opening she hadn't planned but recognized as necessary. "However, there's something we should talk about."

Both boys stilled in their chairs.

She took a deep breath, choosing vulnerability over pride. "Guys, we have to be honest about our finances. I've tried to shield you from worries, but today showed me that maybe you need to understand our situation better. So we can start acting like a team."

She explained, as gently as possible, the delicate balance of their budget. How her job at the café provided stability—as long as she put in the hours there—but her design work paid for the extras and by summer would hopefully replace the waitressing income completely.

How every unexpected expense—like their baseball stuff or today's laptop replacement—meant cutting back elsewhere like delaying Brian's new glasses. Again. How she'd been willing to make most of the sacrifices so they could focus on school.

On being kids.

"But there are going to be bad days—like today." She offered a weak smile. "Days where we have to search for something to be thankful for. Everything with the laptop crash and needing to redo my entire enormous college project before Thursday has been a nightmare—and reinforced that you need to tell me about things even if you think you might get in trouble. But it also showed me that I have friends to count on."

She started listing blessings, her voice growing stronger. "We have a home and each other and food. We have matching team shirts and a big job that will pay for other things we need."

Timothy's earlier frustration seemed to have softened. "I'm thankful I made the team as a freshman when a dozen others got cut."

"I'm thankful I might get to play for the All-Stars if the coach likes me enough." Brian wiggled a bit on his chair.

Tension melted from the kitchen as their list evolved from sincere to silly. From ice cream and pizza to the fact Timothy didn't have to clean his room because Brian was still doing Timothy's chores for another week.

Clarissa snorted at that last one. "Not a chance you weasel out of that or any other cleaning. Not when there's still a sticky spot on the table from earlier."

As the boys cleared their dinner mess, laughter replacing the earlier friction, Clarissa's gratitude mingled with determination. Despite everything, she was keeping her promise—keeping them together, keeping them whole.

It might mean endless days and sleepless nights, especially with her class assignment to recreate, but she'd do whatever necessary to make the Ridge project successful and build a financial safety net.

Just one more challenge to overcome. One more burden to carry.

Chapter Eleven

Guilt provided the fuel as Zeke pitched to Timothy Miller, adjusting the speed and placement of each throw as the satisfying crack of an aluminum bat against a baseball echoed across the practice field.

Saturday morning sunlight slanted through the chain-link backstop, creating diamond patterns on the dusty ground where another nine JV players waited their turn in the batting rotation.

Like Timothy had pointed out last weekend, Zeke had allowed the varsity team to be first in line while his younger players scraped by with leftovers. No more.

These boys deserved the same development opportunities, the same chance to reach their potential.

Hence today's intensive session.

Timothy connected solidly with the next pitch, driving the ball to deep center field where it would have cleared the fence in game conditions.

The improvement in his mechanics after a little coaching was remarkable now that his shoulders were squared, hands positioned correctly, and weight shifting with proper timing.

"That's it, Miller!" Zeke noted the satisfied grin spreading across the boy's face. "Feel that connection?"

From the outfield, where varsity players ran conditioning drills, Andrew Henderson jogged past in his fourth punishment lap for arguing with Devon. For violating the team value of respect.

The entitled attitude that earned him the extra exercise reminded Zeke why he preferred working with the hungrier JV players who still played for love of the game.

"Last round." Zeke waved the next player forward. "Everyone gets five more swings. Focus on what we've worked on—see the ball, trust your swing."

Practice concluded with the usual equipment breakdown and field maintenance duties. Most players dispersed, eager to claim their Saturday freedom, but Timothy lingered as Zeke loaded baseballs into their mesh bag.

"Thanks, Coach." The boy adjusted his cap. "This really helped. I can't wait to get more reps at the batting cages this afternoon."

The mention of batting cages triggered a memory from Thursday night's game—Clarissa approaching him after their victory, asking quietly if he knew where Timothy could get additional hitting practice.

Her exhausted appearance had concerned him; she'd looked like someone operating on willpower alone after missing Tuesday's game for what he'd heard was some sort of a work emergency.

He'd fought the urge to ask about her well-being. Professional boundaries and all that.

Zeke focused his attention on the current Miller. "Keep working on that follow-through. And trust the mechanics we practiced."

He watched Timothy jog toward the parking lot where Clarissa waited beside her sedan. She handed him the keys and retreated to the passenger side, visibly taking a deep breath before getting inside.

The sight almost made him smile despite his efforts to maintain appropriate emotional distance.

As they pulled away—Timothy behind the wheel with careful movements and multiple mirror checks—Zeke made an impulsive decision. Cage time sounded like the perfect way to work out the frustrations of the past week and test his surgically repaired shoulder's current limitations.

The fact that he might encounter the Millers there was purely coincidental.

At least, that's what he told himself.

An hour later, Zeke approached the batting complex where eight metal chain-link enclosures were arranged like pie slices around a central hub of pitching machines.

He scanned the occupied cages, noting a few teenagers he didn't recognize and a father-son pair working on bunting technique.

No sign of the Millers yet, though Timothy had mentioned coming this afternoon.

"I'd like an hour of cage time." Zeke handed the attendant his card. That should keep him here long enough to justify the drive.

Or long enough to run into Timothy and his sister, if circumstances aligned that way.

Leaving his equipment bag outside the gate for cage three, Zeke fed tokens into the machine, selected his preferred speed, and settled into his stance.

The first pitch came fast and straight. He let it pass, timing the delivery, feeling the familiar anticipation build in his muscles.

The second pitch met his bat with a solid crack that reverberated through his hands and up his forearms—a sensation he'd never tire of experiencing.

For twenty minutes, he lost himself in the rhythm. See the ball. Time the swing. Connect. Follow through.

Each successful hit reminded him why he'd fallen in love with this game as a scared kid desperate for something to be proud of.

His shoulder began to ache—a reminder of limitations imposed by surgery and imperfect healing—but he pushed through until muscle memory overcame discomfort.

The sound of applause broke his concentration. He turned to find three figures watching from outside the cage—Clarissa flanked by her brothers, all wearing expressions of impressed appreciation.

"Don't mind us." Clarissa's voice carried a teasing note. "We were just enjoying the show."

Heat crept up Zeke's neck, though he couldn't deny the satisfaction her admiration stirred. Had he known they were there, he might have put a little extra power behind his swing.

Might have showed off a bit more.

Turned out he hadn't needed to.

Zeke propped his bat on his shoulder and approached the gate. "Thought I might work on my swing a bit even though I'm just a coach now."

"You played professionally, didn't you?" Timothy's eyes were bright with hero worship. "The way you crush the ball is way too good for high school or even college."

"For a while."

A very short while.

Zeke deflected the memory with a question of his own. "How many tokens did you get?"

"Twenty." Clarissa consulted her watch. "But we can only stay a half hour at most since I need to get Brian to his practice by three."

An opportunity presented itself—one that felt natural rather than contrived. "I could work with Timothy here, then drive him over to Brian's practice. Where is it?"

Surprise flickered across her face. "The LBA fields on First and Taft. But are you sure? That's a lot of driving and we don't want to take up all your Saturday."

"It's a nice day for a change." He shrugged, then tipped his head toward Timothy. "Besides, a half hour isn't quite enough time to make real progress. At least twice that would be better and I've got time remaining in addition to his tokens."

Relief softened her expression. "That would be amazing. Thank you."

Watching her navigate the logistics of her brothers' schedules and seeing her gratitude for any assistance, only reinforced his growing admiration for her strength. She managed complexities that would challenge most adults, all while maintaining grace under pressure.

For the next hour, they worked on refining the mechanics they'd practiced that morning—weight distribution, bat path, timing. Timothy's natural athleticism responded well to focused instruction, and by the session's end, his consistency had noticeably improved.

"Feel the difference?" Zeke asked as they walked toward his SUV.

"Huge difference." Timothy practically glowed. "It feels natural now instead of like I'm fighting the bat."

It wasn't long before Zeke reached the sprawling Loveland Baseball Association compound. He'd intended to drop Timothy off, but something about the place drew him from his vehicle.

Six diamonds were arranged around a central hub containing restrooms, concessions, and administrative offices. And dozens of boys ranging from eight to sixteen were engaged in various practice activities.

There was something infectious about watching the young players discover fundamental skills, coached by others who shared their enthusiasm.

The sight reminded Zeke of the pure love of baseball before scholarships and professional aspirations complicated the joy.

As they approached the nearest diamond, looking for Brian's team, Zeke couldn't help but assess the instruction being provided.

Solid fundamentals, positive reinforcement, age-appropriate drills.

Though he noticed a few technical adjustments that might benefit the younger players, he was impressed by the organization's commitment to player development.

"This is a great setup." He followed Timothy toward another field. "How long has the LBA been operating?"

"At least since I was little." Timothy grinned. "This might be Brian's first time, but I've been playing here for years. Until this year of course when I made the school team instead."

One field later, they found Clarissa seated on aluminum bleachers behind home plate, watching Brian take ground balls at shortstop.

Her face lit up when she spotted them approaching—a reaction that sent warmth spreading through Zeke's chest despite his efforts to remain detached.

"I thought you were just dropping him off," she said as they settled beside her on the metal seats.

"Got curious about the facility." Zeke shrugged. "Impressive operation. I might look into volunteering this summer."

"The kids would love having a real coach." She turned her attention back to the field where Brian attempted to turn a double play. "Though I'm not sure how much 'real' coaching twelve-year-olds need."

"More than you might think." Zeke watched the practice with professional interest. "These are the years when good habits form. Fix mechanics now, and they'll carry forward forever."

Practice concluded with the traditional team cheer and equipment collection. Brian jogged toward them, dusty uniform and bright smile testimony to a successful session.

"Did you see my diving catch?" he asked. "Coach said it was Major League quality!"

"I saw." Clarissa reached out and ruffled his hair. "Very impressive."

Brian attempted to frown as he smoothed his hair back into place, but the high energy from a solid practice had his smile peeking through again.

"Since everyone needs to eat..." Clarissa stood, brushing dust from her jeans before turning to Zeke. "How about joining us for an early dinner? There's a nice park adjacent to this complex, and I already ordered a pizza delivery. Should have plenty and it's my treat. It's the least I can do after all your help with my transportation issues last weekend."

Zeke hesitated, weighing the wisdom of extending their time together. The boys would provide natural chaperones, and a public park hardly constituted anything inappropriate.

Not if he kept things friendly on the surface.

"Okay." He followed the Millers in the mass migration of families back toward the parking lot.

Was it bad that he already looked forward to more time with the family that had somehow become so important to him? Guess he'd been alone for too long.

Outside the baseball-quote-engraved arch marking the end of the complex, Clarissa turned left toward a vacant picnic table beneath mature cottonwoods adjacent to a playground.

Between the baseball fields and the community park, the place must attract families every weekend.

Clarissa had planned ahead—a cooler in her car trunk yielded cold drinks while she pulled paper plates and napkins from a tote bag. Minutes later, a pizza delivery driver located them and deposited two steaming boxes.

"This is quite the operation." Zeke twisted open his sports drink.

"Experience with impromptu family meals." She offered a self-deprecating smile. "Though I don't often splurge on pizza and we don't usually have company for them."

Although casual, her comment carried implications about their finances. And social engagements.

He'd been invited into something precious as their normal family routine expanded to accommodate him.

"Should we say grace?" Clarissa extended her hands toward her brothers.

Zeke joined their circle, Timothy's calloused palm gripping his right hand while Clarissa's smaller, softer fingers intertwined with his left. The simple contact sent an unwelcome jolt of awareness through him that he worked to suppress.

"Father, thank You for this beautiful day and for friends to share it with." Her voice carried genuine gratitude. "Thank You for helping me get my college assignment recreated and submitted just in time, and for letting me hit that first milestone on my big job so I got paid."

Her words revealed struggles he'd been unaware of, adding another layer to his growing understanding of her daily challenges.

Timothy picked up the prayer thread: "Thanks for helping my batting improve, and for Coach taking extra time with me."

"Thank you that I'm finally going to get new frames for my glasses." Brian touched his slightly bent wire-rimmed spectacles. "Plus that Timothy has to do his own chores again starting Monday."

Clarissa chuckled, then all eyes turned to Zeke, expectation clear in their expressions.

"Thank You for this nice day and for new friends." He meant every word.

But mostly he was thankful to be welcomed into something remarkably like family—an experience he'd forgotten he'd been missing.

The pizza was excellent—a local place he hadn't yet tried—and the conversation flowed from baseball observations to school updates with a healthy dose of teasing between the brothers.

When Brian attempted to demonstrate his diving catch using his pizza slice as a baseball, both Clarissa and Zeke reached to prevent disaster, their hands colliding mid-rescue.

Their eyes met across the table, shared amusement creating a moment of almost parental connection.

As if they were co-conspirators in managing these energetic boys.

The realization should have triggered alarm; instead, it felt surprisingly natural.

"So where did you learn to hit like that?" Timothy asked between bites, curiosity evident in his expression. "I mean, that was impressive."

Zeke soon shared more than he'd intended—college baseball on a full scholarship, dreams of professional play, the sports management degree pursued as backup insurance.

The campus ministry group that had shown him true faith and the Heavenly Father who was so different from Zeke's alcoholic abusive dad.

The minor league draft, the shoulder injury that ended everything, and the long recovery that had redirected his entire future.

"My mom died three years ago. So she never got to see my dreams fall apart. Or get put back together." He was surprised by his own candor.

Would Mom see that he'd kept his promise to be a better man than his father's poor example?

Clarissa's eyes held compassion that tightened his chest. "I'm sorry about your mom. But we're grateful God brought you here for this season."

The simple statement, delivered with quiet sincerity, affected him more deeply than elaborate condolences might have.

She leaned forward. "What made you want to teach?"

"Honestly? I never imagined myself in education and it's turned out to be very different than I'd thought. But getting teaching credentials was the only way to access coaching opportunities, and so when Loveland's position came available mid-year..." He balled up his used napkin. "Sometimes God puts you exactly where you're needed."

"Even when it's not where you thought you wanted to be." She glanced at her brothers, understanding evident in her expression.

At that moment, Zeke could almost believe that God's plans for this chapter of his life were better than his original goals.

Especially if it had brought him here.

To her.

Their eyes met again—another connection charged with possibility. Until Brian's enthusiastic reenactment of his teammate's base-running mishap demanded their attention, breaking the spell.

As the shadows lengthened across the park, Zeke relaxed in ways he hadn't experienced since arriving in Loveland. For a few hours, he was simply Zeke—not Coach Matthews with all the associated pressures and limitations.

Yet while he enjoyed their company, reality intruded.

Every moment spent with Clarissa deepened his appreciation for her character, her strength, her quiet faith. Every shared laugh with her brothers strengthened connections that complicated his coaching responsibilities.

While he'd been honest about his reasons for going into teaching, it was also true that the real job hadn't turned out to be what he'd expected when he'd accepted it.

Teaching physical education extended far beyond games in the gym to mind-numbing staff meetings and tedious record-keeping.

And coaching? He'd imagined developing young talent and sharing his passion for baseball. Instead, he also navigated entitled parents, administrative scrutiny, and professional boundaries that felt increasingly restrictive.

He was stuck by his own word for the rest of this season and school year.

Had to stay the course even if it created a barrier keeping him from something precious he only began to understand.

Because he wanted nothing more than to stay and be a part of the Miller family.

God, give me wisdom. I don't know how to resist them anymore.

And when he eventually walked toward his SUV later, the glaring truth rose up to taunt him.

Getting close could cost him everything.

Chapter Twelve

Rain pelted Zeke in the face beneath the inadequate awning as the opposing team's bus disappeared into the furious storm hammering the parking lot while frustration built in his chest.

The game should have been canceled hours ago.

Any coach—or person—with half a brain could have read the forecast and made the call before teams traveled across the county. But Vaughn had insisted they "wait and see," more concerned with avoiding scheduling headaches than practical decision-making.

Now Coach Morrison was livid about the wasted trip, and Zeke couldn't blame him. Almost two hours of travel for a game that lasted just twelve minutes before the first lightning strike forced officials to clear the field.

"Next time, Matthews, check your weather app," Morrison had snarled before boarding his bus. "Some of us don't enjoy driving through monsoons for nothing."

Not like Zeke enjoyed his current predicament, either.

Lightning split the darkened sky, followed by thunder that almost shook the gymnasium windows behind him.

The gym where they'd all taken temporary shelter until a final decision was made.

The gym where dozens awaited his leadership.

Zeke blew out a slow breath, then turned. He'd rather face a line drive without a glove.

The door slammed behind him as he entered, the sudden warmth a stark contrast to the wind-driven rain outside. The familiar scent of floor wax and perspiration enveloped him, along with the echo of voices bouncing off the cinderblock walls.

His players milled around the near end of the basketball court, their discarded cleats lying in a pile of wet jackets and equipment bags. At the opposite end, parents clustered in the bleachers, obviously reluctant to venture back into the storm.

An opportunity presented itself. What if he had an impromptu practice for the players and an equally impromptu meeting with the parents?

Cut through the red tape and bureaucracy that usually slowed every booster club decision to a crawl.

"Devon." Zeke waved his assistant coach closer. "Get them into tennis shoes, then take them through warm-ups, followed by fielding practice. Grounders first, then pop-flies. If we have time, we can set up base-running simulations—might come in handy in a tight spot later this season."

Devon nodded, already gathering the players. The sound of his whistle pierced the gym's ambient noise as Zeke turned toward the bleachers.

"Parents." His voice carried in the enclosed space as he approached. "Since we're all here, this seems like perfect timing to discuss our next fundraising initiative."

Thunder boomed outside, as if the storm itself emphasized his point.

"As you can see—and hear—weather is always a factor in spring baseball. We need an indoor batting cage to maximize practice time when Mother Nature doesn't cooperate." He pointed to the vacant corner of the gym where old wrestling mats were stacked against the wall. "That space could accommodate a portable cage system if we can raise the necessary funds."

He located Karen Henderson on the front row, complete with her fancy handbag clutched to her midsection. "How much have we raised so far with the merchandise sales?"

She lifted her chin and gave him a number.

He nodded. A decent amount, but not nearly what they might have gotten with a better pricing strategy.

Clarissa had been right about the markup. With cheaper quality shirts in bulk and sold at a more reasonable price point, they should have moved twice as many units. But that was behind them now.

"That's a good start, but not enough." He eyed the other parents. "We need to think bigger. And like I'd suggested to the booster club board, I'd like to see us host a youth baseball skills camp. One afternoon. Multiple age groups. And our varsity players assisting as instructors."

Murmurs of interest rippled through the small crowd.

"When were you thinking?" Mr. Ramirez pulled out his phone to check his calendar.

Zeke consulted his coaching notes. "Next Monday works best with our game schedule. I know that's a quick turnaround, but if we organize efficiently..."

Mrs. Henderson sat up straight. "That's a lot of work and moving pieces to coordinate. Are you sure—?"

"I have no doubts we can get it done." Zeke's mind scrambled. "We'll need an online registration form and some sort of flyer to hand out or other way to spread the word fast."

"I can design promotional flyers." Clarissa raised her hand on the third row, her voice cutting through the overlapping conversations. "And in addition to giving them to the local elementary and middle schools to send home to families, what if the players themselves handed them out on Saturday morning?"

"Where would you propose doing that?" Mrs. Henderson had half-turned to address the group. "We can't just go door to door and expect—"

"I say we target the LBA fields, which are already full of young baseball players, parents, and their coaches." Clarissa stared back. "We could also visit our team sponsors and ask for their help spreading the word."

Her practical thinking impressed him again, though he kept his expression neutral.

"Perfect." Zeke smiled. "So those basic ideas take care of bringing kids in. But then we'll need more volunteers to—just brainstorming out loud here—set up for the event, run a check-in table, maybe have some concessions for parents, and get more dads to supervise the various stations since my coaching staff will be spread thin."

Hands began rising around the bleachers as parents claimed responsibilities.

Mrs. Henderson attempted to insert herself as the coordinator, but Zeke asked her to record who had volunteered for what. It would keep her busy without bogging down the rest of their planning.

"What about registration fees?" Mrs. Torres half-stood from the back row to be heard. "And how many kids do we need to make this worthwhile?"

"Just a minute." Zeke switched to the calculator app on his phone. "If we factor in two lanes plus a couple pitching machines, the special balls, and mats to protect the gym floors... Minus what we already have... That leaves us with..."

He looked up. "Speaking in theoreticals, fifty registrations at twenty-five dollars each would give us our target. But someone asked a good question earlier. Are we providing enough value at that price without giving them a T-shirt too?"

"How much would a shirt cost to make?" Mr. Ramirez had his own calculator app open.

"If we order in bulk with a basic shirt instead of the premium quality, we should be under ten dollars for sure even if we have to pay a small fee for a faster turnaround." Zeke ignored Mrs. Henderson's glare because he'd done his research.

He turned to Mr. Ramirez instead. "We'd need more registrations to cover that added expense. But could you see if Murphy's Printing can fit us in before we finalize anything?"

Mr. Ramirez nodded, then stepped away to make the call.

Zeke glanced at Clarissa. "If the numbers work, can we use that stylized diamond with player silhouettes you created?"

Her eyes widened, but then she nodded. "Of course. And I can put the same image on the promotional flyers."

Mr. Ramirez returned with the go-ahead and a preliminary quote of seven dollars per shirt if they only printed on the front and only used one color of ink.

The energy in the room shifted as parents broke into smaller groups, organizing details with the efficiency of people who'd been given clear direction. Sign-up sheets passed from hand to hand. Phone numbers were exchanged. Tasks were claimed and subdivided.

Across the way, the rhythmic sound of baseballs hitting gloves provided a steady soundtrack. His assistant coaches' voices carried as they corrected fielding positions and encouraged effort.

As the various groups continued their planning, Zeke noticed the Hendersons huddled together on the front row, their expressions tight. He hadn't meant to neutralize Karen's leadership, but sometimes things had to move faster than taking time to coddle her ego.

Movement near the gym's entrance drew his attention.

His athletic director leaned against the door frame, arms crossed and brow furrowed as he observed.

How much had he heard of their plans? The team already had access to the fields on Monday for practice, so surely Vaughn couldn't object to parents working together to raise money to help their kids.

Although Zeke vowed to make a trip to the athletic secretary in the morning to fill out any required paperwork. The political ramifications and ruffled egos would have to be dealt with later.

For now, they'd made a lot of progress in thirty minutes of focused discussion.

A sharp crack of thunder interrupted his thoughts, followed by a lightning flash that illuminated the gym's high windows. The storm wasn't finished with them yet.

"Indoor batting cages are looking more necessary by the minute." Mr. Ramirez glanced toward the windows.

"Exactly the point," Zeke chuckled. "But since it seems you've got everything under control here, I'm going to rejoin practice before Devon starts enjoying being head coach too much."

Laughter followed his comment as he returned to where his players rehearsed a double-play drill with impressive precision.

Weather might derail games and administrators might complicate simple decisions, but this was why he'd gotten into coaching.

For the kids.

To develop their skills but also teach life lessons through sport. To build character that would serve them well long after their playing days ended.

Even if some days he waged a battle simply to do his job.

The Loveland High School parking lot buzzed with organized chaos as Clarissa approached the cluster of coffee-clutching parents and team-shirt-wearing players, Brian on her heels.

Steam rose from paper cups in the crisp Saturday morning air, creating small clouds that dissolved in the light breeze. The storm from earlier in the week had passed, leaving behind the fresh, clean scent of rain-washed pavement and budding trees.

"Clarissa! Perfect timing." The varsity shortstop's mom brandished a clipboard. "I've got your group assignment and downtown route here."

She accepted a thick stack of colorful flyers along with a hand-drawn map marking potential locations throughout Loveland's business district.

"Elementary and middle schools got theirs yesterday." Mrs. Torres addressed the group, checking items off her list. "Today we're hitting parks, baseball fields, family restaurants, and downtown businesses. Cast the widest net possible."

"Thirty-seven registrations online already!" One of the other dads waved his phone. "We're well on our way to our goal, especially since we'll take walk-ups too."

Excited murmurs rippled through the gathering.

"Where's my group?" Clarissa read off the names in the corner of her map.

Timothy appeared at her elbow, along with three other JV players she recognized from recent games. Brian bounced beside her, thrilled to be an honorary team member for the morning.

"We've got the downtown cluster." She plotted a logical path. "I see Peterson's Hardware, Murphy's Printing, The Flower Basket, and several others. Plus if we end at Hope's Café, you can have your parents pick you up there after we get ice cream. My treat."

"Ice cream for breakfast?" One of Timothy's teammates did an awkward jig.

"Ice cream after we finish our job." She soothed the correction with a smile. "And remember, several of these businesses already sponsor our team, so we can also thank them for their support."

Her comments carried to nearby groups, sparking similar promises of post-flyer treats.

Apparently the idea of ending with food held universal appeal for all teens, especially boys.

And she'd still have plenty of time to get Brian to his team practice this afternoon.

Twenty minutes later, her group settled into an established rhythm.

At each business, Clarissa let the boys take the lead—asking permission to hang flyers, explaining the skills camp, expressing gratitude for sponsorship when applicable. Their genuine enthusiasm proved far more effective than any adult sales pitch.

At Peterson's Hardware, the owner's face lit up when he spotted Clarissa behind players.

"There's the young lady who designed our new logo." He gestured toward a painted sign above the register featuring a stylized hammer and wrench design. "Look at that—clean, professional, and it fits on our business cards now."

He pulled a crisp card from his shirt pocket, displaying the same logo in miniature. "Thirty years with my dad's old clip-art mess, and now we look like we belong in this century."

"I'm glad you like it." It might not have been paying work, but it still brought a reward.

A customer examining paint samples turned with obvious interest. "That's beautiful work. Really eye-catching. Did you do those team shirts, too?"

"My sister designed everything." Timothy puffed out his chest, accentuating the artwork there, then tapped the top of a camp flyer.

The woman's eyes lit up. "I've been thinking about updating my pottery studio's branding. Can I get your contact information?"

"Sure." Clarissa handed over one of her business cards.

"This baseball design is so dynamic." The woman studied the flyer more closely. "There's real movement in those graphics. Exactly what I need, so I'll be in touch."

"Thank you." Warmth spread through Clarissa's chest at the casual acknowledgment.

Leave it to God to bring in business in unexpected ways while she'd been using her artistic passions for a good cause.

Her group moved on and were approaching Murphy's Printing when footsteps caught up with them from behind.

"How's it going?" Coach Matthews fell into step beside her, slightly out of breath, as if he'd been hurrying to catch them.

"Good progress." Clarissa tried to ignore the flutter his sudden appearance triggered. "The boys are doing great with the presentations."

"Just checking on all the groups. Making sure everyone has what they need."

It made sense. And yet she noticed he made no move toward other locations. Or other groups.

Were they the last one? Or was it just a handy excuse to be there?

Either way, she wasn't complaining.

As they continued down Main Street, the boys fell back into a continuing conversation about their season so far. And Timothy's batting—and home run—in the JV's last victory became the latest topic.

"Miller finally figured out how to connect." Danny, a sophomore pitcher, jabbed her brother in the ribs. "Must be getting extra coaching somewhere."

"Just doing what Coach taught us." Timothy shoved his friend back.

"And hitting the batting cages." Brian smirked.

Clarissa wrapped an arm around Brian's shoulders and pulled him back, placing a hand over his mouth before he said much more. It wasn't exactly a secret, but nothing more needed to be said.

Other than a whispered "thank you" to that same coach as they trailed behind the others.

"Hey, Tim." Her brother's friend Jake grinned. "Is your crush Monica working at the cafe today?"

Timothy's face reddened instantly. "How should I know?"

Monica? As in Debbie's daughter? If so, they probably also knew Monica's twin brother Mark, although he'd probably hide in the kitchen rather than let his peers see him hauling tubs of dishes around.

Jake shook his head in exaggerated shame. "Because I heard you asking about her schedule at lunch Wednesday."

Beside her, Zeke coughed into his hand as if to cover a laugh.

Clarissa bit her lip and squeezed Brian tighter, willing him to stay out of it. At least until they got home. Because right now, these teens were her source of gossip.

Danny did a little shuffle down the sidewalk. "When you gonna ask out your older woman?"

"She's only a sophomore!" Timothy protested.

"Yeah, but she can drive," the normally quiet Cole chimed in.

Danny spun to walk backward and face the group. "That's like dating royalty. Especially when you're still getting rides from your sister."

"At least I don't spend my time making googly eyes at the concession stand girl from the dugout." Timothy's comeback sent Danny into defensive sputtering and the others laughing.

Clarissa couldn't help but smile at the typical teenage banter, but time to change topics. "Leave it alone, guys. You all have plenty of time for romantic complications later in life."

"Says the person who doesn't have time for a boyfriend." Timothy tossed the comment over his shoulder. "Doesn't make you the expert on dating advice."

Heat flooded Clarissa's cheeks. His verbal punch found its mark as only a brother could.

"Enough." Zeke's voice held a bit of a growl. "Let's focus on the flyers for a couple more stops."

Of course the cause of *her* personal crush had to be walking beside her.

But as they continued their mission toward Hope's Café, her mind wandered.

Timothy wasn't wrong—she had no time for dating, no energy for the complications of romance. Between work, school, and her brothers' needs, there weren't enough hours in the day.

Yet if she dreamed up the perfect man—patient enough to understand her responsibilities, faithful enough to share her values, kind enough to care about her brothers—he'd look remarkably like the coach walking beside her, listening to teenage chatter with good-humored tolerance.

The bell above Hope's Café door announced their arrival, bringing Clarissa back to the present. Her four assigned players commandeered a booth while Zeke pulled over an adjacent table so they could all sit together.

Lauren approached with a coffee pot in hand and barely concealed amusement. "Well, well. Looks like someone's family expanded."

Clarissa rolled her eyes. Although she couldn't deny how they looked. Five energetic boys with she and Zeke as the token parental figures.

She dropped onto the remaining empty chair opposite Zeke. "I promised them ice cream once our flyers were handed out."

At the mention of flyers, Timothy remembered their initial purpose and soon Lauren had one to hang on the community bulletin board and the rest to hand out to customers who fit the demographic.

The instant Lauren left, Monica appeared to take their drink orders, her attention focused on Timothy and his teammates. It was a wonder the girl managed to get all the ice cream requests as well.

Clarissa caught herself exchanging an amused glance with Zeke at one particularly giggly response to a mediocre joke. She'd need to have a serious talk with Timothy later.

The bell over the door clattered and another group of players entered the cafe, led by none other than Karen Henderson and accompanied by Coach Devon.

Zeke stood and crossed the room. "Coach. How did the groups do on your side of town after I left? Got any flyers left?"

Hmm. Seemed the story about checking on groups was true, so she shouldn't read anything into Zeke's time with her group. Or her.

He was just doing his job as the head coach and lead organizer for Monday's event.

Karen's sharp gaze zeroed in on the location of Zeke's abandoned chair. The woman's raised eyebrow and pointed look reeked of disapproval. As if accusing Clarissa of monopolizing his time and attention for personal gain.

Clarissa turned back to the boys and their arriving sundaes. She'd done nothing wrong and so had nothing to feel guilty about.

Zeke sought them out on the street. Then situated himself at their table for a treat. They'd been completely professional in their mission. Surrounded constantly by teenage chaperones and in full view of the community.

Still, the moment served as a sharp reminder of the scrutiny Zeke endured in his position.

Their growing friendship—if that's what it was—existed under a microscope, subject to interpretation and judgment from those only looking for reasons to criticize.

Exactly the kind of complication she didn't have time for.

Chapter Thirteen

Zeke stuffed his hands in his jacket pockets and surveyed the controlled chaos spread across Loveland High's baseball facility, still amazed that they'd pulled this together in under a week.

Sixty-three kids ranging in age from eight to fourteen filled the central diamond and surrounding practice areas with the infectious energy that only came from pure love of the game.

The afternoon sun cast everything in golden light, a perfect backdrop for what could only be described as a minor miracle of organization.

Thank you, God. For the weather, for the turnout, for everything coming together.

At the cage nets, his varsity players demonstrated proper batting stance while younger groups rotated through fielding drills and first and third base. At second base, they'd set up a sliding station now occupied by a cluster of middle school boys.

Zeke spotted Brian Miller among them, his new glasses catching the sunlight as he attempted to mimic the safe sliding techniques being demonstrated.

It had been easy enough to stay busy in the outfield during registration, avoiding any appearance of special attention to the Miller family.

No need to provide ammunition if anyone wanted to accuse him of favoritism.

Though there was one Miller who kept drawing his attention despite his best efforts to remain professionally detached.

Clarissa managed what appeared to be a one-woman command center at a folding table positioned near the home plate backstop.

The registration rush had ended hours ago, but once she arrived, she'd transformed the station into everything else the event needed—sales table for the remaining camp shirts, lost-and-found depot, donation collection point, and a concession stand stocked with sports drinks and water bottles.

All donated by other parent volunteers.

As he watched, a small boy approached her, tears streaming down his dirt-smudged cheeks as he cradled his left hand against his chest. Clarissa came around the table to kneel at his eye level.

Zeke couldn't hear her words, but her body language spoke volumes about patient kindness. She examined the child's scraped palm with gentle efficiency, produced a first aid kit from beneath her table, and cleaned the wound while maintaining a stream of what appeared to be reassuring conversation.

By the time she'd applied a bandage, the boy's tears had stopped and his shy smile emerged. A woman —probably his mother—appeared, offering profuse thanks that Clarissa waved off.

The entire interaction—from crisis to resolution—had taken less than five minutes, but it revealed everything Zeke admired about her character. Grace under pressure. Natural caregiving instincts. The ability to make others feel seen and valued.

Giving in to impulses he no longer wished to deny, he found himself walking toward her table. If anyone asked, he was just checking in on the event's logistical needs.

"How are supplies holding up?" Up close, he spied the dwindling stack of camp shirts and the half-empty cooler of beverages.

"Better than expected." She cleaned the table where the first aid incident had left smears and then tossed the bandage wrapper along with the sanitary wipe. "Though I think we underestimated how thirsty sixty kids and their parents would get on a sunny afternoon."

Her smile carried the satisfaction of someone watching a successful event unfold.

"The turnout exceeded all our projections." Zeke tucked his hands in the pockets of his coaching jacket.

A burst of high-pitched giggles erupted from a group of cheerleaders who'd claimed a spot on the nearby bleachers. Their attention was focused on the older varsity players, underscoring the kind of adolescent drama that always accompanied teens.

Especially with prom later that week.

"Looks like we've attracted a few spectators only here to flirt." Could he use their presence as a conversation opener? Zeke cleared his throat. "On Saturday Timothy made it sound like you don't have much time for dating."

It was a clumsy transition, but Clarissa either didn't notice or chose to ignore his lack of subtlety.

"Hard to compete with homework and chauffeur duties." She gave a self-deprecating laugh. "Then again, my social calendar peaked at about age nineteen."

The opening was exactly what he'd hoped for, though he kept his expression neutral despite the spike in his pulse. "College social life was different?"

"More casual. Less complicated." She reorganized a stack of camp shirts with unnecessary attention to detail. "High school dating was always...cautious for me. My dad walking out when I was twelve made me pretty wary of trusting guys with big promises and charming smiles."

The admission revealed more vulnerability than he'd expected, creating the intimacy that lingered both precious and dangerous given their public setting.

"College was safer somehow." Her voice grew thoughtful. "Less pressure, more honest about expectations. But once I came home to help Mom..."

She shrugged, the gesture encompassing everything that had changed in her life. "Between caregiving and online classes, meeting people became nearly impossible."

Zeke absorbed the information with growing certainty about what it meant.

She was single. Had been for years, by necessity rather than choice. And despite her practical focus on family responsibilities, a wistfulness in her tone suggested she hadn't entirely closed the door on romance.

His pulse skipped at the possibilities.

"That must have been isolating." He moved a step closer under the pretense of examining the donation jar's contents.

The scent of her perfume—something light and floral—mixed with the afternoon's warmth.

"Sometimes." She looked up and met his gaze. "But some things are worth the sacrifice. My brothers needed stability more than I needed a social life."

The quiet strength in her voice made something tighten in his chest.

She'd given up what most people their age considered essential—freedom, spontaneity, the luxury of putting herself first—and somehow emerged with more character than people twice their age.

The kind of character he wished for himself.

"Still..." Was he standing closer than necessary for this conversation? "Everyone deserves..."

He wasn't sure how to finish that sentence. *Everyone deserves companionship? Love? Someone who appreciates their sacrifice?* All of it simultaneously true and inappropriate to voice.

The space between them crackled with unspoken possibilities. With the sense they were on the verge of crossing a line that couldn't be uncrossed.

Her eyes widened and her pulse beat rapidly at the base of her throat. Whatever boundaries he'd been trying to maintain seemed far less important than the woman standing before him.

"Coach Matthews!" A voice cut through the moment like a baseball through a window. "We need you at the batting cages! Some of the kids are arguing about proper grip technique!"

Devon's call jerked Zeke back to reality—to the dozens of children depending on his leadership, the parents who'd entrusted their children to his supervision, and the professional responsibilities that couldn't be ignored.

"On my way!" He stepped away from Clarissa despite every instinct urging him to stay.

Their eyes met one more time, her expression reflecting the same mixture of disappointment and understanding he felt churning in his own chest.

"Duty calls," she said softly, managing a smile that didn't quite mask the moment's lost potential.

•♥•♥•♥•♥•♥•

Clarissa watched from her table as Zeke gathered all sixty-three camp participants in a loose semicircle around home plate, his voice carrying across the infield as he delivered what appeared to be closing remarks.

The late afternoon sun caught the gold in his hair, and even from this distance, she saw the genuine enthusiasm in his gestures as he spoke to the young faces turned toward him.

Her mind kept drifting back to their interrupted conversation, replaying the moment when he'd essentially asked about her dating history. The questions had been deliberately personal, carefully casual in a way that suggested deeper interest.

Was he working up to asking her out?

The possibility sent a flutter through her chest that she tried desperately to suppress.

Even if he were interested—and that was a significant if—what could she possibly offer right now?

She was barely a third of the way into the Rocky Ridge Development project, working hard to stay on pace with the demanding timeline. If she somehow worked ahead and finished a week early, she could make her college graduation into an extra celebration.

But until then, every waking hour was accounted for.

Still, the way he'd looked at her earlier, the careful way he'd stepped closer during their conversation...maybe timing wasn't everything.

"Rissa!" Brian's voice broke through her reverie as he jogged toward her table, grass stains on his knees and a satisfied grin on his face. "Mrs. Evans is here for Cameron and said she'd give me a ride home, too. Is that okay?"

"Did you finish your math homework during study hall?" She fell back into guardian mode despite her distracted thoughts.

"All done. And I already put my gear in their car." Brian grinned.

She spotted the family near the parking lot, Cameron's mother waving in acknowledgment of Clarissa's thumbs up. "Tell her thank you for me. And Timothy and I will be home as soon as we're done here."

As Brian bounded away, she made a mental note to find something special to thank the Evans family for their ongoing help with transportation. Once she survived the next month, she'd have both time and money to express her gratitude.

And to feed her brothers more than another fast food dinner.

The camp participants continued dispersing as parents collected their children, leaving behind the discarded remnants of the afternoon's event—orange cones and empty water bottles in addition to the clutter of her command center.

Working quickly, she consolidated the unsold extra camp shirts into a single box and loaded the remaining drinks into another. Zeke would have to decide what to do with both.

She dragged the borrowed cooler to a grassy area and dumped the icy water before propping the lid open to dry. Hopefully the son of whichever family had loaned it would claim it. Otherwise, it could be stored in the baseball shed until the next home game.

Meanwhile, Zeke directed his players toward their usual field maintenance tasks, his coaching voice carrying across the diamond. "Equipment in the shed, bases secure, infield drag because it really needs it after today. Plus we've got some extra items to handle. Most of these cones and the registration table will go back to the gym storage."

When he approached her table, Clarissa became acutely aware of his presence in a way that made her pulse quicken. Especially the quiet strength in his movements as he examined her consolidated items.

"Looks like we'll need a few trips." He stacked the box of unsold camp shirts atop the drinks and jutted his chin toward the first aid kit as if asking her to add it to his pile. "Equipment shed first?"

Hating to leave anything behind when she had two functional arms, she placed the first aid kit, cash box, and plastic donation jar inside the cooler, then lifted it all. "Lead on."

Walking beside him toward the small building behind the home team dugout, Clarissa found herself drumming up courage she wasn't sure she possessed. If he could ask personal questions, maybe she could too.

"Can I ask you something?" Good. Her voice held steady.

"Shoot."

"Earlier you asked about my dating history. What about yours?"

He glanced at her with surprise, then seemed to consider his answer as they reached the shed.

"Plenty of female attention during college and my time in the minor leagues." His tone stayed casual. "But nothing serious."

He propped the door open with his foot, creating a small space of relative privacy amid the organized chaos of stored equipment.

"There was one girl who got close." He slid the shirt box onto a metal shelf. "Super devoted fan, always at games, always talking about our future together."

She held her breath, sensing a *but* coming.

He dropped the box of drinks near the wall with a thud. "Until I injured my shoulder. Amazing how quickly *forever* disappeared when the dream of major league wives' lounges evaporated."

Clarissa set down the cooler she'd been carrying, studying his profile as he arranged the items it held with unnecessary precision.

"She only wanted me for what I might give her someday." The hurt beneath the forced lightness in his tone was impossible to miss. "Turns out nobody dreams of dating a high school coach."

The vulnerability in his admission made her chest ache.

Without thinking, she reached out to touch his arm. "You might be surprised."

Her quiet words hung between them, loaded with implications she hadn't intended to voice so directly. Heat crept up her neck as she realized what she'd just admitted.

She pulled her hand back, tucking them into the back pockets of her jeans where they'd keep her out of trouble.

He turned to face her, something shifting in his expression. "C larissa..."

A strand of hair had escaped her ponytail, falling across her face in the breeze that swept through the open shed door.

Zeke reached up, his fingertips gentle against her temple as he tucked the piece behind her ear.

The simple gesture created a moment of such charged intimacy that the rest of the world faded. His hand lingered along her cheek, thumb tracing the curve of her jaw with care.

"I shouldn't..." His actions contradicted his murmured words as he stepped closer.

"Shouldn't what?" she whispered, her voice barely audible over the thundering of her heart.

Instead of answering, he lowered his head until his lips met hers in a kiss that started tentative, questioning, then deepened with a certainty that made her forget every reason this was complicated.

His mouth was warm and gentle, worshiping her lips with a patience that spoke of restrained desire.

Her hands found the front of his shirt, fingers curling into the fabric as she kissed him back with years of loneliness and longing.

The callused fingertips that framed her face belonged to a man who worked with his hands, who made everything better just by touching it.

It was perfect. Everything she'd dreamed a kiss could be but had stopped believing she'd ever experience before the boys were grown.

A sudden male voice shattered the moment. "Coach, where do you want the—"

Zeke jerked back as if he'd been burned, horror replacing tenderness in his expression so quickly that Clarissa absorbed the loss like a physical blow.

The approaching footsteps and teenage laughter grew louder.

Zeke stepped away from her, creating a deliberate chasm between them.

"We can't—" He ran a hand through his hair. "This was—"

But he didn't finish the sentence, leaving Clarissa to fill in the blanks with her worst fears.

What have I done?

Had she misread the signals? Just destroyed whatever fragile friendship they'd built by crossing a line he'd never intended to cross?

The shed door creaked wider as the first player appeared.

Have I ruined everything?

Relief flooded through Zeke as three of his players entered the equipment shed with armloads of cones and bases, their chatter filling the space with blessed normalcy.

They hadn't been caught.

No one had witnessed him kissing Timothy's guardian on school property during a school-sponsored event.

But God help him, he couldn't bring himself to regret it.

Not when he could still taste the sweetness of her lips, still feel the way she'd melted against him with a response that suggested she'd been thinking about this possibility as much as he had. That kiss was like coming home to something he hadn't realized he'd been searching for.

"Where do these go, Coach?" Cole Morrison hefted a bag of practice balls.

"Third shelf, next to the batting helmets." Zeke held his voice steady despite the chaos in his chest.

This would take the greatest acting job of his life, pretending nothing had changed when everything felt fundamentally different.

From the corner of his eye, he caught Clarissa's strained expression—confusion mixed with hurt that he needed to address. He had to fix this and fast.

He'd put the rest of the piled equipment away by himself just for a moment of privacy.

"That's good enough for now, guys." He waved them out of the shed and paused in the doorway. "Someone grab the registration table on your way back in to the locker rooms, but all in all, good work today."

The rest of the team dispersed, chattering about the camp's success with fading voices as they retreated back to the school and the locker room inside.

Only then did he turn to the pretty woman who was unnecessarily reorganizing items on a storage shelf.

"Clarissa." He closed the gap, but still maintained a careful distance. "Can we talk for a second?"

She turned, wariness evident in her green eyes.

"I'd really like to see where this could go between us." He kept his voice barely above a whisper in case anyone circled back. "But it's going to have to wait until after the season is over."

The words felt like both a promise and a prison sentence.

Once his coaching contract ended, the surveillance and professional constraints would disappear. He could romance her properly, without risking his career or her reputation.

Hurt flickered across her features before understanding replaced it. "My schedule is completely crazy right now, anyway. College projects on top of everything else."

"So we wait. And have to just be friends for now." An aggravating status that was both necessary and impossible.

Her slight nod carried a disappointment that matched his own.

"But friends can text, right?" The question emerged more hopefully than he'd intended.

"Friends can text," she said softly, her gaze flickering to his lips before she caught herself, color rising in her cheeks.

The blush sent heat spiraling through him, confirmation that whatever had ignited between them wasn't one-sided. His palms dampened as he fought the urge to reach for her again.

The sound of car engines starting in the parking lot broke the spell. Timothy would be among the students heading home, which meant Clarissa needed to leave too.

They separated with careful casualness, gathering their remaining belongings with the studied indifference of people pretending not to notice each other's every movement.

Walking to his SUV alone later with the cashbox under his arm for safekeeping, Zeke begged God for wisdom.

Had he made the right choice?

Yes, he was guilty of one unprofessional moment in the shed during a team event, but did that prevent him from building a future with a single woman on his own time?

His phone buzzed in his pocket and he pulled it out, heart racing. Had his new friend already texted?

The message on the screen from the athletic director made his blood run cold. ***Please see me first thing tomorrow morning. Important matter to discuss.***

Had someone seen them in the shed after all?

Was he about to lose everything for one perfect, impossible kiss?

Chapter Fourteen

The scent of stale coffee and the musty aroma of old filing cabinets did nothing to calm Zeke's nerves as he settled into the uncomfortable plastic chair across from the empty desk.

The cramped space seemed more like an interrogation room than an administrative office.

Fear clawed at his stomach as he waited, hands clasped tightly around the thick envelope in his lap to prevent fidgeting.

Yesterday's kiss replayed over and over with vivid clarity—the softness of Clarissa's lips, the way she'd responded to his touch, the devastating moment when footsteps had approached the equipment shed.

Had someone seen more than they'd thought? Was his career about to end before it truly began?

Keep an open mind. Don't give him ammunition.

The door opened with a sharp click, and Vaughn entered carrying a steaming mug and a manila folder thick with papers. He settled behind his desk with practiced efficiency, fixing Zeke with the kind of stare that suggested this conversation wouldn't be pleasant.

"Let's get right to it." Vaughn frowned. "How much did you raise yesterday?"

Relief washed through Zeke like cold water on burning skin.

Fundraising.

Vaughn wanted to talk about the fundraiser, not inappropriate relationships with players' guardians.

"We had an excellent turnout for such quick planning." Zeke tossed the envelope of cash onto the desktop in front of Vaughn. "These are the walk-up registration fees, shirt sales, and additional donations to add to the online registrations your secretary already tallied. Bottom line, we exceeded our projections."

Vaughn nodded, though his pursed lips suggested the response wasn't enough. "That's nice, but there's a problem."

The qualifier hung in the air like a high fly ball.

"A problem?"

"You might have covered the nets and mats, but you didn't budget for the pulley system to hang everything or a storage cabinet to house it for the off-season. Liability issues during gym classes, you understand."

Disappointment crashed through Zeke's chest. Of course there would be additional costs. There always were when it came to bureaucracy.

"However..." Vaughn's smirk seemed a bit too satisfied as he prolonged the moment. "Consider yourself lucky the Hendersons found a new sponsor to cover those expenses."

The name hit Zeke like a fastball to the ribs.

The Hendersons. Of course.

"You ticked Karen off by railroading the skills camp planning, no matter how well it turned out." Vaughn took a slow sip of his coffee, then shrugged. "Obviously I needed to soothe some ruffled feathers. Promised we'd add a plaque to the storage cabinet thanking Rocky Ridge Development for their generosity."

Irritation flared white-hot in Zeke's chest. The entitled attitude he'd been witnessing from Andrew Henderson on the field now made perfect sense. Just toss a little money at an obstacle and make it disappear.

How long before playing time became the next demand?

Zeke pressed his palms on his knees and worked to keep his voice level. "I don't believe one sponsor should get all the credit when the entire booster club and parent community contributed just as much if not more. This was a team effort."

Vaughn raised a single eyebrow. "How badly do you want those batting nets, Matthews?"

The implied threat loomed, impossible to miss.

Play ball with the Hendersons, or play without equipment.

His boss set his coffee down with a thunk. "You'll keep the Hendersons happy if you know what's good for you. They have considerable influence with the school board. The same board members who vote on educational budgets and employment contracts."

The words settled in Zeke's stomach like lead weights.

Compromise his values—even play the politically connected kid over more deserving players—or risk his job.

Whatever happened to living with integrity? About developing the whole student's mind, body, and character?

Guess Vaughn's catchphrase from Zeke's interview only applied when convenient.

God, give me a solution. Or provide a new job, because I won't become what I despise.

Vaughn's phone rang, interrupting Zeke's internal crisis. The assistant principal's expression shifted from annoyed to alert as he listened to the voice on the other end.

"I see," Vaughn said finally. "And this witness is reliable?"

Witness? Witness to what?

Ice formed in Zeke's veins as Vaughn ended the call.

"Coach Matthews." Vaughn narrowed his eyes. "I've received a report that a student witnessed you getting *cozy* with a player's sister during yesterday's event."

The accusation hung between them.

Only one particular student came to mind, but Zeke wasn't one to accuse without proof.

While he knew for a fact no one had seen the actual kiss, anyone could have seen him talking to Clarissa. One of their topics might have drifted into past relationships, but from the outside everything should have appeared innocent.

Meaning his automatic deflection—denial—was both necessary and fundamentally dishonest.

Zeke forced his expression to remain neutral, though his heart hammered against his ribs. "I can't say there was anything *cozy* about talking to Ms. Miller at the registration table since I also talked to Mrs. Torres and several other parent volunteers throughout the afternoon."

All of which was technically true.

He might have wished to get closer to her before being called away to help with the batting station, but he hadn't.

"Is that the only interaction you had with Ms. Miller?"

What exactly had the supposed witness said?

Zeke frowned, hoping Vaughn would take it as confusion. "She helped with clean up at the end since she had to stay to give her brother a ride home. I believe she was one of multiple people carrying supplies and equipment to storage..."

To the shed where their kiss burned in his memory like evidence begging to be discovered.

Vaughn studied him with the kind of penetrating stare that suggested he wasn't convinced but lacked sufficient proof to pursue the matter further.

Zeke kept his breathing steady. His return focus unwavering.

"Let me be clear, Matthews," Vaughn said. "The fraternization policy isn't a suggestion. One perceived impropriety, and you're finished. We cannot afford any scandal that might jeopardize community support like that from Rocky Ridge Development."

The warning landed with crushing finality.

Stay away from Clarissa, play favorites with the Henderson kid, and bow to wealthy donors.

"Understood." The word tasted like clay in Zeke's mouth.

"Excellent." Vaughn's smile returned, cold and satisfied. "I trust yesterday's success will continue throughout the season. Dismissed."

Walking toward the gymnasium for his next class, the weight of impossible choices pressed down on his shoulders.

If Vaughn had his way, Zeke would never speak to Clarissa again and instead spend his career catering to the whims of entitled parents who viewed athletics as a path to college scholarships rather than a prime opportunity for character development.

But playing it safe wouldn't advance a runner around the bases toward home.

There had to be a middle ground—a way to maintain his integrity while still exploring the most promising relationship he'd encountered in years.

He could certainly be professional in public. Keep all baseball talk off-limits during personal interactions.

But there was nothing inappropriate about two God-fearing single adults getting to know each other better.

And if that friendship eventually developed into something more after the season ended...well, that was between them and God.

Zeke paused at the entrance to the gym and pulled out his phone.

He'd promised Clarissa they could text. Now the question was what to say that would be appropriately casual while opening the door to deeper connection.

His thumbs hovered over the keyboard.

The bell would ring in three minutes, flooding the hallways with students. He didn't have time for hesitation. Not now.

But as he composed his first message, Zeke couldn't ignore the truth that friendship felt like both a beginning and a barrier to everything he actually wanted to say.

The cheerful ping of her phone cut through the clatter of dishes as Clarissa scraped the last of the spaghetti sauce from Brian's plate.

Her heart gave that familiar flutter—the one that had become as regular as breathing these past few days whenever she heard that particular notification sound.

Stop it. But her lips curved upward as she dried her hands on the faded dish towel.

She glanced toward the living room where Timothy sprawled on the couch, controller in hand and fully absorbed in his video game. Brian sat cross-legged on the carpet, surrounded by scattered papers and textbooks getting a jump start on homework so the rest of his weekend would be free.

Since both boys were occupied, she could steal a few precious moments for herself.

Sliding her thumb across the phone screen, her pulse quickened at Zeke's name.

Zeke: Just finished watching a documentary about the history of baseball. I think you'd really like it. Might teach you something. ;-)

Clarissa: Very funny. But how long is it? Not sure I can carve out time before summer.

Zeke: An hour. But speaking of summer, when things slow down maybe you can show me some of those hiking trails you mentioned. I keep hearing about Horsetooth Rock but haven't made it up there yet

Her breath caught.

The casual invitation sounded like so much more than two friends making summer plans. Not when she already imagined the two of them exploring the trail above the reservoir, sharing quiet conversation.

And maybe something deeper.

Clarissa: I'd love to! It's one of my favorite spots. The view from the top is incredible

Zeke: Can't wait. Though I should probably warn you—I'm more of a "take my time and enjoy the scenery" hiker than a "race to the summit" type

Clarissa: Perfect. That's exactly my speed too

The exchange felt intimate somehow, planning something weeks away as if they both believed this fragile connection would still exist.

She pressed the phone against her chest, remembering all the moments that brought them here.

The weight of his jacket around her shoulders when she'd gotten caught in the rain. How he'd driven to her rescue in the sporting goods parking lot. Their shared laughter over pizza in the park.

And then there was the skills camp. When he'd asked about her dating history. When she'd been close enough that the scent of his cologne made her want to lean in.

When he'd kissed her in a way that left her dizzy and hopeful and terrified all at once.

"This is crazy," she whispered to the empty kitchen. When was the last time she'd been this giddy about a boy?

Definitely before Mom got sick and her life collapsed to encompass their household alone. And there hadn't been time or energy for emotions beyond grief or worry ever since.

Until Zeke.

Zeke made her imagine a life beyond the endless cycle of work, school, and keeping her brothers safe and fed and—

Beep. Beep. Beep.

She glanced at the reminder alarm on her phone and sighed.

Family and friend time was over. Time to get back to work on her senior capstone portfolio.

She hadn't come this far to fail now.

Two more weeks. Just two more weeks until her graduation ceremony, followed by an additional week to finish up the Rocky Ridge Development project. Then maybe—just maybe—she could have a life that included more than scrambling to keep up.

She typed quickly, her fingers suddenly clumsy on the small keyboard.

Clarissa: I hate to run, but I need to tackle my portfolio analysis for graduation. Rain check on the texting until after the boys are in bed?

The response came faster than expected.

Zeke: Of course. Good luck. I'll be here whenever you're free

His accepting tone shouldn't have made her heart race, but it did. Everything about him pushed the boundaries of their agreed-upon friendship.

Clarissa forced herself to walk to the card table that doubled as her office. Ignoring the presence of her brothers in the same room, she turned on the laptop.

Now all she needed was to focus.

After pulling up the document she'd started earlier, she squinted at the cursor blinking on the half-finished page.

Over the past four years, she'd collected a representative sampling of her art and graphic design assignments, but had fallen woefully behind in the written component.

Now, in addition to a description of the techniques used on each individual piece, she needed to write a reflection on her entire journey through graphic design, an analysis of her growth as an artist, and a professional assessment of her strongest pieces.

Who really cared how she'd applied the classroom concepts and what she'd do differently in the future? It wasn't like any of her new clients would ever read it before hiring her.

As Clarissa worked her way through the portfolio images one at a time, her mind wandered occasionally to the next season of life. To her freelance business and the types of projects she'd be adding to her professional credits.

Her education certainly impacted the logos she'd designed for the cafe, hardware store, and the baseball team shirts. But taking that same art to online platforms like websites might be her true moneymaker.

Especially if she landed more clients like Rocky Ridge Development.

Could anything she'd learned make an immediate difference there?

Clarissa reached for her sketchbook.

As requested, she'd created a solid foundation for their website with clean navigation and a professional layout. But now it was time to take it to another level to justify the hefty payment and showcase her creativity.

Time to add interactive elements and animations and other polished touches.

She sketched the wireframes to represent the current structure, then tapped her pencil against her lips as the ideas began to stir. A hover effect here. Maybe a slideshow gallery there.

Something to show how the company's divisions took a location from start to finish and beyond. The necessary coding wouldn't be too difficult to make it workable across multiple viewing platforms.

Nothing she couldn't handle using a few techniques from her Advanced Web Design class. In fact, that nightmare of a project she'd replicated in just two days would be the perfect solution with just a couple tweaks.

She scribbled notes faster than her hand could keep up. This was her sweet spot finding creative solutions and thinking outside the box. Imagining something and then leveraging her newfound skills to bring it to life whether that was with a paint brush in fine art or computer coding.

Time blurred as she switched between portfolio analysis paragraphs and her website notes, the steady click of keyboard keys mixing with the distant sounds of Timothy's video game and Brian's occasional questions about his science homework.

The house settled around them, creaking and sighing like an old friend as she continued to make steady progress.

At some point, her neck began to ache from hunching over the laptop. She rolled her shoulders, trying to work out the knots, and blinked at the bright display.

When had her eyes started burning? The words blurred and she re-read the same paragraph for the third time.

Just a quick rest. She'd close her eyes for five minutes, stretch out the crick in her neck, then tackle the final section with fresh energy.

The last thing she remembered was the gentle whir of the laptop fan and the distant murmur of Timothy's baseball game...

Sharp pain lanced through her neck and shoulder, jolting her awake. The pointed corner of the laptop keyboard pressed into her jawline and something beeped insistently nearby.

She blinked in confusion, her vision swimming as she tried to orient herself.

The laptop screen had gone dark. Her phone lay beside her elbow, its battery warning flashing red in the darkness. And there, glowing on the lock screen, was a preview of a text that made her stomach drop to her toes.

Zeke: Guess it was too much to hope you might actually...

No. No, no, no.

With fumbling fingers, she unlocked the phone and opened their conversation thread. The timestamp on her last message glowed accusingly: 6:47 PM.

It was now 2:14 AM.

Zeke: Of course. Good luck. I'll be here whenever you're free

Zeke: Hey, just wanted to check in. How's the portfolio coming along?

Zeke: I know you said after the boys are in bed, but it's getting pretty late. Hope everything's okay

Zeke: Timothy mentioned you've been burning the candle at both ends lately. Don't forget to take care of yourself too

Zeke: Guess it was too much to hope you might actually follow through on staying in touch

As his tone shifted from supportive to concerned to disappointed, she absorbed the sense of betrayal. Sensed the hurt beneath his words and her chest ached in a way that had nothing to do with sleeping on a hard table.

Her cheek throbbed, and she touched it gingerly, feeling the ridged impression of keyboard keys pressed into her skin.

Perfect. As if this night couldn't get any worse.

But maybe...

Before she lost her nerve, she switched to her camera and took a quick selfie, making sure the ancient mantle clock was visible in the background.

The image was hardly flattering—hair mussed from sleep, keyboard marks decorating her face like some bizarre tattoo, eyes squinting in the phone's harsh flash—but it told the story better than any lame explanation ever could.

She attached the photo and typed:

Clarissa: I am SO sorry. Fell asleep at the table on top of my laptop. Which is why my face looks like this right now (note the time on the clock). I promise I didn't blow you off on purpose. Forgive me?

She hit send before she second-guessed herself, then stared at the screen, willing him to respond.

The refrigerator hummed in the kitchen and Timothy's soft snoring came from the back bedroom. But as the minutes ticked by, her phone remained stubbornly quiet.

Of course it did.

It was the middle of the night and he had a team practice in the morning.

Clarissa forced herself to stand, her stiff body protesting every movement. She needed real sleep. The kind that came from an actual bed, not a card table.

She'd have to finish her capstone portfolio later.

But as she shuffled down the hall clutching her phone in her hand, doubts crept in like cold fingers around her heart.

This was what she'd been afraid of. Why she'd warned him that her time was limited until graduation.

Except warnings and reality were two different things.

God, please don't let this end before we even had a real beginning.

Then again, maybe some things were too good to last.

Chapter Fifteen

The satisfying snap of leather meeting leather should have been music to Zeke's ears. Instead, the sound grated against his already frayed nerves as he watched Andrew Henderson botch another double-play turn at second base.

"Henderson!" Zeke couldn't hold back his irritation any longer. "Right foot on the bag and left on the ground. *Left foot.* We've only gone over this fifty times."

The morning sun beat down on the infield dirt. Sweat trickled between Zeke's shoulder blades beneath his coaching jacket, but the heat building inside him had nothing to do with the weather.

His jaw ached from clenching it, and he still tasted the bitter remnants of too much coffee consumed on too little sleep.

Three hours. That's how long he'd stared at his phone last night, waiting for a text that didn't come until nearly two-thirty this morning.

The image of Clarissa's exhausted face, keyboard marks pressed into her cheek like some kind of battle scar, had simultaneously melted his frustration and twisted his gut with concern.

How was she supposed to maintain that pace until graduation?

But that was a problem for later. Right now, he had twenty players depending on him to keep his head in the game.

"Reset the drill." He forced his voice to remain level. "Torres, you're fielding and tossing to second. Henderson, I want to see that foot planted solid this time so you can pivot toward first."

The shortstop jogged back to his position, shooting a quick glance at Henderson that spoke volumes.

Even the other players were getting tired of watching their teammate's sloppy fundamentals. This was supposed to be varsity baseball, not little league instruction.

Zeke crossed his arms and watched as Coach Devon fed a ground ball between second and third base. The junior varsity player running the bases took off for first like he'd just hit a ground ball.

Torres scooped it cleanly and fired to Henderson, who caught the ball with his left foot still dangling off the base like he was testing pool water.

The ball sailed over the first baseman's head with the runner a good stride past the base.

"Come on, man," Torres muttered under his breath, just loud enough for Zeke to catch. The disappointment in the junior's voice hit harder than any lecture Zeke could deliver.

Henderson shrugged, that infuriating smirk tugging at the corner of his mouth. "My bad, Coach. Guess the throw was a little high."

The blood rushing in Zeke's ears nearly drowned out the words. *My bad.* Like fundamental failure was just an oops moment. Like the rest of the team's time didn't matter.

"Miller!" Zeke's voice cut across the field sharper than he'd intended. "Take second base. Henderson, you've got laps. Give me a mile while you figure out where your left foot is."

"What?" Henderson's voice cracked. "Coach, I was just—"

"You were just disrespecting your teammate and this team." Zeke strode toward the boy, feeling every muscle in his shoulders coiled tight as fence wire. "Torres made a perfect throw. Don't you dare blame him for your footwork."

The field went silent except for the distant hum of traffic and the rustle of cottonwood leaves beyond the outfield. Even the maintenance crew working on the visitor's dugout paused, as if sensing the tension crackling in the air.

Henderson's face flushed red beneath his cap. "You can't punish me for one bad throw. My dad—"

"Your dad isn't your coach. I am." Zeke kept his voice low, but every word carried the weight of everything he wanted his players to learn. "And this isn't about one bad throw but a pattern of ignoring correction. This is about respect. This is about taking responsibility instead of making excuses."

The boy's jaw worked silently for a moment before he spun on his heel and jogged toward the warning track, his body language radiating sullen defiance with every step.

Zeke turned back to find Timothy Miller already approaching second base, glove in hand and eyes bright.

The contrast couldn't have been starker. Where Henderson approached every repetitive drill with almost boredom, Timothy moved with the intensity of someone who understood what an opportunity looked like.

"Hope you've been paying attention. You ready?" Zeke asked quietly as Timothy settled into position.

"Yes, sir." The freshman's voice didn't waver, but Zeke caught the slight tremor in his hands as he adjusted his cap.

Good. A little nerves meant he understood what was at stake.

"Torres, let's run it again."

This time, the drill clicked like precision machinery. Timothy's right foot found the bag, his body already turning as he plucked the ball from his glove. The pivot was smooth, the throw crisp and accurate. The first baseman barely had to move his glove, easily beating the baserunner.

"That's what I'm talking about!" Torres pumped a fist.

The entire infield seemed to exhale, tension bleeding away like air from a punctured tire.

They ran the drill five more times. Five perfect executions that had the whole team nodding and calling out encouragement. Even the outfielders drifted closer to watch, caught up in the rhythm of good baseball being played the right way.

The sharp pop-pop of ball meeting leather sounded like music again.

"Beautiful work, gentlemen!" Zeke clapped his hands together, feeling his first genuine smile of the morning spread across his face. "That's how you support each other. That's how you make your teammates better."

As their practice time transitioned to the usual field maintenance—raking the infield, checking the bases, touching up the pitcher's mound—Devon joined Zeke by the home dugout.

"Nice drill." Devon folded his arms and rocked back on his heels.

"Yeah, it was." Zeke pulled off his cap and ran a hand through his sweat-dampened hair. "Funny how much smoother things run when everyone's focused."

Devon glanced toward the warning track where Henderson still jogged through his required laps—leaving all the tedious fieldwork to his teammates—then back to Zeke. "Look, I agree the kid's attitude stinks. But are you sure promoting Miller is the right move?"

The question settled in Zeke's stomach like a lead weight. "Meaning?"

"Meaning he's still a freshman, regardless of how well he looked out there just now. Varsity pressure is different. What happens when he makes a mistake in a close game and the Henderson family starts calling for your head? You think Vaughn's going to have your back when Richard Henderson is breathing down the school board's neck?"

Zeke watched Timothy smooth out a rough patch in the dirt around second base, his movements precise and focused. The kid had been begging for extra batting repetitions plus staying after regular practice to field additional ground balls with a friend.

He'd earned this chance.

"What are you suggesting?" Zeke kept his voice neutral, though his jaw started to ache again. "That I let Henderson's attitude poison the whole team because his daddy has connections?"

"I'm suggesting you think about all the angles before you make a move this bold." Devon's voice dropped even lower. "Wait until Monday. Give Henderson a weekend to cool off. Maybe have a conversation with his parents. Try to fix the problem before you create a bigger one."

The smell of fresh-cut grass and raked clay drifted in the air, usually one of Zeke's favorite scent combinations. Today it just reminded him of all the politics lurking beneath the surface of what should be a simple game.

"The decision about who plays is mine to make," he said. "I have to do what's best for this team—not what's easiest, not what's most convenient. What's best."

Devon was quiet for a long moment, watching Henderson trudge through his final lap. "Just... be careful, man. Some battles aren't worth fighting."

After Devon walked away to supervise the equipment storage, Zeke wandered over to inspect the pitcher's mound, caught between two versions of the future.

His gaze bounced from Henderson's resentful glare to Timothy's infectious enthusiasm as the freshman helped rake the infield with the same intensity he brought to every task.

This was the kind of situation where he'd love to bounce ideas off someone he trusted. Someone who understood complicated family dynamics and tough choices. Someone like...

He cut the thought off before it fully formed.

Asking Clarissa's advice would cross every professional boundary he'd sworn to maintain, not to mention the conflict of interest.

The sun climbed higher, promising afternoon temperatures in the eighties. Around him, the field hummed with purposeful activity from boys who called him Coach.

All of their success depended on him making the right choice.

God, I really need some wisdom here. There are no easy answers, and every choice comes with consequences I can't control.

Henderson finished his laps and stalked toward the equipment shed without making eye contact with anyone.

Timothy looked up from his raking just long enough to flash Zeke a grateful smile that reminded him why he'd gotten into coaching in the first place.

Some decisions shouldn't wait for Monday.

Monday afternoon, Clarissa tapped her pen against her notebook, fighting the urge to check her phone again.

Where was Timothy? Practice had ended fifteen minutes ago, and as usual, she still had a mountain of work waiting at home.

The wind whipped through the parking lot, sending bits of trash skittering across the asphalt and making her grateful she'd grabbed a jacket this morning.

Gray clouds hung low over the mountains, pressing down like a weighted blanket and turning the afternoon light flat and colorless. Even the red brick of Loveland High looked dull under the overcast sky.

She scribbled another note about the database integration ideas she'd discussed with Mr. Ridge's assistant earlier.

The project was finally clicking into place, each piece of code falling into logical sequence in her mind. If she could just get home and test a few theories on her laptop—

A car door slammed with enough force to rattle windows.

Clarissa's head snapped up to see a figure by a silver Mercedes three rows over, hands gesturing wildly as angry words carried on the wind. She couldn't make out the specifics, but the tone was unmistakable—pure teenage fury mixed with words that would have earned her a mouth full of soap growing up.

None of my business.

She ducked her head back toward her notebook. But another door slam, followed by what sounded like something metallic hitting pavement, made it impossible to ignore.

A stream of players emerged from the school, gym bags and backpacks slung over shoulders.

Their body language told a story as some hurried past the drama, others slowing to rubberneck. Only a few brave souls approached the angry figure.

The wind shifted, carrying fragments of conversation her way. "...not fair..." and "...coach doesn't know..." and something that definitely included words she wouldn't repeat in church.

At last, she caught a glimpse of the boy's face as he spun toward his audience, and her stomach dropped.

Andrew Henderson. The booster club president's son.

The same woman who'd been throwing attitude around since the first parent meeting, treating everyone like hired help.

Whatever had set him off, it was baseball-related. And if the other players' mix of sympathy and discomfort was any indication, no one was surprised by the meltdown.

"Hey, sorry I'm late."

Clarissa jumped, nearly dropping her pen as Timothy appeared beside her open window.

His face was flushed, hair damp with sweat, but his eyes sparkled with excitement.

"No problem." She gathered her notebook and purse, glancing back toward the Henderson drama. "Everything okay?"

Timothy shrugged, tossing his equipment bag into the backseat. "Can we take a detour on the way home? I want to practice my parallel parking for a little bit."

She climbed out to trade places, noticing how Timothy deliberately avoided looking at the silver Mercedes even as the shouting continued.

"So what happened at practice?" She buckled herself into the passenger seat and set her things at her feet, trying to keep her tone casual.

"I'll tell you in a minute." Timothy adjusted the rear view mirror, then the side mirrors, his movements precise and focused. Just like she'd taught him. "Let me get us out of here first."

More voices joined the parking lot drama. Deeper, adult voices that carried the unmistakable authority of coaches.

Clarissa spotted Zeke striding across the asphalt with Coach Devon close behind. Despite the distance, she saw the tension in Zeke's shoulders, the way his hands clenched and unclenched at his sides.

When he reached the cluster of players, his voice carried. "Way to prove my point."

The words were quiet, controlled, but they hit like a slap.

Henderson's response was lost in the wind, but his gestures grew more animated, more desperate.

Zeke said something else, then jerked his head toward the exit.

The remaining players scattered like startled birds, some jogging to their cars while others cast uncertain glances back over their shoulders.

One boy—maybe the catcher?—shot a look at Zeke filled with pure teenage resentment before climbing into a beat-up pickup truck.

"Okay, I think we're ready to go." Timothy's voice drew her attention back inside their car as he shifted into drive and pulled away from the curb.

"So," she said once they'd cleared the school zone, "are you going to tell me what that was about? Because Henderson looked about to spontaneously combust."

Timothy's grin could have powered the whole engine. "Coach Matthews moved me up to varsity. I'm starting tomorrow."

Clarissa's heart leapt into her throat. "Timothy! Oh my gosh, really?"

"Really." He checked his mirrors again, then glanced at her with eyes bright as Christmas morning. "Henderson got sent down to JV for attitude problems. Coach said I earned the spot."

Pride swelled in her chest so fast it almost hurt. This was what all those extra batting practices had been for, all those evenings spent working on footwork in their tiny backyard. "I'm so proud of you. You've worked so hard for this."

"I know it might not last," Timothy said quickly, as if he needed to manage his own expectations. "It might be for just one game, you know? But still."

"But still, it's varsity baseball." She squeezed his shoulder, feeling the solid muscle that had developed over the past month. He was growing up so fast. "And I'll be there. No matter what, I'll be in those stands tomorrow watching you play."

The promise slipped out before she could think about it, but she meant every word.

Her capstone portfolio was due Wednesday and she had a lot of work still to do before the Ridge project deadline. But Timothy was going to play varsity baseball, and she wouldn't miss it for the world.

"I know it's an away game so there's added travel. You don't have to—"

"I want to." She pulled out her phone, calculated the drive time, and set a series of alarms so she'd leave the Rocky Ridge offices on time. Might have to pull Brian from school early in order to make it all work.

Such an opportunity for Timothy as a freshman.

All because the Henderson boy had an attitude problem?

Her fingers hovered over the screen. Every impulse begged her to ask Zeke for the inside story. But that would cross lines she had no right to cross.

She had to trust he had his reasons.

As he drove, Timothy continued talking about practice. About how he was finding the sweet spot on the bat. About how the shortstop had given him good advice on reading the pitcher's timing.

But underneath his excitement, Clarissa caught the nervous edge that came with opportunity. The knowledge that this chance could disappear as quickly as it arrived.

Just like it had disappeared for Andrew.

As they pulled into their neighborhood, she found herself thinking about Karen Henderson and her perfectly manicured nails and designer handbags. The way she'd looked at Clarissa during that first booster club meeting like something unpleasant she'd found on her shoe.

The way she held court as queen bee of the varsity parents' social circle.

A woman like that would see her son's demotion to junior varsity as something personal. She wouldn't take such public humiliation lightly and was bound to lash out.

Clarissa's stomach clenched as she imagined the phone calls that were already underway, the connections being leveraged, and the pressure that would be applied.

Would Timothy get to keep his new varsity spot after all?

She opened her phone and typed: ***Couldn't help but see the situation in the parking lot. Know that I'm praying for you. For wisdom and help to survive the fallout.***

She hit send before second-guessing herself, then slipped the phone back into her purse.

Whatever political firestorm Zeke had triggered by benching the booster club president's son, he was going to need all the support he could get.

Because she wouldn't wish Karen Henderson's wrath on her worst enemy, let alone a... friend.

Chapter Sixteen

The familiar hum of the computer filled Clarissa's temporary workspace as she settled into the ergonomic chair, then spread open her notebook of website sketches beside the keyboard like a roadmap to success.

With only limited access to their system, she needed to maximize her time by doing most of her brainstorming outside these walls.

Around her, the Rocky Ridge Development offices still smelled faintly of leather and expensive cologne, a constant reminder that completing this project on time could change everything for her family.

She pulled the flash drive from the pocket of her black skirt, the small device warm from her nervous grip earlier.

Her Advanced Web Design assignment had earned high marks for the clean code and efficient database integration reflecting the kind of sophisticated functionality Mr. Ridge would appreciate for the interactive elements of his website.

Once she uploaded and adapted the framework, she'd be that much closer to meeting the next project benchmark. To receiving that next paycheck.

She slid the drive into the USB port. The computer accepted the device with a soft click, and she flipped her notebook to the page where she'd sketched out the integration plan.

Step one: transfer the foundational code. Step two: customize the database fields for actual property listings. Step three: add the visual elements that would make Mr. Ridge's company look cutting-edge and professional.

She was reaching for the mouse when the computer emitted a sharp, electronic shriek.

The screen flashed red, bold text appearing in a dialog box that made her blood run cold: **SECURITY BREACH DETECTED. UNAUTHORIZED DEVICE. QUARANTINE PROTOCOLS INITIATED.**

"No, no, no," she whispered, clicking frantically at the error message.

A moment later, similar alarms began wailing from computers throughout the office, a cascade of electronic panic that sent her heart hammering against her ribs.

"What have you done?" The voice cracked like a whip behind her.

Clarissa spun to find Mr. Ridge's assistant, Ms. Reeves, striding toward her with eyes blazing.

"I didn't—I just plugged in my flash drive." Clarissa's hands shook as much as her voice. "I brought some code from my college assignment to adapt for the website. I thought—"

"You thought you'd install unauthorized software? From a private device? With a potential virus onto a secure business network?" Ms. Reeves' voice rose with each word, drawing stares from other employees who'd emerged from their offices to investigate the commotion.

Clarissa bit her tongue, the taste of copper flooding her mouth. "I can show you the file. It's just basic database code, nothing—"

"Step away from the computer." The new voice belonged to a security guard who'd appeared as if from thin air. A mountain of a man in a crisp uniform who looked like he'd been hoping for this kind of excitement to spice up his day.

His hand rested on what looked suspiciously like a taser. "Ma'am, I need you to move away from the workstation immediately."

Clarissa stood, her legs like water and her notebook clutched to her chest like a shield. "There's been a misunderstanding. I was just trying to—"

"Phone." The guard extended a meaty palm. "And any other electronic devices. Earbuds. Smart watch. Anything that can transmit or receive data."

As if the code on her drive was designed to...what...download and transmit files?

The overhead lights seemed too bright, washing everything in harsh, unforgiving white.

This had to be a nightmare.

With trembling fingers, Clarissa handed over her phone, watching her lifeline to the outside world disappear into the guard's pocket.

The suffocating silence that followed was broken only by the continued electronic whining from the network of affected computers.

"The notebook, too." Ms. Reeves snatched the sketches and ideas Clarissa had spent hours upon hours developing. "We'll need to analyze it all to determine what proprietary information might have been compromised or infected."

Proprietary information?

Clarissa wanted to laugh. Or scream.

She was building a basic business website for a small town construction company. Not designing nuclear weapons for the Pentagon.

But the expressions around her were deadly serious. Faces that had already tried and convicted her of corporate espionage.

"There's been a mistake." She hated how small her voice sounded in the cavernous office space. "If you could just look at the file on the flash drive—"

"Ms. Miller." Mr. Ridge's voice cut through the chaos.

The crowd of employees parted as he strode toward her. His expensive suit was immaculate, his hair perfectly styled, but his eyes held the cold fury of a man who'd been personally betrayed.

"I trusted you with access to our systems." His voice was low and dangerous. "And you repay that trust by attempting to steal our development plans? Hack into our accounting programs?"

"I didn't steal anything!" The words burst out, louder than she'd intended. "There's only one file on that drive, and I created it myself for a college assignment on web design frameworks. You can check the file's metadata."

Mr. Ridge's smile held a sharp edge. "We'll see about that. But if I find out you've violated our contract by engaging in industrial espionage, you'll be responsible for full restitution. Plus punitive damages for the disruption to our business operations."

The world tilted.

Restitution. Punitive damages.

Legal terms that might as well have been a death sentence for someone living paycheck to paycheck. She couldn't afford a lawyer to fight accusations like these.

Plus she needed this job. Not just the remaining payments to keep her family afloat, but also the potential recommendation to launch her freelance business.

Oh, God. Help me!

"Please." Her stomach cramped. "Just have someone look at the file. You'll see—"

"Someone will." Mr. Ridge's voice was arctic. "Our on-call IT specialist is on the way and he'll also be checking everything else you've done on our system. Until then, you'll wait right here where we can keep an eye on you."

He gestured toward a chair positioned squarely in the center of the office, visible from every workstation.

The ideal location for public humiliation.

Clarissa's skin went clammy, cold sweat beading on her forehead despite the office's aggressive air conditioning.

God, please. She sank onto the chair, her legs giving out completely. *Please let them see this is all a mistake. Please let my motives be clear. I was just trying to do good work, to provide for my family.*

Someone finally silenced the shrill network alarm, but the following minutes crawled by with agonizing slowness.

Ms. Reeves sat at a nearby desk, flipping through the notebook with the intensity of a forensic analyst like the ones Clarissa had seen on television.

The security guard positioned himself within arm's reach, his eyes never leaving her face.

Other employees shot furtive glances in her direction before looking away, as if failure might be contagious.

When her phone buzzed in the guard's pocket, the sound made everyone jump.

"What's that for?" Ms. Reeves glared.

The guard checked the screen, then swiped. "Looks like she set an alarm for something."

Clarissa's lips went numb. "A reminder to start wrapping up because I needed to leave early today."

Ms. Reeves snorted. "No chance of that, sweetie."

The casual dismissal hit like a slap, but it was nothing compared to the growing dread in Clarissa's chest as the implications began to sink in.

Timothy's game. Her promise to be there for his first varsity start. The hour-long drive to the away venue. And before that, her plan to change into comfortable clothes and pull Brian out of school so he could watch his brother play.

The longer this nightmare continued, the more promises she'd have to break.

Fifteen minutes later, another alarm sounded from her phone.

This one her signal to pack up her things, grab her keys, and head for the door.

Instead, she was trapped in the chair of shame, watching strangers rifle through her work while her world crumbled around her.

When the IT specialist arrived—a thin man with wire-rimmed glasses and the demeanor of someone who'd rather be anywhere else—Clarissa felt a spark of hope.

Surely a professional would see that her file was exactly what she claimed it to be and cut the investigation short.

"Please just look at the metadata and the database structure." She leaned forward as he settled at her workstation. "I was going to adapt the code from my Web Design class. The framework is standard. Nothing proprietary about it."

The specialist grunted, his fingers flying over the keyboard.

Clarissa held her breath, watching his expression for any sign of vindication.

Another alarm.

Her final call of sorts. The absolute last minute to leave the building, do all the things, and still make it to Timothy's game on time.

She bit her lip hard enough to taste blood, already imagining her brother's face when he looked up at the empty stands.

"I didn't even get here until noon." Clarissa turned to Ms. Reeves. "You saw me arrive. I barely sat down before this happened. How could I have stolen anything?"

The assistant's expression flickered—just for a moment—with something that might have been sympathy. "That's...that's true. You weren't here long before the system locked down."

Clarissa's phone rang this time.

The guard frowned as he eyed the screen. "Brian's school?"

"Please." Tears stung her eyes. "That's my little brother. I'd sent a note that I was picking him up early today. He's only twelve and needs to know someone's coming for him."

As if Clarissa had the first clue who that might be. Hopefully she'd be out of here in time to meet his bus. If not...

The guard handed the phone to Ms. Reeves.

The assistant sighed heavily, then brought the still-ringing phone closer. "Fine. But put it on speaker so I can monitor every word."

The conversation was thankfully brief since everyone else also heard every mortifying moment of her exchange with a very confused secretary.

Yes, there had been an emergency at work. Yes, Brian would need to wait for the regular dismissal and ride the bus home. No, she couldn't explain more right now.

When Clarissa's phone buzzed again five minutes later—a text from Brian wondering where she was—the first tear spilled over.

"Can I please just—" Her voice cracked.

"One text." Ms. Reeves's tone had softened. "That's it."

With shaking fingers, Clarissa typed the most inadequate message of her life: ***Emergency at work. Ride the bus and head to Cameron's house. Will explain everything when I pick you up later. So sorry.***

Brian's response came immediately: ***What about Timothy's game?***

She stared at the screen, fresh tears blurring her vision.

What about Timothy's game? What about her promise to be there no matter what?

What about the little brother who'd been so excited to watch his older brother play varsity baseball?

"I need to call his friend's mom," she whispered. "To arrange child-care. Please."

That call was even more humiliating. Trying to explain an *emergency* without being able to say what kind. Begging a near-stranger to watch her brother because she was trapped in what felt increasingly like a corporate prison.

Thankfully Mrs. Owens agreed, but Clarissa heard the judgment in her voice.

Another Miller family crisis. Another time when their guardian couldn't quite handle the responsibility.

Clarissa vaguely registered the blinking low battery light on her phone as Ms. Reeves reclaimed possession.

Of course. Because nothing was going her way today.

At least she had a charger in the car.

But the fact remained that reliable communication was rising to the top of her wishlist. Secondhand phones and a prepaid plan could only carry them so far even if it were all she could afford.

Please, God? You know that I really need to be able to finish this job and get paid.

She wiped her tears and then her nose with a tissue Ms. Reeves grudgingly provided, then clasped her shaking hands in her lap.

Meanwhile, the IT specialist continued working in complete silence. His expression was maddeningly neutral, giving away nothing about what he was finding or what conclusions he might draw.

Every few minutes he'd make a note on his tablet, but he hadn't spoken once since sitting down at the computer.

Clarissa watched the office clock tick ever closer to the moment when Timothy would take the field for his first varsity start.

She imagined him looking up at the stands, searching for her face in the crowd. Would he believe she'd had another emergency? Or would he be angry, like the day her laptop crashed?

Would Zeke understand when she didn't show up? Would he think she was flaking again, like Friday night when she'd fallen asleep working?

The fragile trust they'd been building would shatter completely. How was she to explain that she'd been accused of corporate espionage without sounding like she was making excuses?

Finally—finally—the IT specialist stood up from his chair, his expression unreadable as he gathered his notes.

Clarissa's heart hammered so hard she was sure everyone in the office heard it.

"Stay here while I give my report to Mr. Ridge," he said, his voice neutral.

And then he disappeared into the owner's private office with her future clutched in his hands.

•♥•♥•♥•♥•♥•

Zeke shifted on his feet in the coach's box near third base as his varsity players went through their warm-up routine.

The familiar sounds of cleats crunching on the gravel warning track and the thump of the ball into leather mitts should have been calming, but today they only heightened his awareness of everything riding on the game.

Nearby, the arrival of more Loveland High parents filtering into the visitor's bleachers only added to the pressure sitting heavy on his shoulders.

A combined three voicemails from Richard and Karen Henderson. Plus two from Mike Vaughn.

He'd been an idiot to listen to them. To hear their threats masked as concerns about the program and questions regarding coaching decisions. His jaw ached from clenching it.

A sharp crack drew his attention as Devon sent a grounder toward second base. Timothy stretched for it, leather meeting dirt as the ball skipped off the heel of his glove and rolled into right field.

"Shake it off, Miller!" Zeke forced encouragement into his voice. "Next one's yours!"

Torres jogged over from shortstop, clapped Timothy on the shoulder and said something that made the freshman nod and square his shoulders.

Good. The kid needed all the support he could get, especially from the team captain.

Timothy glanced toward the bleachers for just an instant before turning his attention back to Devon.

The next grounder came harder, but this time Timothy's footwork was perfect, his glove secure as he then fired the ball to first base with crisp precision.

From the dugout behind him came a snide voice that carried despite its low volume: "Finally does something right."

Zeke spun to face the bench, his gaze finding Andrew Henderson slouched against the dugout wall with his arms crossed. "Henderson. You're still here to support your teammates. Period."

The boy's face flushed, but he pressed his lips together in sullen silence.

The JV game had ended earlier and while many players had already left with their parents, those who stayed now lined the end of the bench, eagerly eavesdropping.

Zeke stepped closer, lowering his voice. "I'd hoped you could show me you can be a team player."

Henderson's glare could have melted the team's aluminum bats, but he didn't say another word.

The kid's effort and contribution to the JV's victory had been impressive. Too bad his attitude didn't match. The blatant resentment might be new, but the entitlement remained, spewing the same poison that had forced Zeke's decision in the first place.

"I'm not sure you fully comprehend the real consequences of making such a reckless decision."

Zeke shoved the echo of Vaughn's voicemail aside. Yes, he'd have to answer for his decision.

But at least he had someone on his side. A friend praying that he'd have wisdom and help to survive the fallout.

He lifted his gaze to the bleachers, scanning for a flash of red hair among the growing crowd of parents. Nothing.

Where was she?

Timothy had been chattering earlier on the bus about how Clarissa was picking Brian up early from school and they'd both be there for his first varsity start.

The drive from Loveland was just over an hour with road construction, but with the way she usually planned ahead, they should be here by now.

A cold knot formed in his stomach.

Car trouble? Family emergency?

"Play ball!"

The umpire's call snapped Zeke's attention back to the field as his starting pitcher took the mound.

The familiar ritual of the first pitch, the crack of bat meeting ball, the pounding thunder of cleats on dirt.

It should have been pure baseball. Instead, Zeke tracked Timothy's movements with the intensity of a hawk watching prey.

The freshman handled his first fielding chance cleanly, but Zeke saw the tension in his shoulders. The way his head turned toward the stands between pitches. When another grounder took a bad hop and skipped past his glove in the third inning, Timothy's whole body sagged with disappointment.

One run scored.

Then another as the error opened the floodgates.

"Time!" Zeke jogged to the mound, gathering his infielders around him. "Forget that play. It's over. Next batter, fresh start."

But Timothy's eyes were distant. Unfocused. The mental side of the game was already eating him alive.

Back in the dugout after they escaped the inning, Zeke pulled Timothy aside. "Talk to me. What's going on in your head?"

The boy's jaw worked silently for a moment before the words tumbled out. "She said she'd be here no matter what. Clarissa always keeps her promises. She would have texted if she was running late, or if something came up, or..."

A glint of moisture appeared in his eyes before he blinked it away fiercely. "Something's wrong, Coach. She wouldn't just not show up."

The raw worry in Timothy's voice hit Zeke like a fastball to the chest.

He was tempted to check his own phone, but team rules existed for a reason. No distractions during games.

"I'll do better." Timothy squared his shoulders with visible effort. "I promise."

The kid headed for the bench and Devon appeared at Zeke's elbow.

"You're too invested in this kid," Devon hissed. "Looks like you're making excuses for your decision. And both of you looking for his sister in the stands every five seconds isn't helping your cause."

Panic flashed through Zeke's chest. Were his emotions that obvious?

Devon had promised to keep the coaching staff accountable to the fraternization policy, but having his judgment questioned mid-game stung.

The fourth inning brought more disaster when Timothy bobbled another routine play. This time the error led to three runs.

The visiting crowd's murmurs grew louder, fingers pointing toward the dugout. Zeke caught fragments of conversation.

"...the freshman is in over his head."

"What was Matthews thinking? Coach Brenner never would have..."

As he'd feared, the tension spread to the rest of the team, causing more uncharacteristic mistakes.

He'd needed Timothy to perform under pressure, but that was asking too much while his support system crumbled around him.

In the fifth inning, a flash of movement in his peripheral vision had Zeke glancing to the bleachers. A woman in a dark skirt hurried up the metal steps, red hair catching the afternoon sun as she searched for an empty seat.

Relief flooded through him so fast it made him dizzy. Clarissa was okay.

But as she settled into the stands, smoothing her skirt and checking her watch, questions replaced relief.

Why was she dressed like that? And why was she so late to the game?

Didn't she care that her brother had been worried out of his mind?

The crack of the bat brought his attention back to the field, but the damage was already done.

Timothy's head was still in the clouds. Their team was falling apart one error at a time. And Zeke's decision was to blame.

Some days, being right felt a lot like losing.

Chapter Seventeen

Clarissa pressed her palms flat against the aluminum surface of the bleachers, trying to stop the trembling that had started hours ago in that hostile office and hadn't let up during the frantic drive across two counties.

Her hands still ached from gripping the steering wheel like a lifeline, knuckles white as she'd leaned forward at every red light and construction zone, willing traffic to move faster.

Breathe. She forced air into lungs constricted by invisible bands.

By God's grace, she'd been cleared of wrongdoing.

The IT specialist had checked all of her previous files on the network servers, actually complimented her coding skills on the forbidden flash-drive file, then handed her a list of new restrictions for the remainder of her work.

Bottom line, the website project would continue. There would be a paycheck instead of a lawsuit.

But sitting here now, that victory felt hollow because of her broken promise.

She lifted her gaze to the scoreboard, squinting against the afternoon sun.

The numbers made her stomach clench. Bottom of the fifth inning and they were down by six runs. With several errors also recorded on the board.

Her eyes found Timothy, his familiar shock of red hair sticking out beneath his baseball cap as he crouched near second base. Looked like he'd need another haircut soon.

But everything else about him was wrong.

His shoulders curved inward like he tried to make himself smaller. His jaw set in a grim line that reminded her of their father during his worst days, before he'd eventually walked away from all of them.

Please don't let him blame himself. Except the sick feeling in her gut told her it was already too late.

A sharp crack echoed across the field as someone connected with the ball. The center-fielder made the easy catch to end the inning.

The Red Wolves jogged toward their dugout, Timothy trailing behind his teammates.

While the others clustered together near the fence, calling encouragement to those donning batting helmets, Timothy moved to sit alone at the far end of the bench.

"I don't know what Coach Matthews was thinking." Karen Henderson's voice carried from three rows below, dripping with the kind of authority that expected to be heard.

"Your Andrew would never have made those errors," another woman chimed in, her voice also pitched to carry. "At least he has his family's support. You can see why the Miller boy is struggling since no one bothered to show up for him until it was too late."

Clarissa's cheeks burned with shame and anger in equal measure, her hands clenching into fists in her lap.

Obviously they'd seen her late arrival and wanted her to hear their opinions.

"Poor Coach Matthews." Karen's tone suggested anything but sympathy. "Despite the scandal, at least Coach Brenner knew how to evaluate talent. He never would have benched a quality player for some freshman charity case."

Coach Brenner? Clarissa frowned, filing away the unfamiliar name.

There was history there—including some kind of scandal—but right now she couldn't focus on anything beyond the venom in the women's voices.

At least Brian wasn't here to witness his brother being called a charity case.

She'd raced to the Owens house after being released from her corporate lockdown, only to find Mrs. Owens frowning on her front porch.

"You just missed him, dear. I sent him to the hardware store with Cameron and his father. You really should have called ahead."

"My phone died."

And of course her charger had also vanished from the car, probably *borrowed* by one of her brothers and never returned.

Mrs. Owens' expression suggested that excuse wasn't nearly good enough. So much for Clarissa being a responsible adult.

At least she'd remembered the basic directions to the sports complex from an earlier search and was able to find it without a functioning navigation app. Only one wrong turn before she'd spotted the outfield light towers rising above the suburban sprawl and followed them like a beacon.

She'd found a parking spot close enough that her run to the bleachers hadn't required removing her work heels.

Should she have come at all? Part of her wondered if showing up this late only made things worse—a harsh reminder of her failure rather than a gesture of support.

But she'd made a promise.

Timothy deserved to know she'd tried to keep it, even if she'd fallen short.

The Red Wolves' batters went down one right after the other.

As the teams swapped sides and the visiting players jogged back onto the field, Clarissa focused on her brother, willing him to look up into the stands.

To see that she was here. That she cared. That his first varsity start mattered to her.

He settled into his crouch at second base, glove ready, eyes fixed on home plate. But he never once looked toward the bleachers.

Surely he'd looked earlier? How many times had he searched for her before giving up and believing the worst?

The realization stole what little breath she'd managed to regain.

She'd let him down and destroyed his trust.

What should have been a celebration—his first varsity game, the culmination of hard work and extra practice—would forever be tainted.

He'd remember this day not as the moment his baseball dreams came true, but as the moment his sister proved she couldn't be counted on.

"I'm sorry, Mom," she whispered, her voice barely audible over the crowd noise. "I promised to keep us together, but somehow I'm tearing us apart."

The failure tasted bitter on her tongue, sharp as the tears she refused to let fall.

She'd worked so hard to be a sister and guardian and provider all rolled into one. But there weren't enough hours in the day, enough energy in her body, or enough pieces of herself to go around.

And now she didn't know how to fix what she'd broken.

Didn't know if it could be fixed at all.

The home team's victory celebration echoed across the diamond as players chest-bumped, coaches shook hands, and parents cheered from the stands.

Zeke had to give them credit for being well-coached, disciplined, ready for every situation. The game should have been competitive, maybe even winnable. At least on another day when his team showed up with their heads screwed on straight.

Instead, they'd been carved apart like a Thanksgiving turkey.

Zeke's jaw ached from clenching it for seven innings.

Losing always stung, but today was different.

Personal.

When error compounded upon error. When mental mistakes snowballed into an eight-run deficit. And when the young player at the center of it all was only in that position because Zeke put him there...

That decision weighed heavy as he turned toward his own dugout, where players moved with sluggish dejection.

Cleats clattered against concrete as they changed into street shoes, the sharp sound mixing with the rustle of equipment being stuffed into canvas bags. The air hung thick with disappointment and the infield dirt that clung to their uniforms.

They needed him to say something.

To deliver some sort of speech about learning from mistakes, about bouncing back, about how this loss would make them stronger. The usual coach-speak intended to transform devastation into motivation.

He'd heard it all before as a player, but now the words stuck in his throat.

Especially when his gaze caught Andrew Henderson's face.

The kid wasn't even trying to hide his smirk—a twisted expression of satisfaction that his teammates had lost.

As if their collective failure validated his importance to the program.

Zeke curled his hands into fists at his sides.

This was the toxic attitude that had earned Henderson a spot on the bench, and apparently nothing had changed.

If anything, today's disaster had only fed the boy's arrogance.

Behind Henderson, his assistant coaches Devon and Grant huddled together in animated whispers, their body language radiating the kind of frustration that came from watching a train wreck in slow motion.

No support there, either.

Devon had warned him this would happen, had practically predicted this exact scenario.

Just be careful, man. Some battles aren't worth fighting.

Well, too late for that wisdom now.

Zeke cleared his throat, and twenty pairs of eyes turned toward him with varying degrees of expectation and wariness.

"I'll keep this short because I hate losing just as much as you do." His voice emerged rougher than he'd intended. "And while we always want to learn from our mistakes, there are plenty of fingers to point today."

A few snickers rippled through the group before dying under his steady glare.

Timothy Miller sat hunched at the far end of the bench, staring at his hands like they held the secrets of the universe.

Zeke's stomach cramped with guilt, but he focused on the others. "We've got a long drive tonight, so I won't make you stay for a debrief. But I'll expect your full attention during our ride to tomorrow's away game."

He stuffed his fists into his jacket pockets. Hopefully by then he'd have found enough distance for objective advice.

He nodded at the cluttered area. "Make sure you've got all your stuff, and if you're riding home with family instead of on the bus, check out with a coach."

The dismissal was met with relieved exhales and the immediate resumption of movement as players scattered like startled birds.

Zeke couldn't blame their eagerness to escape.

Grant stepped forward, taking charge of the final equipment sweep.

Leaving Zeke to collect his own things, then shoulder his bag plus the bulky duffel containing the team's batting helmets. The familiar weight of responsibility felt heavier today, like everything else.

But as he emerged from the dugout, he realized he'd forgotten about running the gauntlet.

Parents clustered in groups along the chain-link fence, their voices a murmur of consolation mixed with criticism. With arms crossed and foreheads creased, they shot glances in his direction that ranged from sympathetic to openly hostile.

The latter from those gathered near the Hendersons.

He had to give most of them credit for trying to console their dejected sons, but underneath the parental comfort lurked something too close to that of an angry mob—minus the pitchforks and torches.

He aimed for the narrow path between the dugout and the parking lot. *God, give me strength. Help me face this with integrity.*

He'd done what he believed was in the best interest of the team.

Sure, it hadn't worked out like he'd hoped—mostly because of circumstances beyond his control—but his intentions were pure. That had to count for something, right?

The sharp buzzing of his phone in his jacket pocket made him jump.

He pulled it out, but at the sight of Vaughn's name flashing on the screen, Zeke sent the call straight to voicemail.

Whatever the athletic director had to say could wait until he was back in Loveland and had time to think. To distance himself from the emotions swirling in his gut.

The phone vibrated again. A text this time.

I can't begin to defend your decisions if you won't explain them. Call me.

Another buzz followed seconds later.

I tried to warn you earlier. Reckless decisions have consequences.

Zeke shoved the phone back into his pocket without responding.

The consequences were becoming clear.

If only Andrew Henderson had learned something. Anything.

Because after today's debacle, Zeke would have a harder time justifying keeping the roster switch in place.

Was his hope to shape the team's character worth the battle? Was this job worth the constant political maneuvering and second-guessing? Would he even still have a job after Vaughn finished fielding phone calls from angry parents?

The questions swirled in his head like storm clouds, darkening his mood with each passing second.

He'd thought coaching was his future, his calling, the perfect intersection of his love for baseball and his desire to mentor young athletes.

But the Henderson situation slowly poisoned everything he'd once loved about the game.

A few players jogged past him toward the bus, equipment bags bouncing against their legs. Their subdued chatter sounded forced, like they were trying to convince themselves the loss wasn't that bad.

"Coach Matthews." The voice behind him dripped with venomous satisfaction.

Zeke turned back to find Karen Henderson approaching, her handbag clutched like a weapon.

"We'll be seeing you in Principal Vaughn's office tomorrow morning." She raised an over-plucked eyebrow.

A flicker of his old defiance sparked to life. "Can't say I'm looking forward to it."

Her eyes narrowed at his tone, but she must have decided she'd delivered her message. With a dismissive sniff, she brushed past him and stalked toward the parking lot.

Leaving Zeke standing still with his jaw clenched so tight he was surprised his teeth didn't crack.

Every fiber in his body screamed for physical release. The satisfying jolt of a bat in his hands as it connected with a baseball. The burn of muscles pushed to their limit. Anything to work off the frustration and anger coursing through his veins.

The batting cages would have to wait until after practice later in the week, assuming he still had a team to coach by then.

A few families brushed past him on their way to the parking lot, voices a murmur. Probably a mixture of disappointment and speculation or accusations.

Behind them, Timothy trudged alone, his tattered equipment bag dragging like a dead weight.

Guilt held Zeke in place.

This was his fault. He'd put Timothy in an impossible situation. And when the kid needed support most, his sister had been nowhere to be found.

Speaking of which, where was she now?

Zeke pivoted, finally spotting her beside her beat-up sedan.

At least she was out here instead of standing with the other finger-pointing parents who'd clustered near the fence.

But why was she smiling?

Her expression looked almost... expectant. As if she had no idea what she'd put Timothy—and him—through today. As if nothing was wrong and her brother should be grateful for her belated attention.

A spike of anger kindled in Zeke's chest, slow and hot like coals catching fire.

Too little, too late.

Maybe he'd been wrong about Clarissa Miller. Maybe the woman he'd been falling for was just another person who made promises they couldn't keep.

Timothy deserved better. They both deserved better.

The anger spread, feeding on hours of accumulated frustration.

He'd defended her to himself all afternoon, made excuses for her absence, worried about her safety. And for what? So she could show up at the end looking like she'd stepped out of a business meeting, oblivious to the damage she'd caused?

Zeke took a step forward, then another.

Someone needed to confront Clarissa Miller.

Because people shouldn't make promises at all unless they were going to keep their word.

•♥•♥•♥•♥•♥•

Clarissa kept her smile in place as she leaned against the warm metal of her car door, waiting as Timothy shuffled his way toward the team bus.

Any other day, she'd scold him for dragging his equipment bag behind him, but not today. Not when he had yet to spare her a glance.

Tears stung in the back of her nose and she blinked the sensation away.

She only hoped that the moment he spotted her, that he'd see her love. Her pride in him no matter the outcome.

That he'd detour her direction.

Beyond her brother, Zeke followed at a distance, a bulky bag of gear slung over his shoulder and his expression unreadable from across the parking lot.

Had he also heard the toxic commentary from the bleachers?

Clarissa had been too happy to escape the vicinity since Karen Henderson and her minions spent the final innings dissecting every coaching decision—and her family situation—with surgical precision.

Unfortunately for Timothy—but fortunately for her—it sounded like he'd be back on JV for the next game.

At least then she could watch with the nicer parents for a change, instead of enduring another onslaught of whispered character assassinations and pointed glances.

Timothy's head lifted, scanning the parking lot with the mechanical movements of someone going through the motions. When his gaze finally found her, Clarissa straightened and widened what she hoped was an encouraging smile.

The emotions flickered across his face like a slideshow.

Relief first—a split second of pure joy that lit up his features before reality crashed in. Then anger, sharp and immediate, tightening the muscles around his eyes. Betrayal came next, raw and cutting, making him look older than his fifteen years.

Then, nothing.

His expression went blank, as if he'd flipped a switch and decided he didn't care that she'd come at all.

The transformation lasted maybe three seconds, but was like watching someone die.

Timothy changed direction, his shoes crunching on gravel as he approached their car.

He yanked open the back seat door, threw his equipment bag inside, then slammed the door. At least it appeared he'd be riding up front instead of climbing into the back like she was some sort of chauffeur.

Thank God for small mercies.

"When did you get here?" His voice sounded dead, weary in a way that made her chest ache.

"Fifth inning. I'm so sorry—"

"Save your excuses." He opened the passenger door. "Let's just go."

Tears blurred her vision as waves of guilt and exhaustion crashed over her.

It had been the longest day of her life, starting with that nightmare at Rocky Ridge Development and ending with this—her brother's trust lying in pieces between them like shattered glass.

And the day wasn't over yet.

They still had the long drive home ahead of them, possibly in complete silence if Timothy decided to give her the full freeze-out treatment.

Her hands already shook from stress and caffeine withdrawal; the thought of navigating an hour of hostility made her stomach clench.

She was fumbling for her keys when more footsteps approached on the gravel behind her.

"Clarissa." Zeke's voice made her turn, hope flickering in her chest despite everything.

For a moment, she thought he might have seen Timothy's cold rejection and be sympathetic. Might understand that whatever had kept her away hadn't been a choice.

But when she met his eyes, the hope died.

His expression was controlled, but she saw the storm underneath—disappointment mixed with something harder. Something suspiciously like judgment.

Gone was the friend texting about summer plans. The one who'd made her believe in possibilities again.

Instead, the person in front of her now was like a stranger wearing Zeke's handsome face.

"Why did you miss most of the game?" His tone was conversational, almost casual, but steel lay beneath the surface. "Timothy said you'd promised to be here no matter what?"

The question hit her like a slap, and she flinched.

"I—" She started to explain, then stopped. What could she say that wouldn't sound like another excuse? That wouldn't cast her in an irresponsible light, even if that were true?

Timothy slammed the car door from inside, the sound echoing like a gunshot. The message was clear: whatever explanation she had, he didn't want to hear it.

And judging by Zeke's expression, neither did he.

Chapter Eighteen

Clarissa stared at Zeke across the gravel parking lot, her throat tight with unshed tears at his implied accusations.

Why had she missed most of the game?

It wasn't like she wanted to admit she'd been accused of corporate espionage. That she'd spent four hours trapped in an office while a security guard watched her every move and the battery on her confiscated phone slowly died.

"There was a crisis at work." She wrapped her arms around her waist, her voice barely above a whisper. "They took my phone and—"

"Work." Zeke rolled his eyes, dismissing the truth. "The cafe closed hours ago and nothing else could be more important than your brother. He was so excited about today."

"No, you don't understand. I never said I was at the cafe. It was a freelance job and I was accused of—"

"I understand perfectly." He slashed a hand through the air, then pointed a finger at the passenger seat of her car. "I took a risk on Timothy. Put my reputation on the line because I believed in him. And when he needed support most, his guardian couldn't be bothered to show up."

The words landed hard, each one finding its mark in the tender places where her deepest fears lived. "I made it here. And my phone was dead so I—"

"There are pay phones. You could have asked someone—anyone—with a phone to call hours ago."

Heat flooded her cheeks.

Yes, she should have had Brian text his brother. Except he hadn't been at the Owens house when she arrived and by then the game had started.

Timothy would just now be reading the message.

"It was too late by then." Shame and anger warred in her chest. "I was trapped! I couldn't leave, couldn't communicate, couldn't—"

"Enough." Zeke took a step closer, his knuckles white around the strap of his bag. "You could have done a lot... if you'd actually cared enough to try."

"I cared. I care..." Her voice cracked.

"You cared about yourself without thinking of anyone else." Zeke's eyes were hard as flint. "You were selfish. While I got to watch that kid implode out there because he was worried sick about you. Because he trusted that you would keep your word."

Selfish.

The accusation hung in the air between them like poison gas. Something shattered inside her chest, stealing her breath.

How was putting her family's financial security first selfish? How was working multiple jobs while finishing college selfish?

She'd sacrificed everything—her social life, sleep, and sanity—to keep her brothers safe and fed and together. Surviving on caffeine and determination alone for months.

But the words stuck in her throat, too raw and complicated to explain to someone who'd already made up his mind.

"I can't trust you to keep your word." Zeke's voice grew quieter and somehow more devastating. "Not to Timothy. Not to Brian. And not to me."

The parking lot tilted. She opened her mouth to defend herself, to explain, to beg him to listen.

But he'd already turned away. "I can't be with—let alone risk my job for—someone who makes promises they won't keep."

The words landed like a death sentence.

Zeke jogged toward the team bus without looking back, his shoulders rigid. A moment later, his silhouette appeared inside and out of reach.

Clarissa stood frozen while around her car doors slammed and engines started, the sounds muffled and distant.

Zeke's last words sounded like a breakup.

But how did one break up with someone they'd never really been with? How had she lost something she'd barely allowed herself to want?

She'd clearly failed as an almost-girlfriend.

Failed in a relationship that existed in stolen moments and careful text messages and the fragile hope that maybe, just maybe, she could have something good for herself.

Turned out Zeke was just like the rest of the judgmental crowd in the bleachers—quick to condemn without knowing the facts, ready to assume the worst about her character based on a single afternoon.

She'd thought he was different. Thought he saw something in her worth waiting for.

God saw the truth, but that wasn't enough to keep her heart from shattering.

A sob clawed its way up her throat, and she pressed her hand to her mouth to hold it back.

She couldn't fall apart here. Not in this parking lot with curious eyes watching and Timothy already disgusted with her failure.

Clarissa fumbled for the door handle, her hands shaking so badly it took three tries to get it open. The driver's seat foreign beneath her, like she borrowed someone else's life. The steering wheel was still warm from the afternoon sun, but her fingers were numb as she gripped it.

"Can I explain?"

Timothy stared out the passenger window, his body angled as far away from her as the seat belt would allow. Then he stuck his fingers in his ears like a toddler having a tantrum.

The gesture was so juvenile and yet so heartbreaking that fresh tears spilled down her cheeks.

Her little brother, who'd always believed she could fix anything—who'd trusted her to be both sister and parent and provider—had given up on her completely.

All she could do was turn the key and pull out of the parking lot, her vision blurred by the tears that kept coming no matter how many times she wiped them away.

Zeke heaved the bag of batting helmets onto an empty seat with more force than necessary, the dull thud echoing through the bus like a punctuation mark on the day's disasters.

He tossed his own bag onto a bench seat three rows behind the driver.

Far enough from where his assistant coaches usually sat to avoid conversation but close enough to maintain the illusion of leadership.

A few subdued players came down the aisle and Zeke side-stepped into the narrow leg space of his new seat to allow them to pass.

He didn't want to talk to anyone right now.

Didn't trust himself not to say something he'd regret more than he already did.

But he was still the head coach, whether he felt like it or not.

"Devon?" Zeke forced his voice to hold steady. "Can you make sure we've got all the bats secured? And check that the water cooler was drained this time before it was loaded?"

"Already done." Devon avoided his gaze, his tone neutral.

The kind of professional distance that spoke volumes about how today's game had gone.

Zeke pulled out his phone and scrolled through the attendance sheet, checking off names as a couple more players claimed their seats.

Even when everything else fell apart, someone had to make sure all the kids were accounted for, the equipment loaded, and no one left behind in a parking lot over an hour from home.

He gave the driver the go-ahead signal, then scanned the bus one more time.

Two JV players huddled near the back, their faces flushed with the awkward embarrassment of being stuck in the same space as the handful of disgruntled varsity players and their equally upset coaches. They looked uncertain and a little lost.

Zeke dropped into his seat, recalling the same feeling with painful clarity.

He'd been in their shoes. Knew well the stigma of being the kid whose parents couldn't get off work for afternoon games, especially the away ones that required extra travel time.

The isolation of standing on the sidelines while teammates got picked up by families, wondering if anyone would notice if he just disappeared.

The bus lurched into motion, the diesel engine rumbling as they pulled out of the parking lot.

Zeke fumbled for his earbuds, desperate to drown out the hushed conversations among his coaching staff. He couldn't escape their glances but didn't need to hear their discussions about lineup changes and damage control.

Outside the window, suburban Colorado rolled past in a blur of strip malls and housing developments. The soon-setting sun pierced the glass, casting everything in harsh golden light that made his eyes water.

Or maybe that was something else entirely.

A lingering edge of anger still burned in his chest. Fury at being almost sucked into the Miller family mirage.

He'd been there before, living with a man who specialized in broken promises and elaborate excuses. Even after the divorce—and between rehab stints—his dad would swear he'd be somewhere.

Then never show. Never call. Never apologize.

Zeke had learned not to trust his father's word. Learned that some people were just unreliable. No way was he ever climbing on that emotional roller coaster again, not for anyone.

He'd given Clarissa her chance when she'd fallen asleep instead of texting. But for her to do it to her own brother? That was a pattern he couldn't afford to ignore.

Part of becoming the man his mother had wanted him to be meant not repeating her mistakes either. Not getting tangled up with someone who couldn't follow through when it mattered.

As the light outside dimmed, his reflection stared back at him from the window glass, revealing a jaw still tight with residual anger and eyes shadowed with exhaustion. But as the image came into focus, he remembered the look on Clarissa's face as he'd unloaded on her in the parking lot.

The same expression he'd seen on his mother's face during those final months before the divorce.

The pain of being attacked unfairly by someone who should have been a defender. The helpless bewilderment of someone trying to explain themselves to ears that had already stopped listening.

A knot formed in his stomach, guilt mixing with the anger until he couldn't tell them apart. He'd reacted like his father used to—lashing out when things didn't go his way, making assumptions, refusing to hear explanations that might complicate his narrative.

Maybe he'd gone too far.

His fingers moved across his phone. ***I'm sorry I lashed out like that. It was a rough game.***

He stared at the message, waiting for the three dots indicating she was typing back. The screen remained dark.

Because she was driving?

Or just ignoring him.

Zeke slumped deeper into the vinyl seat, the aroma of aging upholstery swirling around as he folded his arms over the ache spreading through his chest. An ache that grew as he took a hard look at himself and his claims to be a man of integrity.

What he saw wasn't particularly flattering.

He'd gotten too caught up in Clarissa Miller's world, too invested in the fantasy of belonging somewhere.

Had almost broken his promise to himself to maintain professional boundaries. Had edged dangerously close to violating the fraternization policy that kept his job secure.

Maybe he should be relieved that he'd escaped that trap just in time?

Instead, he was mostly disappointed that he hadn't seen her for who she really was—just another person who talked a good game but couldn't deliver when the stakes were high.

He tried texting again. ***The fact I got so upset tells me that maybe I was moving too fast.***

The words rang hollow even as he typed them.

Moving too fast toward what? Toward the dream of finding a family to call his own? Toward believing he could have something real with someone who understood the weight of responsibility?

His phone remained dark and silent, hope dwindling with each passing mile.

However, as the immediate anger and regret over Clarissa began to fade, his thoughts returned to her brother.

Timothy had such raw potential, flashes of brilliance that reminded Zeke why he'd gotten into coaching in the first place. The mental errors today had been about pressure and distraction, not a lack of ability.

He wasn't completely sure what to do about his varsity lineup moving forward. Henderson's attitude remained toxic while Timothy's confidence had been shattered.

No easy answers there.

Yet whatever had—or hadn't—happened with Clarissa, Timothy deserved to have someone stand up for him. And the rest of the players deserved to be surrounded by teammates who gave their best effort while having each other's backs.

Zeke checked his phone one more time.

No reply from Clarissa, but Vaughn's earlier text glowed accusingly on the screen.

Reckless decisions might have consequences, but Zeke knew he had not been reckless.

He blew out a long breath and started typing: ***Despite the loss, I still stand behind my decision.***

A moment later, his phone rang. Vaughn's name flashed on the display like a threat.

Zeke declined the call, then sent a quick text: ***On the bus, can't talk.***

He powered off his phone.

He'd deal with Vaughn and the Hendersons tomorrow, when he could think clearly and defend his choices without the emotional baggage of today's disasters clouding his judgment.

For now, all he could do was watch the dimming Colorado landscape roll past and wonder how everything had gone so spectacularly wrong.

Clarissa glanced at the dashboard clock. With the miles stretching ahead, it would be a long time until they reached home.

Time to endure Timothy's silent treatment.

Time to come up with a way to explain to a disappointed Brian where she'd been and why his plans had changed so suddenly.

She sighed.

Make that another disappointment to add to the growing pile. Another way she'd failed as a guardian and sister.

And it all started with the freelance website job she'd thought was a blessing from above.

Crazy that the reason for today's cascading disaster was the only bright spot waiting for tomorrow. The only reason they still had income instead of a lawsuit and financial ruin.

Oh, but tomorrow held another milestone.

Her capstone project sat at home, needing only a final proofreading pass before the deadline. Her last remaining requirement for graduation.

At least that was one promise she could still keep to herself. To her mother.

God had been faithful to bring her to the end of that chapter.

Like Greta had reminded her not all that long ago during another crisis, God kept his promises, even when people didn't.

So God saw everything that happened today—the accusations, the panic, the desperate drive. Timothy might be ignoring her but God listened. He forgave.

And He would continue to carry her burdens when they were too heavy for her.

God, I know You're good and You have a plan. Please help me mend the broken relationships somehow. Starting with the one in this car.

The sun sank behind the mountains and fields gave way to scattered houses as they approached the town she'd grown up in.

Her tears had dried into salt tracks on her cheeks, leaving her skin tight and raw.

While Timothy's silence had evolved from angry to sullen to something that might have been exhaustion.

His head rested against the window, eyes closed, looking younger than his fifteen years. The lines around his mouth softened into something that looked more like defeat.

Once they reached city limits, she nudged his knee. "Can you text Brian? Let him know we'll pick him up soon and ask if he wants us to get him anything to eat since I'll get us fast food for a late dinner?"

Timothy opened his eyes, and for the first time since the parking lot, he looked directly at her. His gaze fell to the cupholder where her dead phone sat like evidence of her failure, then to the vacant spot where the car charger should have been.

"Guess that explains why you didn't text."

His observation was so matter-of-fact, so painfully accurate, that she let out a combination hiccup-snort-sob-laugh that probably sounded as broken as she felt.

"If only that's where it started today."

Timothy's fingers flew across his phone screen, the simple gesture feeling like the first crack in the wall he'd built between them.

Not everything was as easy to fix as a dead battery, but she'd find a way to rebuild the trust she'd lost.

Hopefully.

Maybe.

Chapter Nineteen

The school's main office smelled like industrial disinfectant and old carpet, a combination that always reminded Zeke of detention halls and disciplinary meetings.

Ironic considering his destination.

He paused just inside the glass doors, checking his phone for the time—8:56 a.m., four minutes before he was supposed to face the firing squad.

One unread message waited on his screen. Clarissa's name made his heart skip.

Would she forgive him? Hope and dread warred in his chest as he opened the text.

You might be sorry now, but you meant what you said, and that hurts. Especially since you refused to listen. It's not a bad idea to step back for a while. Pray about whether there should even be an us...

The words hit like a punch to the solar plexus, stealing his breath and leaving him standing frozen in the middle of the office hallway.

What else did he expect after the way he'd treated her yesterday?

He hadn't listened at all, instead cutting off her explanations and throwing accusations like fast balls without caring about the collateral damage.

And now he'd have to find a way to make it up to her and build bridges again.

A raised male voice filtered through the closed door of Vaughn's office, sharp and indignant even through the thick wood. Probably Richard Henderson warming up for the main event.

The void created after losing Clarissa settled into a lead weight in the pit of his stomach.

He approached Vaughn's door on legs that felt disconnected from his body, catching a glimpse of the secretary's sympathetic expression before she ducked her head back to her computer screen.

Did she know something he didn't?

Had the outcome of this meeting already been decided?

Zeke tugged at his coaching jacket, bracing for the coming battle. But in the lingering aftermath of Clarissa's text, there were holes in his defenses.

Weak spots where doubt and regret crept in.

God, give me strength to stand my ground. And wisdom to know what to say.

No more stalling. He raised his hand and knocked twice before turning the handle.

Inside, an extra chair had been squeezed in beside the two that normally faced Vaughn's desk, creating a cramped triangle that would force everyone to sit closer than comfort allowed.

Too bad he couldn't just stand.

The air conditioning struggled against the combined heat of bodies and tempers, leaving the room stuffy and warm.

Zeke nodded to Vaughn who sat hunched behind his desk, looking like he'd rather be anywhere else in the world.

Before Zeke had settled onto the remaining chair, the onslaught began.

"Coach Matthews." Richard leaned forward with his arms crossed and his expensive suit jacket straining across his chest. "We need to discuss your unfortunate decision to bench our son in favor of a freshman who clearly wasn't ready for varsity play."

Karen perched on the edge of her chair like a bird of prey, as for the next ten minutes, the Hendersons took turns unloading their grievances.

Their son Andrew had been a varsity player since last season. Timothy Miller was a lousy freshman who'd lost the game for the team and could have cost them their playoff chances.

And Zeke's decision must have been personal, vindictive, and based on some imagined slight rather than objective evaluation.

Each time Zeke tried to interject explanations, he was steamrolled by fresh accusations.

After about ten minutes, Karen fixed him with a withering stare. "Well? Aren't you going to say anything in your defense?"

Zeke drew a deep breath, tasting the stale office air and something that might have been fear. "As I said from the very beginning to both players and parents, as head coach I am the final voice in the roster for each game, and I will continue to make those decisions with the team in mind."

He held up a hand to stop the argument already forming on Richard's lips. "As for your son, I have observed—and tried unsuccessfully to correct—a deteriorating attitude and lack of effort over the course of multiple practices and games. As you so loudly pointed out, it's not fair for one player to bring down the other eight, so I decided to shake things up."

"Is Andrew on varsity for today's game or not?" Karen's voice almost screeched with barely controlled hysteria.

"I will continue to evaluate both performance and attitude for all my players. And will make today's roster announcement on the bus."

After all, he needed to see Timothy's confidence level and gauge whether yesterday's disaster had broken the kid's spirit.

Karen slumped back in her chair with an audible huff.

Richard's expression shifted to something craftier, more calculating. He reached into a leather briefcase and withdrew a large bronze plaque that caught the overhead light.

"We had this made." He handed it across the desk to the so-far silent observer Vaughn. "As a way for the program to show appreciation for the very generous donation the Henderson family solicited. You know, for those indoor batting cages."

Zeke read the inscription upside down: *Donated by Rocky Ridge Development*.

The Hendersons exchanged pointed looks with Vaughn, the implication hanging in the air like smoke from a house fire.

Money had changed hands. Gifts came with expectations. And playing time could be purchased if one knew the right people.

Zeke clenched his fists as the Hendersons brushed past him and out the door.

After the door clicked shut, Vaughn cleared his throat. "Look, Zeke, maybe we—"

"If you hang that up, I will personally rip it down." Zeke stabbed a finger in the direction of the plaque. "Accept his money if you want, but I will not discount the sacrifices of all the others who raised the majority of the funds. Giving false credit reeks of bribery and I won't be part of it."

"It's not a bribe." Vaughn's token protest was as weak as the hands he lifted. "It's just recognition—"

"Delivered in the same meeting where they demanded varsity playing time for their son?" Zeke shook his head. "It's sickening."

The silence stretched between them, heavy with unspoken threats and ultimatums. Zeke stood, his chair scraping against the industrial carpet.

"Maybe I'm not a good fit for the Loveland High program," he said, surprised by how steady his voice sounded. "I'm here for baseball and the kids, not to play political games with donors and boosters."

Vaughn's eyes narrowed, and he muttered something under his breath that sounded suspiciously like, "Should have hired Devon to keep the peace."

The words hit Zeke like ice cold water.

Devon. His assistant coach and supposed ally.

The man who'd been giving Zeke advice about handling difficult situations and warning him about the consequences of bold decisions.

Had Devon applied for the head coaching job? Was there an underlying rivalry Zeke had been too naive to see? Could he trust Devon's guidance going forward, or would the man try to sabotage him to claim the position he'd wanted all along?

As Zeke walked out of the suffocating office and back into the hallway, one thought echoed in his mind: if he couldn't trust his assistant coach and he'd already lost Clarissa's respect, exactly how alone was he in this fight?

·♥·♥·♥·♥·♥·

Clarissa moved through her morning routine at Hope's Cafe like a sleepwalker, muscle memory guiding her hands while her mind remained trapped in the emotional wreckage of yesterday.

Another sleepless night—this time not because of too many responsibilities clamoring for attention, but because of the aftermath that kept replaying behind her closed eyelids.

Nightmares of frowning security guards treating her like a criminal, sneering queen bee mothers dissecting her failures in stage whispers, and finger-pointing coaches who refused to listen to explanations.

But above all, she couldn't escape the agonizing image of Timothy turning away from her, sticking his fingers in his ears like a child desperate to block out painful truths.

She clung to the few remaining shreds of hope.

The first being Brian's quick forgiveness last night when she'd finally made it to the Owens house with her stumbling explanation about work emergencies and dead phones.

Zeke's apology texts also helped a little. Although she wasn't entirely sure when he'd sent them since it was well after midnight before her phone had recharged enough to power up.

Had her response been too harsh?

No. Wisdom said to press pause. To pray about whether there was enough of an *us* to salvage.

Meanwhile, despite her mental fog, life around her continued its relentless forward motion, punctuated by the clink of silverware on plates and the murmur of voices.

Maybe she just needed more coffee?

Clarissa combined half-pots of brew on the warmers, then set about starting another batch. Through the pass-through window, she caught bits of conversation as Frank barked out an order, only to have Trevor respond calmly as the lead chef.

Debbie certainly had her hands full mediating between them with her diplomatic and soothing tone. Years of experience with her twin teenagers must come in handy.

Clarissa would miss this place when the time came to move on. Miss the controlled chaos, the family dynamics, and the way everyone had each other's backs despite their differences.

From the dining room, she caught fragments of conversation about the craft fair the church ladies had organized in the space next door.

Something about extending it another month and splitting proceeds between Frank's medical fund and other community causes. Someone suggested it might evolve into a permanent indoor flea market that paid rent to the Dawson siblings.

Considering Clarissa's emotional fog, all of it blended into background noise.

But as she refilled water glasses and delivered plates, she spotted Amanda standing in the entryway, running her fingers along the surface of the newly restored antique buffet.

The dark-haired waitress seemed transfixed by the piece, her expression soft with something like wonder.

"It's beautiful, isn't it?" Clarissa said, approaching with a fresh pot of coffee. "I heard Matt delivered it yesterday afternoon."

Amanda nodded, her touch reverent against the rich wood grain that almost glowed in the morning light filtering through the front windows. The intricate carved details spoke of old-world artistry. Of hands that took pride in their work.

"You should have seen the wreckage after the truck came through the window." Clarissa could still picture the splintered wood and damaged leg that made the piece look beyond repair. "But Matt's a talented carpenter. It looks like he put it back together better than before."

"I heard him say something interesting yesterday," Amanda whispered, glancing around to make sure they weren't overheard. "That despite all the damage, it never lost its value. He said the same thing about the old house he's restoring."

Clarissa grasped at the fragments of conversations from weeks ago. Matt had mentioned floors or staircase woodwork or something similar, his eyes lighting up when he talked about breathing new life into forgotten places.

Could God take the wreckage of Clarissa's life and do the same thing?

The thought triggered fresh tears that she tried to blink away.

But Lauren noticed—Lauren always noticed—and appeared at her elbow with the kind of gentle concern that didn't pry too much. "I'm not going to ask what's wrong this time, but you need to take a break. Go sit in the office for a few minutes. "

Clarissa welcomed the rare reprieve from gossip. Not because she hated to burden her friends with complaints after all they'd done for her, but the scary level of paranoia over a website was enough to buy her silence.

If they asked, she'd just say she ran into a snag with a freelance job and leave it at that. In the meantime, the small office off the kitchen welcomed like a sanctuary, quiet except for the muffled sounds of breakfast service.

Before she could sit, she had to move a dusty box off one of the mismatched chairs around the small table that now held a mixture of framed photographs that used to hang on the cafe walls, a rainbow pile of colored papers, markers, stickers, and other craft supplies.

Lauren appeared in the doorway with a cup of coffee and a warm cinnamon roll, then hurried to gather the scattered items. "Sorry about the mess. I got this stuff from that little scrapbook store two doors down—though I think I was the only customer they had all day. I'm not sure how much longer they'll stay in business."

Joel paused in the doorway, grinning at his fiancée. "Please tell me again how you'll have all of Grandma's old photos and letters organized before our Christmas wedding? I don't want to be tripping over memory lane during our honeymoon planning."

They shared a quick kiss that made Clarissa's chest ache with longing.

Longing for the way Zeke's callused hands had cupped her face in the storage shed, the way he'd looked at her like she was something precious worth waiting for.

Once the couple left, Clarissa dove into the sugary cinnamon roll, grateful for the momentary energy boost flooding her veins. She'd definitely miss treats like this when she eventually moved on to bigger and better things.

If she ever managed to put her life back together enough to have bigger and better things.

As she prepared to rejoin the breakfast rush, something caught her eye—a few scripted words visible on a letter sticking out from under Lauren's pile of supplies.

Everything has fallen apart since you died, and I don't know how to fix it.

Fresh tears stung Clarissa's eyes, the words hitting like an arrow to the heart.

Nothing had been the same since Mom died, either.

The constant struggle to hold everything together, to be enough for Timothy and Brian, to fulfill promises she'd made to a woman who couldn't see whether she was keeping them or not.

Another argument filtered in through the office door, reminding her that the dining room still contained a restless breakfast crowd eager for food and more coffee.

But Clarissa couldn't resist pulling the letter free. Hope's handwriting filled the page, the ink faded with time, but the emotions as raw as if they'd been written yesterday.

Clarissa folded the letter with care and slipped it into her apron pocket. Later, when she had time to breathe without someone watching, she'd read the rest of Hope's words.

Maybe they'd contain something she needed to hear, like wisdom from a woman who'd faced loss and found a way to keep going.

Maybe they'd even help her figure out how to put the broken pieces of her own life back together, one lonely step at a time.

The bus rumbled with nervous energy as twenty players shifted in their seats, equipment bags jostling together in the back seats and shoes tapping restless rhythms against the metal floor.

Zeke stood in the narrow aisle, gripping the back of a seat for balance as they swayed around a curve.

Outside the windows, farmland rolled past under overcast skies. The forecasters predicted rain much later tonight, but the gloomy weather matched the tension that hung over his team since yesterday's loss.

"All right, listen up." He waited for conversations to die down and earbuds to be pulled free. "I promised you a debrief from yesterday's game, and we need to cover some things before we take the field today."

Before he could begin his prepared remarks about mental focus and execution under pressure, a hand shot up from the middle of the bus.

"Coach?" Timothy Miller's voice carried above the engine noise. "Can I say something first?"

Surprised murmurs rippled through the bus. Players craned their necks to look at the freshman who'd been the center of yesterday's meltdown, their expressions ranging from curiosity to sympathy to barely concealed dread.

Zeke nodded. Whatever the kid had to say, it took courage to want to speak up in front of the entire team.

Timothy stood, his red hair in stark contrast to his pale skin as he faced his teammates.

Despite the slight tremor in his hands at his sides, his voice held steady. "I want to apologize for my level of play yesterday. I know I let you guys down, and that's not acceptable."

He swallowed hard. "After my mom died last fall, it's been just my brother and sister at home. So when she didn't show up at the game, I got scared that something had happened to her."

A few players nodded as if they understood the weight of family uncertainty. Hadn't he heard that one had lost a grandfather last year and another's parents had divorced over the summer?

"I got distracted and made a stupid error that got up in my head and snowballed from there." Timothy's cheeks puffed as he blew out a breath. "Turns out she was safe but had a horrible day that got worse when her phone died. And she couldn't let me know because I'd taken her car charger."

Several players winced and Zeke caught a few guilty exchanges of glances. He guessed Timothy wasn't the only one who'd borrowed family electronics without returning them.

But what was that about a horrible day?

"That's no excuse for letting my team down." Timothy's voice gained strength. "I should have been able to focus regardless of what happened in the stands. I'm sorry for—"

"Hey, man." Torres interrupted from his seat near the front, his captain's armband catching the light as he turned to face Timothy. "That's gotta be hard, dealing with all that. But honestly, we all made mistakes yesterday. I—we—should have been there to pick you up instead of letting the frustration get to us."

"Exactly." Their left-handed pitcher and first baseman Patterson jutted his chin out from across the aisle. "When one guy's struggling, the rest of us step up. That's what teams do."

"We all make errors." Martinez's voice carried the wisdom of someone who'd learned resilience the hard way. "The important thing is we don't stay there. We learn from our mistakes and get better."

A chorus of agreement rose as many of the players nodded, called out encouragement, or reached across the aisle to bump fists with Timothy.

The transformation from yesterday's sullen defeat to today's unified support made Zeke's chest tighten with pride.

He cleared his throat and reclaimed his position at the front of the bus. "Couldn't have said it better myself."

The irony wasn't lost on him.

He'd thought he'd be teaching these boys about character in the context of a game, but here they were demonstrating the kind of grace he'd failed to show Clarissa yesterday.

"Since we're talking about learning from mistakes..." Zeke's gaze swept the interior of the bus. "Let's make this a teaching moment. One of our team values is resilience, and I want to see that in action today. Every error, every bad pitch, every strikeout—we bounce back. We don't let one play determine the next one."

Heads nodded. The energy continued to shift, transforming from nervous anxiety into something more focused and determined.

"Torres, Patterson, and Martinez." Zeke pivoted to make eye contact with the individual members of his team. "Thank you all for taking responsibility and supporting your teammate. That's exactly what I expect from you."

"And Timothy?" Zeke's voice softened. "Thank you for setting the first example this afternoon. Taking ownership, being honest about your struggles, asking for help when you need it—that type of personal responsibility is why I'm keeping you on varsity for at least another game."

The kid's face lit up like Christmas morning, his eyes wide with surprise and gratitude. "Really, Coach?"

"Really." Zeke's gaze swept across the bus, taking in the mixture of supportive smiles and resigned acceptance. "But like I've said before—everyone here has to earn their spot every single day. Attitude, effort, and accountability. Those are non-negotiables."

In his peripheral vision, he caught Andrew Henderson's expression. The boy's mouth dropped open, as if he couldn't quite process that his demotion might stick.

Good.
Maybe a little uncertainty would motivate better behavior.
If only he could say the same for the kid's parents.

Chapter Twenty

A sense of peace settled over Zeke's shoulders like his familiar jacket as he watched his players' faces—some relieved, others determined.

All of them more unified than they'd been less than twenty-four hours ago. Well, most of them.

For now, Timothy's honesty had done what no coaching speech could accomplish, transforming yesterday's fractured team into something solid again.

"All right, spend the rest of our drive getting focused." He tapped his hand on the back of his seat. "We'll be there soon."

As the chatter on the bus resumed, Zeke sank down onto the bench, ignoring the cluster of assistant coaches huddled several rows ahead.

This was his fight now, his line in the sand.

Whatever Devon and the others thought about his roster decisions could wait until after the game.

Zeke relaxed into the vinyl cushion, warmed by the afternoon sun streaming through the windows. Spring was certainly edging toward summer with this weather.

"Coach?" Timothy appeared in the aisle, uncertainty written across his freckled face. "Can I talk to you for a minute?"

Zeke slid over to make room, noting how the freshman's hands trembled as he settled onto the bench. The poor kid was likely still processing the emotional whiplash of the past two days.

"I wanted to thank you for the second chance." Timothy's voice was barely audible over the engine noise. "I know I have to prove myself all over again."

"You will. I have faith in your ability."

Timothy's gaze flicked toward the back of the bus. "I'm worried about Andrew, though. About causing bad feelings on the team."

Zeke followed his line of sight, taking in the player's crossed arms and scowl. "Let me worry about that. You just focus on your position and trust your teammates to have your back."

Timothy nodded, but his expression remained troubled. "I'm glad there was an easy explanation for why my sister couldn't call yesterday. I was starting to think she just...didn't care anymore."

The comment hit Zeke like a fastball to the chest.

He'd been tempted to fish for information about Clarissa's absence, but hearing the raw vulnerability in Timothy's voice made his curiosity feel selfish.

Zeke rested a hand on the boy's shoulder for a moment. "Not a chance of her not caring about you. But what happened?"

Timothy's jaw tightened. "She was working on some freelance project for this rich developer guy who accused her of something she didn't do. Wouldn't let her make any phone calls and treated her like a criminal."

A criminal? Zeke's fingers curled into a fist.

"With a name like Rocky Ridge, it's no wonder they caused a mountain of trouble." The kid shook his head. "Then again, I should be grateful for the income. She's worked so hard to provide for us."

Rocky Ridge? And a developer?

The pieces clicked into place along with the hours-old memory of a bronze plaque honoring Rocky Ridge Development.

What were the chances that the company who'd made Clarissa's life miserable—and therefore disrupted his team's performance—was the same one being used by the Henderson's to buy preferential treatment for their son?

If so, Zeke's decision to fight the bribery attempt felt even more justified now.

But relief was followed by a crushing wave of guilt.

There had been a logical explanation for her absence—a crisis beyond her control—and instead of listening, he'd unloaded his frustrations on an easy target. After she'd already endured hours of being accused and treated like a criminal, his angry words must have made everything worse.

"I need to text her about the roster change." Timothy pulled out his phone, then moved back to his original seat.

Leaving Zeke with an uncomfortable sensation crawling across his skin like ants. The weight of his mistakes pressed down on him, making the bus feel stuffy and claustrophobic.

If only he could escape the shame somehow. Forget the look of pain on Clarissa's face when he'd torn into her in the parking lot.

For a fleeting moment, he understood his father's impulse to disappear into a bottle when the guilt became too heavy to carry. The temptation to numb the feelings rather than face them head-on.

But no. There was only one place to leave the bad feelings—at the foot of the cross. Only one source to fill the hollow ache in his chest.

He pulled out his phone and typed: ***Timothy told me what happened, and once again I'm so sorry I let my past affect how I spoke to you. I can only pray that you'll forgive me someday.***

The message was inadequate, like trying to repair a shattered window with a single piece of tape. But it was a start.

He needed to think and pray about all of this later—about his tendency to jump to conclusions, about the way his father's abandonment still poisoned his relationships, about whether there could ever be an "us" with Clarissa after the damage he'd done.

But for now, as the bus pulled onto a side street and the baseball complex came into view ahead, they had games to play.

The sight of dugouts and warning tracks should have brought comfort, but instead it triggered fresh anxiety.

Clarissa should be here later to watch Timothy. Which meant he'd have to work twice as hard to keep his focus on the team instead of scanning the stands for red hair.

And she wouldn't be the only family member in attendance.

What would the Hendersons do when they realized their son still rode the bench?

The weight of responsibilities sat lighter as Clarissa navigated the winding roads toward the baseball complex, today's drive mercifully shorter than yesterday's marathon.

Brian bounced in the passenger seat beside her. "I can't believe Timothy's message that he's on varsity again. Do you think he'll start at second base?"

Clarissa grinned. "I hope so. He's worked hard, and I'm glad he got another chance."

And a day of second chances was something to be thankful for.

Not just for Timothy on the field. Or for her getting another opportunity to be the supportive sister in the stands. But also at Rocky Ridge Development.

While the new restrictions were annoying but manageable, her time today contained no security guards or accusations. Just several hours of solid work and real progress on the website coding.

Now, instead of rushing home after tonight's game to tackle mountains of college homework, she could simply...breathe.

Everything was done except walking across the stage next weekend to officially graduate. Tonight was just family time for a change, and the novelty of that felt almost surreal.

Once at the complex, Clarissa chose seats that were close enough to cheer from but distant enough to avoid the worst of the toxic commentary that had poisoned yesterday's experience.

And they were at an angle that kept her from seeing the coaches unless they walked out past first base. Somewhere she wouldn't accidentally see Zeke and recall his hard expression and even harsher words.

Yesterday was still too fresh.

Brian settled beside her with his homework, content to work on math problems between innings.

With extra time before Timothy's game, Clarissa dug through her bag for the mystery novel she'd been trying to finish for weeks. Instead, her fingers found the folded letter she'd rescued from Lauren's craft supplies that morning.

The opening sentiment from Frank and Greta's mother Hope Dawson still called for her to read more.

She unfolded the paper, smoothing the creases against her leg.

Dear Harold, everything has fallen apart since you died, and I don't know how to fix it. The kids are grown, and at least I have that to make life easier. Just doing the best I can. Messing up a lot.

However, little Joel is just two years old, and I'd like to help fill in for our grandson when the time comes. Hope Frank remembers learning to catch and throw a ball from you and teaches his son.

Grief is a funny thing to leave such a hole in a family. You made me promise that if anything ever happened to you that I would raise our family to love God and serve others.

I pray I can do that but will have to trust God to fill in the gaps where I'm lacking...

The words blurred as tears pricked Clarissa's eyes.

Hope had experienced the same crushing weight of grief. The same fear of inadequacy.

The same desperate need to fulfill a promise made to someone who could no longer see whether she was keeping it or not.

Just like Clarissa. Except Hope had found a way through.

The Dawson matriarch raised her children to love God and serve others while building a business that became the heart of a community.

And she'd done it by trusting God to fill in the gaps where she was lacking.

The truth settled into Clarissa's chest like a warm embrace.

God had already been filling those gaps—through Greta's motherly guidance, through Lauren's friendship, through the entire café family who'd rallied around when her laptop died.

Through neighbors and friend's parents who provided childcare or gave rides.

Even through coaches like Zeke who taught Timothy skills she couldn't provide.

She might not have a boyfriend or husband to share the load of guardianship, but God would be enough for her and the boys.

She'd have to trust Him, cling to His promise to provide, and hope He wouldn't fail them this time, either.

Clarissa skimmed the rest of the letter, then re-folded it before tucking it into the secure pocket of her bag.

When she pulled out her phone, Zeke's earlier text glowed on the screen. ***I can only pray that you'll forgive me someday.***

There might not be a future between them, but she could at least set him free from guilt and herself free from bitterness by leaving yesterday in the past where it belonged.

Her fingers moved easily over the screen. ***I already have.***

After stashing her phone away, she pulled out her sketchbook, then let her pencil move freely across the page as she imagined what Hope's Café might have looked like decades ago.

Simple booths and counter stools, vintage fixtures, the same warm atmosphere that still drew people in today.

There was joy in the drawing, in the creative process that had nothing to do with earning money or meeting deadlines. She'd have to make time for art again—real art, not just website designs and logos.

The junior varsity game flew by in a blur, and then the varsity took the field.

Even Karen Henderson's dirty looks couldn't distract Clarissa's focus or dim her joy because Timothy played with both confidence and focus.

Tears slipped down her cheeks as he fielded ground balls with precision.

Hope had been right about God filling in the gaps. Timothy had coaches to teach him what she couldn't, teammates to challenge him, and opportunities to grow that she never could have provided alone.

When Timothy jogged toward their car after the victory, his face flushed with joy and accomplishment, he stopped short at the sight of her tears.

"Oh no. What now?" The sharp-toned question was softened by his concerned expression. "Are you okay?"

She laughed, wiping her cheeks with the back of her hand. "I'm more than okay. I'm proud. And grateful. And..."

She struggled to find words for the sense of peace that had settled over her. "I found a letter from Hope today. About grief and promises and trusting God to fill in the gaps."

As she drove them home through the gathering dusk, she shared more of Hope's story. Which in turn led to memories of their mother and how scary it had been to face the future without her.

"I want to thank you both for your patience these past few months," Clarissa said as they pulled into their driveway. "I know I've been stretched too thin, but it'll get better soon. And once I quit the café, I'll have even more flexibility at home."

Timothy paused with his door half open. "You shouldn't have had to give up all your dreams for us. All your sleep. All your time. You deserve to do something just for you."

"Like what?" Clarissa swallowed hard.

Did she dare to dream again?

Timothy straightened. "I'm going to get a job this summer to help save for a car and insurance. It's time I stepped up."

Fresh tears threatened as Clarissa recognized the man her little brother was becoming. "Timothy—"

"I saw how you were around Coach." His voice was both gentle and knowing. "I want that happy feeling for you."

She sighed, reality creeping back in despite the evening's healing. "Maybe someday, with someone. But I don't see it happening as long as you're on his team."

The truth hung between them.

Some complications couldn't be wished away.

Instead of heading to the school parking lot with the last of the departing fans and families, Zeke veered toward the freshly groomed baseball field.

He climbed into the home team bleachers, settling onto a sun-warmed aluminum bench that creaked under his weight.

Around him, the school's sports complex settled into the quiet of a Saturday afternoon. No more cheering crowds or crackling speakers as the announcer gave his commentary.

Just the distant hum of traffic and the occasional bark of a dog from the nearby neighborhoods.

Zeke rested his elbows on his knees and buried his face in his hands.

Ever since Tuesday's debacle, he'd tried to leave his worries with God, but it was a battle. Especially when his world felt like he was just waiting for the next curve ball to leave him swinging at air.

Three regular season games left, and they were balanced on the knife's edge of making the championship playoff bracket.

Timothy was helping for sure—the kid had found his confidence and fit in with the varsity roster. His defensive play was solid, his batting average climbing, and most importantly, his teammates welcomed him completely.

But the Hendersons were fuming.

If it wasn't thinly veiled threats delivered to his voice mail, they were launching passive-aggressive comments from the bleachers. The kind that poisoned team chemistry.

Even their son's attitude festered like an untreated wound, his sullen presence on the bench affecting the younger players who should look to the upperclassmen for leadership.

And when it came to the coaching, more and more fell onto Zeke since Devon grew increasingly distant. The man avoided eye contact and offered only the bare minimum of support during games.

Even teaching PE had become an emotional minefield, knowing Vaughn was somewhere in the building, probably fielding phone calls and pressure from influential parents.

Zeke scrubbed his face, then lifted his head.

His gaze drifted to the row where Clarissa had been just an hour ago. He'd caught glimpses of her red hair throughout the game, fought to ignore the tug of longing every time she cheered for Timothy.

It had been torture to pretend she was just another parent in the stands while Vaughn and Devon watched for any excuse to question his professionalism.

The need to make things right between them was becoming more of a craving than a simple desire. Her text saying she'd already forgiven him had been freeing, but it wasn't enough.

He missed their growing friendship. The way her smile lit up her face. The warmth of her lips beneath his.

But he also missed the family feeling he'd glimpsed in those brief moments when he'd been welcomed into the Millers' chaotic, loving world.

The sharp ring of his phone cut through his brooding. He glanced at the screen, surprised to see his old college coach's name.

"Coach Bryant?"

"Zeke! How are you, son?" The familiar voice carried genuine affection that loosened the knot in Zeke's chest. "You've been on my heart lately, and I felt like I needed to call and check in. How's the coaching life treating you?"

For the next twenty minutes, Zeke poured out the complications of his current situation.

The job that had started as a dream to mold young athletes, but revealed unexpected challenges. The teaching role that wasn't as fulfilling as he'd hoped, bogged down by bureaucracy and classroom management. The talented team with real playoff potential, but the political headaches mounting daily.

"There's this kid—a junior, so I'll get to deal with this for another year—who thinks the world revolves around him. His parents are making my life miserable because I benched him for attitude problems."

Coach Bryant chuckled. "Unfortunately, there will always be those parents with their precious superstars. You either have to move up to the college level for some separation from that drama, or focus on kiddie leagues before parents start believing their child is the next Derek Jeter."

For a moment, Zeke remembered the clusters of elementary kids gathered right here not quite two weeks ago for the skills camp fundraiser. Of the two options, he knew which one he'd prefer.

Coach's tone grew more serious. "I can only advise that you focus on one game at a time with the group you have. Don't worry about anything beyond this season. But I have a feeling that's not all that's bugging you."

The invitation to share more hovered like a lifeline.

In careful terms, Zeke opened up about Clarissa—his attraction to her, the pull toward her family, but also his fear of violating fraternization policies and losing his job.

After a long pause, Coach sighed. "I have to ask. Are you protecting your principles or protecting your heart from the risk of caring too much? Because some things matter more than regulations."

The question hung in the air long after they'd said goodbye, and Zeke slipped his phone back into his pocket.

God, thanks for sending a friend when I needed wisdom the most.

As the afternoon shadows lengthened, Zeke lingered.

Like Coach said, he could only take one game at a time on the field and leave the results in God's capable hands. The same was true for everything else—the Hendersons' threats, Devon's loyalty, and his own uncertain future.

The only thing certain was God's character and promises. The foundational truths that had anchored him through previous storms. God had fed him when he was hungry for purpose, had been living water when his soul felt parched and empty.

God was his Heavenly Father, the best sort of father ever. Nothing like the drunken man who'd abandoned his family when life got difficult.

And God saw it all. The roster decisions that created such chaos, the Miller and Henderson family dynamics, and even the way Zeke messed up with Clarissa.

God saw his heart, forgave his failures, and offered strength for today along with new mercies every morning.

Zeke stood from the bleachers and stretched muscles that had grown stiff during his long contemplation.

The peace that now filled his chest was different from the temporary relief he'd been chasing—deeper, more sustainable, rooted in something bigger than his own ability to fix things.

He'd surrender the future to God. Would let Clarissa remain on the sidelines while he focused on classroom responsibilities and game preparation for these final weeks of the school year.

God had a plan, even when Zeke couldn't see beyond the immediate complications.

And he could only hope that plan included a family somewhere.

Somehow.

Chapter Twenty-One

♥

Surrendering her backpack and phone to Mr. Ridge's assistant when Clarissa arrived had become almost comforting in its predictability.

Almost.

Clarissa bit her lip, leaving the taste of copper on her tongue as she watched the woman rifle through her belongings, supposedly checking for mysterious flash drives that might compromise their precious network security.

As if Clarissa would make such a mistake again.

In fact, the only thing she now took to her assigned work station was her notebook with its dwindling checklist of remaining tasks.

"Everything looks fine to me." Ms. Reeves offered a smile that seemed more genuine than the icy professionalism of last week. "However, Mr. Ridge wanted to review your materials personally today."

The moment of comfort evaporated instantly.

Clarissa's stomach clenched as the imposing man emerged from his office, his hair gleaming under the harsh fluorescent lights.

She held her breath as he flipped through her notebook, then moved to her sketchbook with the methodical precision of someone accustomed to finding fault.

Please God, don't let there be anything inappropriate in there. Had she sketched any doodles of grumpy security guards or unflattering caricatures of entitled mothers from baseball games?

Mr. Ridge paused at one particular page, and Clarissa's heart hammered against her ribs.

It was the sketch she'd drawn at the game—the one inspired by Hope's letter, where she'd imagined what the café might have looked like decades ago.

The drawing had evolved into an idyllic small-town street scene, complete with tree-lined sidewalks and cheerful storefronts that appeared to glow with warmth and community spirit.

A gleam flickered in Mr. Ridge's eyes—so brief she almost missed it—before his expression returned to its usual neutral mask. "You drew this?"

"Yes, sir." Her voice came out smaller than intended. "Just practicing my art. Working on perspective."

He studied the sketch for another long moment, then closed the book with a decisive snap. "I have an additional project for you."

"A what?" After all she'd been through, did she want to spend more time here?

"Our website needs something for the Future Projects page. It's too soon for architectural renderings, but I need something appealing to show potential investors."

Clarissa blinked, trying to process the sudden shift. "What kind of something?"

"A drawing. Something with a small-town vibe like this sketch, but more... ambitious." His fingers drummed against the leather cover of her sketchbook.

"Ambitious?" She almost tripped over the word.

"A multi-story building with shops below and apartments above. No hole-in-the-wall diners or rundown establishments. Think upscale boutiques, chic coffee shops, art galleries. Generic but appealing. The kind of place people would want to live and spend money."

The description sent a tingle of excitement through her despite the clinical way he described it. Especially since it combined her love of art with a practical application.

"It could take up an entire block." His voice gained enthusiasm. "Or feature a central courtyard for residents. Really capture that modern urban village feel."

"That sounds wonderful," she said, meaning it. "When do you need it?"

"By the end of next week, along with the rest of the website. I'll pay extra for the artwork since it falls outside your original contract."

Could she get it all done during the afternoons when Timothy still had baseball games? Or should she ask for additional time... or flexibility?

He passed her the sketchbook. "I'll allow you to work on the drawing at home in the evenings if you prefer. No reason for it to be created here in the office. I'll have Ms. Reeves scan it into a digital file once completed."

Relief flooded through her at the answer to her unspoken prayer. And the knowledge this extra task would not cause any delays.

Even with the unexpected delay of last week's lost work day and having to recreate code from scratch, she was still on schedule to meet the original deadline—possibly even finish early.

And the additional payment would help pay down her credit card balance faster.

"Thank you, Mr. Ridge. I'll get started on it right away."

The gleam returned to his eyes, brighter this time. "Excellent. I have a feeling this project is going to exceed everyone's expectations."

Four hours later, Clarissa found herself in yet another set of bleachers, watching another baseball game unfold.

The uncomfortable aluminum seat was already hot from the sun, making her both glad for the change in weather from the season's earlier rainstorms and concerned about getting burned.

Being a red-head with a propensity for freckles on her pale skin had a downside.

She slathered on another layer of the highest SPF available, then dug one of her brother's old baseball caps out of her bag, threading her ponytail through the gap in the back and tugging the brim low to shade her face.

Two more games after today, and then hopefully some breathing room to figure out what came next—for her brothers, for her career, and for the fragile peace she'd finally found within her own heart.

Then again, with Brian's first scrimmage scheduled for Saturday, she'd be doing this all summer long. Just with younger players on the field and hopefully more civilized parents in the stands.

Half an inning later and she grew bored, her fingers twitching for something to do. It wasn't often that she got to just sit.

Although, didn't the experts say embracing boredom was good for creativity?

It wasn't long before her idle mind drifted back to Mr. Ridge's artistic assignment, and she pulled out her sketchbook.

The one containing her Hope's Cafe inspired artwork that had landed the additional work. The same sketches she'd started in another set of stands.

There must be something magical about baseball games.

She grinned, then flipped to a fresh page, the blank white space full of possibility. Just like her future.

A few initial pencil strokes brought the first building to life from her imagination. Clean lines suggesting modern architecture were then softened by traditional details. She added shop windows that invited browsing with sidewalks wide enough for outdoor café seating.

Who knew where such a development would actually be built without displacing existing businesses, but that wasn't her concern.

Her job was to create something beautiful and appealing, to capture a vision that would excite investors.

Such an illustration would integrate beautifully with the rest of her website design and become the centerpiece of the Future Projects page.

Her heart overflowed as she added more details. Decorative iron railings. Flower boxes that would brim with color once she had access to her pastels at home.

Maybe she could give the impression of warm light spilling out from the windows onto the street?

Lost in the creative process, she hardly noticed the transition between games, the way the crowd shifted and changed as JV parents filtered out and varsity families claimed their preferred seats.

"Nice artwork."

The unexpected voice made her jump, pencil skittering across the page and leaving an unintended mark.

She looked up to find Kyle, the newspaper reporter and cafe regular, settling onto the bench beside her with his ever-present notepad.

"Thanks." She placed her hand over the drawing. "Just keeping my hands busy."

Kyle's sharp eyes missed nothing. "Looks like some kind of development project. Related to your freelance work?"

Her heart pounded and heat flooded her cheeks. "Just... ideas. Nothing specific."

He nodded, but she saw the curiosity simmering behind his casual expression. Kyle made his living noticing details other people missed, connecting dots that weren't meant to be connected.

And with Mr. Ridge already so paranoid about protecting his trade secrets and throwing around accusations of corporate espionage, Clarissa had to do something to deflect Kyle's attention. And fast.

She jutted her chin toward the field. "What brings you here?"

"I might ask you the same thing."

"Huh?" Clarissa frowned. "I'm here to watch my brother and his team."

"Your brother plays for the Red Wolves?" Kyle raised an eyebrow.

"He does. Second base."

She couldn't have picked better timing for her comment because the varsity chose that moment to jog onto the field for their warmups, white home uniforms bright against the green grass.

And Timothy's trademark red hair easily visible.

Kyle hummed. "Guess that makes him the freshman who could help them make the playoffs."

"Playoffs?" Had Timothy said anything about that? Or had she been so distracted lately that she'd tuned him out?

"It's still a bit of a long shot—especially with a rookie coach—but just in case they pull it off, I'll need some background information for a story."

Kyle began taking notes. And in the relative quiet, Clarissa turned to a fresh page of her own.

There'd be no more working on Mr. Ridge's assignment tonight, but she could still sketch her favorite player. Well, at least her favorite player in tonight's game since Brian would soon have his own games.

On the plus side, focusing on Timothy and the drawing taking shape in her lap made it easier to avoid looking at the coaches. At Zeke.

Easier to avoid the complicated feelings that arose whenever she caught glimpses of his profile. Glimpses that reminded her of the way he'd held her in the equipment shed, the way his lips caressed hers, or the way his eyes sparkled with shared laughter over her brothers' antics.

Easier also to ignore the sound of Karen Henderson several rows below, still airing her grievances about coaching decisions and favoritism.

For now, Clarissa had pencil and paper to lose herself in. The opportunity to create while her brother played the game he loved.

The rest of her life could wait.

Friday afternoon, Zeke slipped his phone back into the pocket of his coaching jacket, energy buzzing through his veins like electricity.

Had that really just happened?

He pinched himself, feeling the sharp reality of skin between his fingers while the conversation with Vaughn still echoed in his ears.

His phone vibrated with an incoming text.

He pulled it out again, thumb sliding across the screen to follow a website link. The state athletic association's page loaded, and there it was in black and white.

The championship playoff bracket with the Loveland Red Wolves listed in one of the coveted spots.

His heart hammered against his ribs with the proof that in his first season as a head coach, they'd actually done it.

"Team huddle!" His voice carried across the field where the players had been going through their usual drills with an air of restless uncertainty. Yesterday's final regular season game had left everyone wondering what—if anything—came next.

Cleats churned up dust and blades of grass as twenty players jogged toward the pitcher's mound, their faces showing varying degrees of curiosity and hope.

Like before tryouts, Zeke breathed in the unique scents of the outdoors, clay, chalk, leather, sweat...and possibility. He'd only dreamed of this moment ever since accepting the job.

"First, I want to thank you all for a great season." He fought the smile threatening to give away the news too soon. "This was my first time at the helm of a team, and I'm proud of your growth as players and as teammates."

Zeke folded his arms over his chest, looking each of them in the eye. "You've shown resilience, accountability, and the kind of character that goes beyond baseball."

Torres shifted his weight from foot to foot while Timothy stood to one side, his red hair damp with sweat and uniform streaked with dirt. Some of the others exchanged glances, their expressions suggesting his words sounded like a wrap-up speech.

"I'm especially proud..." Zeke let his smile build, savoring the moment. "Because all that hard work paid off. I just heard from our athletic director and confirmed it on the state website. We made the playoffs!"

The eruption was immediate and glorious.

Players whooped and chest-bumped, jumping up and down like kids on Christmas morning and tossing caps into the air.

This was why he'd fallen in love with sports. With baseball. And now with coaching.

"All right, settle down." Zeke raised his hands for quiet.

The celebration gradually died to eager murmurs, but the energy still crackled through the group like contained lightning.

"JV players, thank you for all your hard work. Keep grinding in the off-season, because next year you'll be competing for varsity spots." He made eye contact with several of the younger players, noting their mixture of disappointment and determination.

"I will be holding over a few JV guys to help with our playoff run since we'll need depth on the bench. Extra infielder, extra outfielder, a bullpen catcher, and another pitcher." He pulled out his notes, though he'd already memorized the names in case today's news happened. "Ramirez, Morrison, Martinez... and Henderson."

Andrew Henderson's face transformed from sullen resignation to smug satisfaction in the span of a heartbeat. The kid lifted his chin and shot a meaningful glance toward Timothy.

Zeke's stomach tightened.

Henderson was the best backup based purely on experience and skill level. Personal feelings aside, Zeke had to make his decisions based on what gave them the best chance to win.

He could only pray nothing happened to his varsity lineup to warrant the need for a bench player. And that just maybe keeping Andrew around for at least another week would make the kid's parents calm down.

Zeke blew out a breath, because he had only one team to worry about now. "Varsity players, expect a long practice tomorrow morning. We'll start earlier than normal to get in extra work on situational hitting for any close games."

Timothy's face had gone white as the chalk dust on the baseline. He looked like he might be sick.

Was it Andrew's presence back on the roster? Some kind of family emergency? He'd need to find out before the kid got into his head again.

"Coach?" Torres raised his hand. "What time tomorrow?"

"Eight o'clock sharp. Any questions before we clean up today?"

The players began to disperse, chattering excitedly about playoff schedules and championship possibilities.

Zeke took one step toward Timothy, but was stopped by Grant and then Dave—and even Devon—with a multitude of questions ranging from practice plans and strategy to equipment transport and travel arrangements for the next weekend's game.

By the time Zeke was free, Timothy had disappeared into the crush of players heading toward the parking lot and the opportunity was gone.

The next morning Zeke arrived early to unlock the equipment shed, then hauled batting practice gear toward the dugout.

The day promised plenty of sun later, but for now the overcast skies were a welcome relief.

Before long, his assistant coaches and players began to arrive, their voices carrying across the field in various octaves as they changed into their cleats and began their stretching routines.

The pre-practice energy built gradually—joking and trash talk mixed with a new focus that came with knowing the playoffs were on the line.

But as eight o'clock approached, one face was notably missing from the gathering crowd.

Timothy Miller was nowhere to be seen.

Zeke's stomach clenched as he scanned the field again. He should have followed up on his instincts yesterday.

The kid had been early to every other practice, eager to prove himself worthy of his varsity spot. Except today hadn't been on the original parent calendar since playoffs weren't guaranteed.

Maybe he should have made the expectations clearer or confirmed everyone had a ride since he'd changed the normal time?

"Devon?" Zeke strode toward where his assistant coach organized infield drills near second base. "Did Miller communicate anything to you about today?"

Devon's expression was neutral. "He sent me a text last night. Said he had a previous commitment he couldn't miss. Didn't give specifics."

The words sat wrong in Zeke's gut.

Timothy wasn't the type to blow off practice for something trivial, not when they were preparing for the playoffs. And something was off about Devon's tone too—too casual, almost rehearsed.

"Coach, that reminds me." Andrew Henderson appeared at Zeke's elbow with the timing of a predator sensing weakness. "Your team rules say that if you skip practice, playing time is affected. So Miller can't start our first playoff game, right?"

The kid's voice carried just loud enough for nearby players to hear. Several heads turned their way, curious and waiting.

Devon's expression shifted to something that might have been a smirk, hidden behind a cough.

Zeke's chest squeezed as he was backed into a corner.

Team rules were team rules and he couldn't change them on a whim now. Missing practice without a legitimate excuse meant reduced playing time.

But something about this whole situation almost reeked of a setup.

Had Devon really received a text message? Had he relayed it accurately?

Except there was nothing Zeke could do without additional information. Not with a dozen boys waiting to start practice.

He clenched his fists at his sides. "Henderson, take second base for now. And use the opportunity to work on your double-play turns the way we've tried to teach you."

Andrew jogged away with barely concealed glee, but not before Zeke caught the satisfied glance he exchanged with Devon.

The pieces of some larger puzzle were shifting into place, but he couldn't quite see the complete picture yet.

Whatever kept Timothy away, Zeke had the uncomfortable feeling he'd missed something crucial.

And now with the kid missing valuable instruction about specific batting situations and the Henderson boy getting those precious repetitions, Zeke's team rules and roster decisions were about to blow up in his face.

If he only knew where Timothy was and what kept him away.

Chapter Twenty-Two

"I'm sorry you had to get up so early and wait so long." Clarissa squinted against the sun streaming through the windshield in that annoying spot the visor wouldn't reach as Timothy navigated the familiar streets toward the Loveland Baseball Association complex.

She sighed. "And then you sat by yourself through the whole ceremony—"

"Are you kidding me?" Timothy shot her an incredulous look before returning his attention to the road. "There was no way on earth I'd miss your graduation, too."

Too.

The word carried the weight of choices they'd had to make as a family without enough adults to go around. Because they'd known for weeks that her graduation ceremony conflicted with Brian's uniform handout, team pictures, and warmups before his first official scrimmage.

Timothy had represented their family well, if not quietly. In fact, his shrill whistle when her name was called had echoed across the entire auditorium, making several graduates turn to look for the source.

She pulled out her phone to reread Brian's text from earlier: ***Watched the whole thing on the live stream! You looked awesome walking across that stage! Don't worry about me - Mrs. Winters is driving me to the game like we planned. Super proud of you sis!!!***

The middle-school enthusiasm in his message made her smile despite the pang of grief that their mom wasn't here to see this milestone.

How many more moments would they navigate without her presence, wisdom, or steady love anchoring their family?

But looking at Timothy—really looking at him as he checked his mirrors and signaled for the turn into the baseball complex—she again caught glimpses of the man he was becoming.

Responsible, thoughtful, loyal to his core. Mom would have been so proud to see him growing up like this.

"Was Coach Matthews okay with you missing practice this morning?" A flutter of worry stirred in her chest. She'd been so focused on her own big day that she hadn't considered the consequences Timothy might face.

Timothy shrugged, his expression too-casual as he pulled into a parking spot. "I let my position coach know I had a previous commitment. I'm fine with whatever happens next."

The worry intensified. What did *whatever happens next* mean? Would this affect his playing time? His spot on varsity?

She opened her mouth to ask, but Timothy was already climbing out of the car.

"Come on," he said, retrieving her cap and gown from the back seat. "You're wearing these, and you're carrying that diploma folder. This is your day."

She indulged him, slipping the polyester gown over her sundress and settling the cap on her head despite feeling ridiculous.

The walk to Brian's assigned field drew amused looks and spontaneous congratulations from strangers who put together the clues, making her cheeks burn with a mixture of embarrassment and pride.

It had been a long journey and she'd worked hard to earn the right to wear this get-up.

As they reached the aluminum bleachers, her stomach growled, reminding her of the afternoon hour and a skipped meal. She sent Timothy to the concessions stand with cash for both of them, then settled back to watch Brian finish warming up with his teammates.

Being here, surrounded by families and couples cheering for their children, brought back vivid memories of the day Zeke had watched practice with her and then stayed for pizza in the park.

The memory was bittersweet—a glimpse of what could have been, of the family dynamic she'd briefly allowed herself to imagine.

She tried to trust God and believe He held good things in store for her future. But sitting here alone in the bleachers, watching other families share their joy, the loneliness was especially sharp.

Please God, will I ever feel as cherished again?

Brian took the field at shortstop, his red hair bright under the afternoon sun.

The coaches had been clear that they'd rotate players through different positions early in the season to develop everyone's skills, but he looked natural at the position, scooping up a quick grounder and firing it to first base with casual precision.

An older man appeared at the end of the bleachers, hands in his pockets as he watched with the practiced eye of someone who'd spent years around youth baseball.

When Brian made another smooth play and Clarissa cheered, the man chuckled.

"Guess I know which kid is yours." He turned a friendly smile in her direction. "That red hair is pretty distinctive."

"Guilty as charged." Clarissa adjusted her graduation cap self-consciously.

"I remember him from tryouts not so long ago. His skills have improved a lot since then."

"His older brother's been helping him at home." She glanced toward Timothy who climbed the bleachers with nachos, a hot dog, and drinks.

"The skills camp and Coach Matthews did a lot more than I did." Timothy sat and handed her a drink. "That guy really knows what he's doing. Studied sports management but also played in college and almost in the pros. He's the whole package."

The older man's eyebrows lifted with interest. "Matthews... I saw his name in the paper about the high school team making the playoffs. Impressive for a first-year coach."

A commotion near the entrance caught Clarissa's attention. A group of familiar faces hurried down the main sidewalk of the complex, and her heart leaped with recognition.

"Surprise!" Lauren called out, practically skipping as she approached with Joel close behind. "We couldn't miss celebrating our college graduate!"

Suddenly Clarissa was surrounded by a deluge of café family—Greta carrying an apple pie with a triumphant grin, Debbie trailing behind with her twins Mark and Monica, and Trevor supporting his mother who looked fragile but determined to be there.

Even Amanda had come, her dark-haired toddler balanced on her hip, the little girl's enormous eyelashes fluttering as she took in all the excitement.

"Let me see that diploma," Lauren demanded, and Clarissa found herself passing around the leather folder like a trophy while comments flew about her cap and gown.

Greta held up her contribution to the celebration. "Nothing's more American than baseball and apple pie. And it's not quite the Fourth of July!"

The laughter was infectious, warm and genuine in a way that made Clarissa's raw emotions swell until tears blurred her vision.

As soon as Brian's scrimmage concluded—and she'd smothered him with compliments and welcomed his congratulatory hug—the group migrated toward the nearby park's picnic tables.

Once there, she saw Timothy approach Joel with a purposeful expression.

"Any chance you might need summer help at the café?" Timothy's voice carried just enough hope that Clarissa's heart squeezed. "I'd like to start contributing more at home."

Joel clapped him on the shoulder. "Let's talk. We can always use reliable people."

Nearby, Monica Palmer shot so many glances at Timothy that her brother Mark started frowning. The teenage dynamics were comically obvious, and Clarissa hid a smile behind her hand.

Trevor settled his mother into a lawn chair, then placed a small plate of pie in her shaking hands.

She looked fairly good for someone who'd been enduring months of chemo. And the gratitude in her eyes when she looked at the café staff made Clarissa understand why Trevor had been so dedicated to this place and these people.

As the impromptu party swirled around her—conversations overlapping, laughter echoing off the cottonwood trees, the playground equipment squeaking as some of the younger kids explored—Clarissa felt so loved she thought she might burst.

Not just by her brothers, but by this entire extended family God had given her to navigate this season without their mom.

There was only one thing missing.

One person whose presence would have made this perfect day complete.

Maybe someday there would be room in her life for that kind of happiness again.

But for now, she'd have to wait. And pray something grew from a friendship that had been cut far too short.

The ground ball should have been routine. A sharp grounder to second base that any varsity player should field in his sleep.

Instead, Zeke watched in dismay as Andrew Henderson bobbled the ball, juggling it like a hot potato before securing it in his glove. Only a superhuman stretch by the first baseman saved the out, his glove barely snagging Henderson's off-target throw.

Relief flooded through Zeke's chest, but it was immediately followed by frustrated disbelief as Henderson pumped his fist like he'd just made the play of the century.

The kid had no awareness of how close he'd come to costing his team. No recognition that he'd been bailed out by a teammate's exceptional effort.

Zeke's gaze flicked to the bleachers nearest their dugout and his jaw clenched so hard his teeth ached.

The Hendersons occupied the front row like visiting royalty, their voices carrying across the infield as they proclaimed that "Coach obviously made the right decision for today's lineup."

A few rows behind them, Vaughn sat in his Friday afternoon suit, representing the school with the kind of political visibility that made Zeke's coaching jacket feel more like a straitjacket.

The mid-May heat pressed down on him, making the fabric stick to his skin. He was tempted to tear it off and toss it aside, but without a jersey underneath, that might give his critics more ammunition.

Being backed into this corner had been eating at him all week.

It hadn't mattered that Timothy had a legitimate excuse for missing practice for his sister's college graduation ceremony that Zeke had somehow forgotten was approaching.

No. Vaughn had made it crystal clear that team rules couldn't be bent this late in the season. Not when parents and boosters were watching every choice with microscopic scrutiny.

Timothy had accepted his demotion with the kind of grace that made Zeke's heart ache. But the decision had divided the team, even before Zeke spent the week practicing Timothy at second base while rotating Henderson around the infield.

The message was clear to everyone: the better player was riding the bench because of politics and technicalities.

He prayed they survived tonight's game with a win so his hands would be untied for tomorrow.

The next batter lined a single to center field, and Zeke forced his attention back to the present moment. Focus on what he could control. Trust his players to execute. Let everything else fall where it would.

"Come on, Torres!" Timothy's voice rang out from the dugout fence, his hands gripping the chain-link as he shouted encouragement to his teammate. "You got this!"

The other bench players joined in, creating a wall of vocal support that energized the entire infield.

It appeared that Timothy was a better team player than Henderson had ever been. Investing in his teammates' success even when he wasn't on the field and leading through service rather than demanding attention.

Other voices from the bleachers caught his ear, and a quick glance confirmed what his peripheral vision had already detected. The other Millers were also there, supporting the team despite Timothy's benching.

However, Clarissa's presence was both comforting and distracting.

The guilt hit him fresh since his belated congratulations text about her graduation had been woefully inadequate.

He hated that he couldn't start Timothy today, but he would have felt worse if the kid had skipped his sister's ceremony for a mere practice.

She'd needed her family there to support her milestone, like she'd always supported theirs.

The crack of the bat snapped his attention back to the field. Line drive to right field, caught on the run for the second out. One more and they'd escape the inning without much damage on the scoreboard.

One game at a time, Coach Bryant's voice echoed in his memory. *One inning. One batter.*

The game remained tight into the sixth inning, each play feeling magnified by playoff pressure. In the bottom of the sixth, with runners on first and third and one out, Henderson made an error that was impossible to disguise—a clean grounder that went right through his legs, allowing the tying run to score.

Zeke stood poised at the dugout entry, ready to signal for Timothy to take over at second base, when the next batter stepped up to the plate.

Then connected with the first pitch.

Torres fielded the grounder cleanly, stepped on second himself, and fired to first to end the inning before more damage could be done. Their shortstop had turned a potential disaster into a double play with no help from Henderson.

And through it all, Timothy's voice never stopped encouraging his teammates from the bench, his energy infectious even as he watched from the sidelines.

They managed to scratch out a run in the top of the seventh and held on for a 5-4 victory, but Zeke felt no satisfaction as his players celebrated on the mound. They'd won despite Henderson's mistakes, not because of his contributions.

In the post-game huddle inside the dugout, the concrete walls amplifying voices and the smell of sweat and dirt thick in the humid air, Zeke tried to focus on the positives. But when he addressed the errors, the kid's response made his blood pressure spike.

"That was a bad hop." Henderson whined like someone who'd never been held accountable. "Then Torres should have trusted me to cover second on that double play instead of taking all the credit himself."

Trust? No. Zeke understood why his captain had made the split-second decision.

Zeke waved off the weak explanations and dismissed the players to pack up their equipment.

Seemed the toxic attitude that had earned Andrew his original benching still festered. Still poisoned the team chemistry even after a victory.

And with the competition only becoming more difficult in the next round, they couldn't afford players who made excuses instead of improvements.

Which made it easy to know where the kid would be during tomorrow's game.

Zeke was willing to take the risk, while already bracing for the inevitable fallout. But at least he was smart enough to save that announcement for later.

As families began infiltrating the dugout area to greet their players, Zeke shouldered his bag and stepped outside, spotting Clarissa wrapping Timothy in a fierce hug.

The kid hadn't played a single inning and had been demoted because of a rule that felt increasingly arbitrary, but his family celebrated his presence like he'd won the game single-handedly.

Some rules—like the ones keeping Zeke from pursuing Clarissa openly—might be worth breaking for the right reason.

"Good game, Coach." Vaughn's voice carried a smarmy tone that had Zeke gritting his teeth. "Glad to see you made the right decision about the lineup after all."

The implication was clear: Vaughn had expected Zeke to play Timothy anyway. To ignore the missed practice rule when it mattered most. To give him a reason to fire Zeke on the spot.

Maybe he should have played Timothy after all.

Maybe integrity sometimes meant knowing when rules served people instead of the other way around.

"I'm just going to keep doing my job and doing what's best for the team until our season ends." Zeke held his voice steady despite the frustration building in his chest.

He turned toward the bus, needing distance from Vaughn's political games and the Hendersons' smug satisfaction.

As he walked, the timeline crystallized in his mind. Just five more days of school. And if they didn't win tomorrow, the season would be over, too.

Ending his contracted obligations to Loveland High School.

Since Vaughn clearly wouldn't offer his support through the inevitable conflicts ahead, Zeke would be looking for a new job instead of signing a contract renewal.

He'd have to trust God to lead him somewhere his principles wouldn't be constantly under attack. Unfortunately, in a small town like Loveland, there might not be other opportunities involving baseball.

But at least his integrity would be intact and that had to count for something.

Except that might also mean leaving Clarissa and the Millers behind.

Unless God worked a miracle to keep him here. Unless both Vaughn and the Hendersons somehow got their due. Little chance of that happening.

Handle the future details, Lord. Starting with tomorrow's game.

Because tomorrow would test more than his team's resilience on the field.

It would determine whether Zeke had the courage to stand by his principles even when the cost was higher than he'd ever imagined.

And prove whether he'd become the kind of man his mother would be proud of.

Or not.

Chapter Twenty-Three

Clarissa's stomach churned as she climbed the stairs into the home team's designated cheering section.

How were the boys handling the pressure of being one of only sixteen teams left in the championship bracket when she battled such nerves just sitting in the stands?

Overhead, the sun beat down while the benches radiated back the heat that shimmered in the afternoon air. It was the kind of scorching Saturday that would leave everyone wilted and sunburned by game's end.

Hopefully the Red Wolves would walk away with a victory for their efforts.

Once seated, Clarissa squeezed a large dollop of SPF 50 onto her still-pale arms, the coconut scent mixing with the smell of hot metal and concession stand popcorn. Her legs, even whiter after months of jeans and long pants, got an extra coating before she tugged her baseball cap low over her eyes.

"Brian, sunscreen." She held out the bottle to her younger brother, who was already turning pink around his ears from his morning game. "You know how you burn."

He groaned but accepted the bottle, muttering something about always looking like a ghost so what difference did it make.

It wasn't long before nervous energy had him fidgeting in his seat, drumming his fingers against his knee as both teams went through their warm-up routines on the field below.

Clarissa checked her phone for the time, then found herself staring at the text exchange still open on her screen. It was ridiculous to read and re-read the same short conversation, but she couldn't help herself.

Clarissa: *Congratulations on a continued season!*

Zeke: *Thanks. It's both good news and bad, because I honestly want this for the boys but also can't wait for it to end.*

She'd been dissecting those words since last night, hope and uncertainty warring in her chest.

Did he mean his feelings were still there? That despite the misunderstanding and hurt, he still wanted to pursue something with her once the season ended?

The memory of their moment in the storage shed surfaced unbidden—the look in his eyes right before he'd kissed her, the rough texture of his fingertips as he'd traced her jawline with such gentle reverence.

Heat flooded her face, and she fanned herself with her program, hoping anyone watching would blame the sun for her flushed cheeks.

Because Zeke's text could just as easily mean he was tired of dealing with pushy parents and administrators.

She caught sight of the Hendersons in their usual front-row seats, Karen's voice already carrying sharp critiques about "questionable coaching decisions" despite the game not having started yet.

Actually, Clarissa didn't care anymore what they might say. She'd spent too much emotional energy worrying about other people's opinions.

Her attention shifted back to the field just in time to see Zeke remove his jacket and toss it aside with a gesture that looked almost defiant.

The short sleeves of his baseball jersey revealed those sculpted arms that had held her so gently, highlighting the athletic build that spoke of years dedicated to physical conditioning and outdoor work.

More fanning.

Definitely more fanning.

At last, both teams took their positions, with the Red Wolves having earned the home team status and the privilege of batting last.

Clarissa held her breath as Timothy jogged out to second base, his red hair bright under the blazing sun.

This start would automatically earn him a varsity letter. She'd looked up the guidelines in the parent handout earlier in the week.

Turned out that players had to start a certain percentage of games to qualify for the honor—with the automatic exception of a state playoff game—and Timothy had been just short after his earlier benching.

Thank You, God, for this additional blessing.

A school jacket to display the letter would be an added expense, but one she'd gladly cover out of the final payment from Mr. Ridge.

Thank God that project was officially finished, too. She was free from the demanding schedule and had even earned a bonus that she'd tucked away as an emergency fund.

Better yet, freelance work was already lined up for the coming weeks, and after Memorial Day—her last day at the café—she'd have complete flexibility to work from home.

Meaning she'd been able to offer to watch Brian's friend Cameron Evans as needed over the summer, a small way to thank his family for their help during her crisis.

The first inning passed without incident, both pitchers finding their rhythm early.

During the break, Timothy looked up toward the stands and she gave him an enthusiastic thumbs up.

His answering grin was quick but genuine before he turned his focus back to the game with the kind of concentration that made her proud.

"I just hope the freshman doesn't mess this up for everyone." Karen Henderson's voice carried over the crowd noise.

"Oh, would you shut up already?" another parent snapped back. "The kid earned his spot fair and square."

Clarissa smiled despite her nerves. Apparently the Hendersons' constant negativity wore thin even among their usual allies.

But by the bottom of the third inning, with the score tied 1-1 and the pressure mounting, the visiting team showed why they'd made it this far in the playoffs.

Clarissa's stomach clenched again with fresh worry.

Two of the home team batters had reached base on a walk and a perfectly placed bunt that hugged the foul line.

Now Timothy was up to bat, the weight of the inning settling on his young shoulders like a physical burden.

From the dugout, Zeke's voice carried across the diamond. "Stay relaxed, Miller! See the ball, trust your hands!"

"Here's where we find out if Matthews made the right choice," Karen Henderson said loudly enough for half the stands to hear. "Kid's gonna choke under pressure."

Someone ought to choke that woman.

Oh. Forgive me, Lord.

Clarissa grasped her knees and leaned forward to watch.

The first pitch came in low and outside. Ball one.

Timothy stepped out of the box, adjusted his gloves, and took a deep breath before settling back into his stance.

The second pitch was a fastball down the middle, and Timothy's swing reminded her of that day weeks ago when they'd watched Zeke at the batting cages.

The crack of the bat silenced every conversation in the stands, and Clarissa found herself on her feet screaming along with hundreds of other fans as the ball sailed over the center fielder's head.

Two runs scored with ease, and Timothy slid safely into second base with what the announcer called a stand-up double that gave the Red Wolves a 3-1 lead.

The grin on Timothy's face was worth every moment of anxiety she'd endured.

But even better was the satisfied smirk on Zeke's face as he clapped from the coaching box, and the absolute silence from Karen Henderson's section of the bleachers.

Take that, critics!

The seventh inning stretched before them like a tightrope walk over a canyon.

Zeke watched his players take the field, their movements sharp with focus despite the heat that had everyone's uniforms clinging to sweat-dampened skin.

They held a fragile two-run lead, but with their starting pitcher showing signs of fatigue and their backup warming up in the bullpen, all it would take was a couple solid hits to blow the game wide open.

Not to mention the opposing team's heart of the order was coming up again, stacked with seasoned players who'd earned their spots through clutch performances just like this one.

While his guys would get the last bats if necessary, he'd much rather end it here.

Zeke's stomach rolled at how little control he had over the next few minutes.

All the strategy and preparation in the world couldn't replace the need to trust his players with the skills he'd taught them and pray they responded to the coaching signals he'd send.

He glanced toward the stands, taking in the sea of red that had grown throughout the afternoon.

The newspaper articles about their playoff run had drawn more than just families. It seemed like half the community made the trip to witness history in the making. After all, the Red Wolves hadn't advanced past this round in well over a decade.

Somewhere in that crowd was Clarissa, whose presence was both comforting and distracting, a reminder of everything he hoped to pursue once the season ended.

Then he spotted Vaughn, his expression unreadable but somehow managing to convey both hope for victory and desire for an excuse to clean house.

Life, like baseball, was full of risks and bad hops and errant pitches that could change everything in an instant. But then again, sometimes the ball hit the sweet spot on the bat and caught just enough air to clear the fence.

God, please carry my team through this last inning. The outcome is in Your hands.

The first batter worked a full count before grounding out to third base.

One down, but it had taken eight pitches from their already-tired pitcher. Zeke saw the strain in the young man's posture, the way he shook out his throwing arm between pitches.

The second batter roped a double down the left field line, the crack of the bat sending Zeke's heart rate spiking. One runner in scoring position with the cleanup hitter approaching the plate.

The third batter drew a walk on four straight pitches, none of them close to the strike zone.

Now there were runners on first and second with only one out, and Zeke sensed the momentum shifting like the wind direction before a storm.

He called time and jogged to the mound, the infield dirt puffing beneath his cleats and the smell of rosin from the pitcher's bag filling his nostrils.

The other infielders surrounded them as Zeke eyed his pitcher.

The kid's face flushed with heat and pressure, but his eyes were still focused. Good.

"You've got this." Zeke placed a steadying hand on the young man's shoulder. "Trust your fastball and let your defense work behind you."

"We got your back." Timothy's voice cracked but the sentiment was echoed by the others.

The kid would make a great team captain someday.

After a quick—habitual more than necessary—reminder of the situation and location of forced outs and another nod to the pitcher, Zeke jogged off the field.

Back near the dugout, he shifted his weight from foot to foot, every muscle in his body coiled with excess energy.

The next batter stepped into the box with the confidence of someone who'd driven in runs all season long.

The pitch came in belt-high, and the batter's swing was smooth and powerful. The crack of the bat sent Zeke's stomach plummeting... until he saw the trajectory.

It was a sharp grounder between first and second base.

Timothy broke toward the bag with perfect timing, his glove snaring the ball on a short hop before firing to Torres on second base.

The shortstop's pivot was textbook perfect, his throw to first beating the runner by half a step.

Double play.

Game over.

The infield erupted in celebration, players mobbing each other in a tangle of dirt-streaked uniforms and triumphant shouts.

The stands also exploded with noise that almost shook the very foundations of the ballpark, hundreds of voices joining together in pure joy.

Zeke's knees went weak with relief and pride.

They'd done it. Advanced to the final eight teams in the state championship bracket, marking an achievement that would be remembered long after these players graduated. And next weekend could take them further.

But as he basked in the moment, he dreaded the week to come.

More pressure. More politics. More scrutiny of every decision he made.

Last night's text to Clarissa still held true. He wanted this for the boys but also couldn't wait for it to end.

Across the field, he caught Vaughn's eye and received a raised eyebrow that suggested grudging respect mixed with continued irritation. So nothing had really changed.

From the dugout, Devon offered a reluctant nod, acknowledgment that maybe—just maybe—Zeke's controversial decisions had been justified.

Even the Hendersons looked almost happy as they hugged other parents, caught up in the communal celebration despite their son riding the bench. Surely they wouldn't still push for Andrew to get playing time next weekend after watching Timothy's stellar performance?

Zeke gathered his team for a post-game huddle, their faces bright with exhaustion and elation. "Enjoy today." He raised his voice to be heard over the noise from the stands. "You've earned it. We'll get back to work on Monday."

As the formal team obligations ended and players scattered to find their families, Zeke was swept into the crowd of well-wishers.

Parents and community members pressed close, offering congratulations that he deflected back onto his players.

"They're the ones who earned this," he said again and again. "I just tried to put them in position to succeed."

A hand touched his elbow, and he turned to find a stranger, an older man with graying hair and the weathered skin of someone who'd spent years outdoors.

"Coach Matthews? I've heard a lot of great things and had to see it for myself." The man extended his hand. "You certainly know your stuff, and I think you're the man for the job."

Zeke blinked. "Job?"

The man smiled and pulled out a business card. Zeke's eyes caught the words *Loveland Baseball Association* along with a too-small-to-read-from-here name and number.

His mind spun with possibilities as hope grew in his chest.

Coach Bryant had said Zeke needed to move either up or down to avoid the parent politics. Was this an answer to his prayers?

"I'd love to set up a meeting at your earliest convenience." The stranger handed over the card, then clapped Zeke on the shoulder. "We can talk details then, but I have a feeling this could be exactly what both of us are looking for."

As the man walked away, peace settled over Zeke like a familiar embrace.

Even when the path forward seemed impossible to navigate, God was faithful, and His promises endured.

Making all the political battles and administrative headaches manageable, as if they were temporary obstacles rather than permanent roadblocks.

Across the field, he caught a glimpse of red hair in the chaos of the celebrating crowd and his pulse skipped.

Soon—very soon—the season would end, and the school year would close.

And then, maybe, he could pursue the life he'd been dreaming about.

Assuming she agreed.

Chapter Twenty-Four

Clarissa balanced three steaming plates as she rounded the end of the counter, her heart squeezing with bittersweet emotion that leaked into her eyes.

Two and a half hours.

That's all she had left as an employee of Hope's Café, and she tried not to think about how much this place meant to her. How God had provided exactly what she needed exactly when she'd needed it.

"Those better be happy tears." Lauren's voice was bright with teasing affection. "Because if you're going to miss us that much, we can always fire your brother Timothy, instead."

"Hey!" Monica's immediate protest came from across the dining room, her cheeks flushing pink as she wiped down a recently-vacated table with unnecessary force. "You can't fire Timothy. He hasn't even started yet!"

Lauren's knowing grin made Clarissa laugh despite the moisture threatening her eyes. "Don't worry, Monica. Your secret crush is safe for now."

Although it wouldn't be a secret for long with their full dining room.

Still, the relaxed Memorial Day crowd created a different rhythm than the usual rush of a Monday morning. Making it easy to pause and breathe in the scents of cinnamon and coffee that carried on the early summer breeze drifting through the propped-open front door.

Clarissa delivered the orders of Trevor's special cinnamon French toast to a few familiar faces who'd made a point of sitting in her section.

And they weren't the first.

In fact, Clay had come in hours earlier than usual, then left a tip that was more than some people made in a day, accompanied by a note about how much her website design had helped his business.

Even their resident reporter Kyle pressed a twenty into her hand with instructions to "keep up the good work, kid."

And the "Best Wishes to Clarissa" jar that Lauren had placed on the restored antique buffet was embarrassingly full, testament to how this little café family had embraced her over the past five months.

The bell chimed from the pass-through window, calling Clarissa back to work.

But as she continued to serve customers with a now-natural efficiency, her attention drifted again and again to the things she'd miss.

Like the way morning light slanted through the front windows, the comfortable chaos of the kitchen during rush hour, and the sense of purpose she'd found within these walls.

The sense of belonging.

Thanks to referrals from her cafe connections, her freelance business was thriving, and she wasn't going far. After all, she'd be driving Timothy to and from the cafe until he got his license and they managed a second car.

Not that anyone could take the co-owner's place, but with Joel doing more and more consulting outside the cafe in a quest to pay down the business debt before the wedding, he and Lauren had created the perfect support position for Timothy.

With a schedule that still allowed Amanda to come in a bit later in the morning.

But oh, how Timothy was going to hate the early wake-up calls.

Clarissa grinned. At least he only had to endure the summer months until school started up again and they gave him fewer shifts. Then again, working alongside Debbie's twins—including Monica—would be a friendly perk.

Unless anything came of the argument she'd overheard between Debbie and her son. If Mark quit, Timothy would be needed even more.

As she made another round of coffee refills, Clarissa watched Amanda wipe down the corner booth near where Matt sat lingering over his coffee, their conversation quiet but intense.

There was something growing between them—she saw it in the way Amanda's guarded expression softened when she looked at him. And the way Matt's eyes followed her movements.

Weeks ago, Amanda had referred to Matt's furniture restoration work, saying "he sees value in damaged things."

But Clarissa suspected the carpenter also saw value in people others had given up on.

Please, God, bring them what they need to heal.

Just like God had turned every single one of these people at the cafe into a family.

Hope's letter had been right. God did fill in the gaps.

There was just one gap left in Clarissa's life. One space left conspicuously empty despite all the blessings surrounding her.

Would she ever find love? A partner to journey through life with?

Now that school was officially out for summer and Timothy's team had fallen in the Final Four round, maybe—just maybe—Zeke would make his move.

If he was still interested.

If their fragile friendship hadn't been completely destroyed.

A moment of insecurity fluttered through her chest before she pushed it aside. She trusted God to work out the details of this next chapter, because He who promised was faithful.

By the time eleven-thirty rolled around, Clarissa found herself dragging out the familiar end-of-shift routine. Counting her tips, marking her time card one final time, then dropping her dirty apron into the laundry basket where it would be washed and worn by someone else.

She shouldered her purse, then stepped out of the office into the kitchen.

"For your boys." Greta pressed a bakery box into her hands. "Apple turnovers and those chocolate chip cookies Brian loves."

"Thank you." Clarissa's throat tightened and tears threatened again.

She turned toward the back door leading to the alley parking lot and her car.

"Oh no, you don't." Joel gripped her elbow.

"Why not?"

Joel's grin reminded her of Timothy at his most mischievous. "Front door exit. It's a new tradition."

Despite her protests, he steered her into the dining room and applause erupted from every table.

Her face heated to probably the exact shade of her hair as customers she'd served for months called out well-wishes and encouragement.

Lauren took pictures, Greta dabbed at her eyes with her apron, and the normally stoic Trevor emerged from the kitchen with the rest of his staff to join the send-off.

Ahead, the front door beckoned like salvation from the embarrassing attention.

Clarissa picked up her pace, eager to escape to the privacy of her car where she could process the overwhelming emotions of this transition without an audience.

But there, through the propped-open door, she caught sight of a familiar profile waiting on the sidewalk and her heart skipped a beat.

Zeke. With his blond hair catching the late morning sun and the same broad shoulders she'd memorized from countless stolen glances across baseball fields.

He stood with his back partially turned, flowers clutched in his hands as he shifted side to side with a nervousness that was endearingly at odds with his usual confidence.

He wasn't wearing his red coaching jacket or any school-related clothing. Instead, he'd dressed in khaki slacks and a crisp white dress shirt with the sleeves rolled up to reveal the corded strength of his forearms.

The deliberate formality of his outfit sent her pulse skittering.

What did it mean? Why was he out here? Were those flowers for her?

Never mind the questions.

He was here. With flowers. Looking like he was on a mission.

Her smile stretched so wide her cheeks ached as she pulled away from Joel and closed the distance, ignoring the chuckles and ribbing from the cafe family around her.

Whatever Zeke had to say, she was ready to listen.

Zeke shifted his weight from foot to foot on the sidewalk outside Hope's Café, his palms sweaty as the sun beat down on his back.

Maybe he should have come up with a different plan, but too late now.

Especially after Timothy had casually mentioned when his sister got off work and then guaranteed she'd leave through the front door.

If only he wasn't hyperaware of the curious glances from passersby who wondered why a grown man clutched a bouquet of mixed wildflowers like his life depended on it.

Movement at the entrance to the cafe had his heart hammering against his ribs, and then Clarissa was there in the doorway with a bakery box in her hands and a smile that made his breath catch.

Genuine and unguarded. And reminiscent of those few perfect moments they'd shared together.

Moments when he'd offered his jacket in the rain. Eaten pizza in the park with her brothers. Or even after that magical kiss in the baseball equipment shed where they'd agreed to text each other.

Back before everything imploded.

Back when he'd thought they had all the time in the world.

Clarissa came to a stop in front of him, her green eyes bright with curiosity and something that looked like hope. "What brings you here, Coach Matthews?"

The formal address reminded him that their last in-person conversation had been filled with harsh words and hurt feelings.

But calling him coach also triggered memories of another conversation from weeks ago about dating.

He held out the flowers, noting the slight tremor in his hands. "I brought a peace offering with hopes to butter you up before asking a very important question."

Her eyes widened with what looked like panic.

Oh. That almost sounded like something else and he rushed to fix his mistake.

"Since the season is over, I have to ask if there's any chance you'd ever date a kids' baseball coach?"

She jostled the bakery box, then accepted the flowers, bringing them to her nose and inhaling.

"That depends on whether *you* are the coach in question." The smile that bloomed across her face reached all the way to her eyes, making them sparkle. "But don't let the high schoolers ever hear you call them kids."

"About that..." He glanced toward the café windows where multiple faces were pressed against the glass, then gently tugged her to a small bench positioned between the café and the storefront next door. "There's something I need to tell you."

Once they were seated, he moved her bakery box and flowers to the ground near their feet, then reached for her hands. Her skin was soft and warm, and when he rubbed his thumb across her knuckles, he registered a slight shiver in response.

"I am not renewing my contract with the high school as either a teacher or a coach." He searched her face for her reaction. "All those headaches with politics and lesson plans and parents who think they know better than the coaches... I'm done with it."

"What will you do instead?" She leaned closer, a furrow between her eyes.

"The Loveland Baseball Association offered me a position as program director. I'd oversee all the age groups and really develop fundamentals like we did with that skills camp fundraiser."

The same event that had led to the best kiss of his life.

His excitement built at the possibilities. "Youth baseball, Clarissa. Teaching the game without political pressure and building skills in kids who still love the sport for its own sake."

She beamed. "That sounds perfect for you."

"It gets better."

"How?"

"They want to partner with a new indoor facility for more skills development, host tournaments, maybe even expand into basketball during the winter months." He paused, studying her face. "The best part is it's all still here in Loveland. I don't have to leave."

"I couldn't imagine a more ideal situation for someone with your experience and education." Her smile faded. "Except now you'll be coaching Brian instead of Timothy. Won't that still cause problems for us?"

"I talked to the Board of Directors before accepting." He squeezed her hands. "Since Brian's already on a team and I won't be coaching any specific teams anyway, there's no conflict of interest. Especially if we're already dating before I start work tomorrow."

Her breath caught, and he drew courage from the heat in her eyes.

"Which brings me back to my original question." He pressed a gentle kiss to her knuckles. "Will you date a kids' baseball coach?"

The twinkle in her eyes made his pulse race. "Dating implies an actual date, but I don't seem to recall you asking me out yet."

He chuckled at the challenge in her voice. "Guess it's time to swing for the fences and pray I don't strike out. Will you go to dinner with me tonight and then explore that hiking trail to Horsetooth Rock this weekend?"

"A double play." She pursed her lips, trying to hide a smile. "Are you trying to steal my heart?"

"Guilty as charged." He grinned at her answering baseball references, then grew more serious. "Although I want you to know I'm not planning on running any bases beyond God's guidelines. I just really want to see where this relationship could go."

Her gaze dipped to his lips, and her voice dropped until it was barely audible above the street noise around them. "Yes, I'll date you."

"Yes!" If he hadn't been holding her hands, he'd have pumped a fist to the sky.

Except his outburst startled a trio of women walking past and drew even more attention.

Zeke eased back, giving her hands a gentle squeeze. "Thank you."

"As for dinner tonight..." Her cheeks flushed pink. "I'm taking the boys to the batting cages later since Timothy wanted to give Brian a few pointers, and then we were going to grill burgers but I suppose—"

"Deal. For all of it." Zeke blew out a breath to slow his pulse. Except he couldn't ignore the eagerness to spend time with her, no matter what it looked like.

They'd wasted enough time already.

"Perfect." She stared into his eyes as if memorizing his face.

Capturing the moment, just like he was.

He gathered her flowers and the bakery box, then pulled her to her feet, lacing their fingers together. "Can I give you a ride? And what can I bring?"

"My car is parked in the back." Clarissa pointed back toward the corner intersection and then left as if they'd take the side street to get there. "And Greta provided a little dessert, but there's always room for ice cream."

"I'll just stop at home to change clothes, then pick some up before coming over." He tugged her along down the sidewalk, ready to set their plans in motion. "But I definitely want to be there for the batting cages. It will give me a chance to win over your brothers in terms of dating their sister."

As they rounded the corner and moved out of sight of the café windows, he paused their progress, turning to face her.

"Before we go any further, I need to say this in person. I'm truly sorry for how I overreacted before. Thank you for forgiving me. I promise I'll never—" He shook his head. "Actually, that's not true. I'll probably break promises in the future."

She bit her lip. "And so will I. After all, we're human. Only God keeps all His promises."

"True." How had he gotten so lucky as to find her? Especially when their shared faith was such a solid foundation for the future.

Her free hand came to rest against his chest. "But what if we learn to face our challenges together instead of alone?"

Together never sounded better.

Could she feel the erratic rhythm of his heartbeat beneath her palm?

He nodded, then reluctantly continued their stroll to her car and helped arrange her belongings in the passenger seat.

The afternoon stretched ahead of them, full of possibility and promise, except there was one thing he couldn't wait for.

He moved closer until Clarissa was backed against her car door. "Since we're likely to have an audience later, I want to make sure nothing gets in the way of a proper post-date kiss."

Her eyes widened before her hands fisted in his shirt, pulling him down to meet her lips.

The kiss was everything their first one had been and more—sweet and breathless and full of hope for the future. She gave as much as she got, and his heart nearly burst with gratitude and joy.

He eased back before they lost control, resting his forehead against hers as they both struggled to catch their breath.

"God truly does put the lonely in families," he murmured, thinking of how perfectly she fit into his arms, into his life, into the future he'd been afraid to dream about.

"I can't wait to see what He does next," she whispered back, her smile bright enough to rival the afternoon sun.

Neither could he.

Especially with her at his side and God leading the way.

What's Next?

♥

The Cafe on Hope and Main Series continues with Book 3, *Where Love Abides.*

•♥•♥•♥•♥•♥•

She's convinced she's too broken for love, but he specializes in restoring what others have tossed aside.

Amanda Yates is drowning under financial pressures after her husband's betrayal and death, terrified that she's failing her special-needs daughter. Waiting tables at Hope's Cafe is barely keeping them afloat and now with the escalation of her daughter's mysterious self-injury behaviors, her prayers feel as empty as her bank account and she fears she's as defective as her in-laws claim.

Cafe-regular Matt Simpson spends his days transforming forgotten furniture and neglected homes into treasures, but his refusal to sacrifice quality for profit has already cost him a fiancée and his family's respect. As his construction business finally begins to gain traction and recognition, pressures also mount to compromise his values in the name of success.

A moment of compassion led to friendship and a working relationship sparked hopes of a future, except past wounds have a way of resurfacing. And without faith, some things might be beyond fixing, especially a broken heart.

Fans of Becky Wade, Denise Hunter, and Karen Kingsbury will fall in love with the charming world of Hope's Cafe.

Continue this heart-warming, faith-filled series today.

If you'd like to receive updates about upcoming books or sales, you can sign up for my email list on my website at CandeeFick.com.

(There might be a few surprises headed your way including a free castle novella.)

Dear Reader

Thank you for spending a few hours of your time with the characters who call Hope's Cafe their second home. There are a lot more stories to come, so I hope you can settle in with a cup of coffee and a cinnamon roll to savor the journey.

There is no greater pleasure as an author than knowing that I've encouraged my readers! If you enjoyed this book, please take a few minutes to let the rest of the world know by leaving a review on Amazon or on sites like Goodreads or BookBub. It doesn't have to be long. Just a few words pointing other readers this direction would be much appreciated. And even a simple star rating goes a long way!

Readers always ask what's real in a story and what's made up. While the town of Loveland, Colorado is real, this particular diner/cafe and its founding family are fictional. I may have placed it on a corner on "Main" street where real locals used to frequent such a restaurant before it closed, but I took creative license with the surrounding businesses and street names in order to set up future story situations.

When it came to the baseball scenes, I definitely drew on my hours and hours in the stands at recreational, competitive league, and high school games cheering on my sons. In fact, my husband was an official assistant coach a few of those years and a backyard coach the rest of the time. The name of the high school, mascot, and colors are real and I used that team's schedule as a starting place when it came to plotting the story. But all of the names and situations (including the past coach's scandal) are pure fabrication. After all, I write fiction woven with truth!

As I continue to write stories of faith, hope, and love, my prayer is that you will experience the amazing love of God and find encouragement for the journey called life. That you will latch onto hope as an anchor for your soul and like Clarissa, learn to rest in the arms of the God who is faithful to keep His promises.

Until we (hopefully) meet again in the pages of a book, happy reading everyone!

Candee

More Fiction

A complete and up-to-date list of all my books can be found on my website at CandeeFick.com

Cafe on Hope and Main Series

(Contemporary small town romance)
Where Hope Begins (Lauren and Joel)
Where Promises Endure (Clarissa and Zeke)
Where Love Abides (Amanda and Matt)
Where Faith Remains (Debbie and Ethan)

The Wardrobe Series

(Contemporary romance in theater settings)
Dance Over Me (Dani and Alex)
Focus on Love (Liz and Ryan)
Sing a New Song (Gloria and Nick)

A Picture Perfect Christmas (Liz and Ryan continued)
Home For Christmas (Grace and Tyler)
Complete Series Boxed Set

Within the Castle Gates Series

(Historical romance in various time periods)
Stepping Into the Light (Moira and Evan)
To Win Her Heart (Emma and Grayson)
The Lost Heir (Kathleen and Reuben)
Finding Home (Susannah and Nicholas)
Saving Grace (contemporary - Grace and Drew)
A Castle in the Clouds (Miranda and Josh)
Books 1-4 Boxed Set

Standalone Romance

Catch of a Lifetime (Cassie and Reed)

About Candee

Candee Fick is a mocha latte fueled author who writes heartwarming, hope-filled Christian romance. She knows first-hand that while life is hard, God is good. That's why her stories show relatable characters overcoming real-life problems through their faith in God and the support of their small town communities. When Candee isn't weaving intricate plotlines at her favorite coffee shop, she can be found spending quality time with her family in Colorado or lost in the pages of a captivating story while letting the dust bunnies multiply.

Visit www.CandeeFick.com to learn more and get a free book by signing up for her newsletter.

www.ingramcontent.com/pod-product-compliance
Lightning Source LLC
LaVergne TN
LVHW100522110826
845146LV00002B/744

* 9 7 9 8 9 5 0 8 5 9 0 0 7 *